Scott lean ... **forehead, brushing hair back** ... **"You okay?"**

She nodded. Smiled. He was there. Still sharing moments with her. Probably not for long. They'd known from the beginning that their liaison wasn't permanent.

No expectations, they'd promised. And she had none that reached beyond the present.

But when Scott lowered his head and kissed her softly, she gave herself fully to that present. Kissing him so completely, she lost her air and sucked his. He touched her everywhere, and she touched him back. Letting her fingertips learn every part of him. And when they came together, lying on their sides, their gazes joined and held, along with their bodies, until the waves had come and gone. Making memories that they could call up at some point in the future if they wanted to do so.

Iris gave Scott the best of her, hoping that the experience would be a place of joy in his memories, too.

Dear Reader,

Welcome to Ocean Breeze! The private beach stretches for two miles, the cottages are everything you'd want them to be, the people accept visitors and newcomers without judgment, and the unofficial dog society...well that's just loads of love waiting to welcome you.

Scott and Iris are two of Ocean Breeze's first residents. Over the years they've lived on the beach, they've become best friends. The kind who see each other every day, hear about work, know what's for dinner, and are privy to weekend and vacation plans. But as it turns out, there's a lot of stuff they don't know about each other. Their story gripped me as I was writing it. And months later, when I did the final read as the book went into production, I laughed. I cried. And I came away feeling as though I'd been enriched. I hope you give these two special people the chance to take a hold of you, too.

And in case you missed it, there's a free novella on Harlequin.com, *Coming Home to Ocean Breeze*, that introduces you to this highly sought-after neighborhood.

Welcome home!

Tara Taylor Quinn

BEACH COTTAGE KISSES

TARA TAYLOR QUINN

SPECIAL EDITION

Harlequin®
SPECIAL EDITION™

Recycling programs for this product may not exist in your area.

ISBN-13: 978-1-335-40221-9

Beach Cottage Kisses

Copyright © 2025 by TTQ Books LLC

 Harlequin Enterprises ULC
22 Adelaide St. West, 41st Floor
Toronto, Ontario M5H 4E3, Canada
www.Harlequin.com

Printed in Lithuania

MIX
Paper | Supporting responsible forestry
FSC® C021394

A *USA TODAY* bestselling author of over one hundred novels in twenty languages, **Tara Taylor Quinn** has sold more than seven million copies. Known for her intense emotional fiction, Ms. Quinn's novels have received critical acclaim in the UK and most recently from Harvard. She is the recipient of the Readers' Choice Award and has appeared often on local and national TV, including *CBS Sunday Morning*. For TTQ offers, news and contests, visit tarataylorquinn.com!

Books by Tara Taylor Quinn

Harlequin Romantic Suspense

Sierra's Web

The Coltons of Owl Creek

The Cottages on Ocean Breeze

Visit the Author Profile page
at Harlequin.com for more titles.

For Phyllis Perryman—you embody in real life
how time spent on Ocean Breeze makes me feel.
Thank you, my friend.

Chapter One

"**I** do."

The threat of tears tightened her throat. Pricked at her eyelids.

Shocked, feeling raw and exposed, Iris Shiprock held her pasted smile as the preacher turned from Sage to Gray. "Grayson Bartholomew, do you take Sage Martin as your lawfully wedded wife?"

Iris barely heard the positive response due to the sudden roaring in her ears.

Leave me alone.

Her best friend was getting married. She was not going to let the past mess up the present.

"Miss Iris, you got a run up your nose. Better catch it 'fore it drips." The loudly whispered words, coming from the four-year-old glancing up at her, created a small rustle in the very full room. Taking the tissue the bridesmaid next to her   an attorney from Sage's office—slid discreetly into her hand, Iris made a quick wipe.

And smiled at little Leigh. Sage's daughter. The love of Iris's life.

Nodding her approval of the fix, Leigh slid her little hand into Iris's and turned back solemnly to watch her mom and new father as they followed formal vows with their own, more personal promises to each other.

Standing just to the side of Sage, Iris could only see Gray's face, and watched the usually collected expression break along with his voice as he finished with "I will never turn my back on you or our family. You can count on me. Forever."

As the roaring in Iris's ears started up again, she averted her gaze. And it ran straight into the pair of blue eyes that were watching her, not the couple getting married.

The best man. Sage's twin brother. Scott Martin.

Iris's second-best friend.

Who had the audacity to wink at her. Right then and there.

As though he knew.

He didn't. No one did. She'd reinvented herself when she'd moved from Northern California to San Diego ten years before.

And had long been over the bouts of panic that used to plague her.

She'd attended hundreds of weddings. All without issue.

Hadn't had a breakdown in years.

And between Leigh and her uncle Scott, she didn't have one then, either.

The groom kissed the bride. They both turned and picked up Leigh, kissed her cheeks, faced the crowd and started down the aisle.

On cue, Iris's arm slid through Scott's. He gave it a little squeeze. And off they went. Just as rehearsed.

Best buds dressed in their finery. At a glorious occasion.

With a fun evening ahead.

She was off the hook.

Weddings were not his thing. Scott had first had the revelation right about the time he'd looked over to see Iris struggling not to cry.

Three years they'd been friends and he'd never seen her look...vulnerable. Emotionally overwrought.

The sight wiped him out almost as much as listening to the vows his twin was making to his best friend, hearing his biggest failure among them.

Once upon a time he'd said, "I do."

But he hadn't followed through on the promise.

Had Iris also been married before? Was that why she'd just had what could only be described as a near breakdown? That initial moment of panic, before she'd seemed to pull herself together...

Three years they'd seen each other more days than not, and not once had she hinted at any heartbreak in her life.

Nor had she ever brought a man home that he knew about. She never mentioned dating. At least not to him.

Had someone promised to love her forever and then broken her heart?

The idea brought an instant flash of anger toward the jerk.

Which quickly turned inward on himself. Molly had been a lovely, intelligent, giving woman. A friend to many. Who'd all rightfully hated him when he'd paid so little attention to his wife that he hadn't even known she'd left him until the day after she'd moved out.

How could he be angry with an ex who broke a friend's heart? He *was* that guy.

As a husband, yes.

But as a friend?

On the dance floor during the maid-of-honor-and-best-man dance with the bride and groom, Scott pulled Iris's sexy body close and teased her about the entire plate of pasta she'd consumed seated next to him at the bridal table.

And grinned when she told him he was just lucky she hadn't dumped it in his lap.

They were good. Fine. The best.

Friend he could do.

As best man and brother of the bride, he was there for the night.

If Iris needed a distraction to keep the stricken look off her face, he'd stick close enough to make sure he provided it.

And if she needed a shoulder to cry on?

He could be that, too. Thirty-one years connected to his twin had him well-versed in that area.

The bride was pregnant and so the bride and groom weren't drinking, but waiters with trays of champagne were everywhere and Scott grabbed a couple of bubbling flutes as he and Iris left the dance floor after that first dance.

The liquid seemed to reflect the purple of Iris's slim-fitting long dress as she lifted the glass he gave her up to her mouth. Took a sip.

From lips that bore the same lipstick she'd had on for the ceremony. Since photos were being taken throughout the evening, Sage had asked the wedding party to remain in ceremony dress mode. For him, that just meant keeping his shirt buttoned up and tux jacket and tie on. For Iris, the charge had meant touching up her makeup after dinner, too.

He knew all the behind-the-curtain details.

And still, those lips against the glass, the liquid passing over them…sent a wave of want down beneath his fly.

The sensation itself was commonplace enough that he didn't instantly take a step back. Until his gaze rose to Iris's deep green eyes.

What the hell?

Iris?

Three years and not once had that happened.

It couldn't happen again, either.

"What?" she asked him, that gaze homing in more specifically on his features, as though she could read his thoughts.

He wasn't completely sure she couldn't. The woman had a way of seeing things that no one else caught. Usually behind the lens of her camera.

Not while standing in a luxuriously decorated, romantically lit room, with only inches between them.

"I was just thinking about the long road Sage and Gray took to get here," he ad-libbed. Pulling out a thought he'd had while on the dance floor.

"Yeah, but I'm guessing that if you asked either one of them, they'd say the destination was worth the trip."

Sage and Gray had both grown a lot since Gray had broken off their first engagement years ago, just a couple of days before the wedding. Remembering his sister's brokenness, he'd never have believed that she could be put back together again with a wholeness that surpassed what she'd been. Still couldn't quite wrap his mind around the depth of her happiness.

"I wish my father had lived to see this day," he said, lifting his glass to his lips as the band struck up another number and the dance floor filled. Randolph Martin III, wealthy, demanding, strict widower father of the twins he'd adored, would be so proud of Sage.

He'd have no doubt that he'd succeeded with at least one of his offspring. He'd be extremely pleased with Scott's courtroom successes, too. But Sage, she'd conquered both the personal and professional worlds.

Iris moved toward a table farther back in the room, away from the band, talking as she walked, so Scott went with her and heard her say, "I think she was happiest having you walk her down the aisle." She slid onto a stool at the high top she'd chosen. "She loved your dad, but it's clear that he intimidated her. With you, it's just unconditional love and acceptance."

Scott glanced at his sister, on the dance floor again, with both Gray and sweet Leigh, and hated himself for the envy he felt along with the joy.

When it had just been single mother Sage, and him as Uncle Scott, his own life had felt full. But with Gray there...

He took another sip of champagne. Needing to get over himself. And saw Iris watching him again. "It's harder than I thought...watching her leave the nest, so to speak," he said. Because she was Iris. Friend to both of them. Almost like a member of the family.

Something he had a sudden need to firmly establish after his little episode moments before.

But as he said the words and saw the deadpan look that passed over Iris's lovely face, he wished he'd held his tongue. Her gaze darkened, and for a second, it looked as though she might cry again before she blinked, took a sip of champagne and said, "Just wait until Leigh gets married..."

Leigh. And the new baby on the way. Gray would be there to give both away. Or to stand beside his son, if the baby turned out to be a boy. Scott would be the doting uncle in the background.

He was generally good with that. Outside Sage's wedding.

Sitting in the midst of it, while feeling like an outsider, watching from the sidelines... Scott took another sip of champagne.

And concentrated on showing his and Sage's friend Iris a completely platonic fun time.

* * *

The music was slow. And loud enough to engulf you if you closed your eyes and sank into the words of deep, undying, forever love.

The cake had been cut. The garter thrown. Leigh had gone up to bed in her room in the bridal suite. Had a sitter with her for the rest of the night, before the three Bartholomews embarked on their month-long family-moon.

And Iris had… Scott. Leaning against him as they danced along with a dozen other couples, she wanted so badly to lose herself and be a woman who believed in happily-ever-after. Who had the capacity to love forever. Just for a little while.

Until she could get back behind the camera lens through which she viewed life. Saw beautiful things. And found deep emotion.

As the only two in the wedding party without dates, Scott and Iris had been dancing partners for the past couple of hours.

She hadn't had a horrible time.

"The crowd is thinning," Scott's voice sounded just above her ear. "Shouldn't be too much longer."

She nodded. Glad to be almost done. And yet, oddly reluctant at the thought of going up to her room alone. "You want to go outside for a few?" she asked him. The fresh air would do her good. Being on the beach, even a public one, was the panacea for pretty much all her pains.

Taking off her shoes, she felt easier inside as her toes slid into the sand.

The only thing that would make the moment better would be having Morgan and Angel with them. Scott's corgi and her miniature collie.

Come to think of it…as they walked…a few inches between them as always…she said, "I think this is the first time we've been on a beach without the girls."

Or on any beach together that wasn't the mile-long private stretch on Ocean Breeze, where they both lived.

"I'm sure they'll let us know about it tomorrow." Scott's chuckle sounded different, somehow. Familiar, and yet new. Because of the waves?

They sounded different, too. More open. As opposed to their beach that was protected on both sides by large walls of mountain rock.

She felt sorry for Scott, who couldn't as easily find the same solace as her, strapped up as he was in dress socks and patent leather dress shoes.

"You feeling better?" she asked him.

They walked as always, staring ahead. Around. Not at each other.

"Are you?" His question unsettled her again.

Sent her back to a place she didn't want to be.

"I'm fine," she told him, purposely lightening her tone, almost as though she was talking to Leigh.

"You weren't."

Scott's strange tone had her looking up at him as she walked. He was watching her, too. Not something they did. She didn't stop it, though.

Instead, she said, "I…don't…believe in love lasting forever." And wasn't sorry that she'd done so. She had a strong feeling she was with a like mind. Other than Sage, Leigh, Gray and Iris, Scott's relationships were all casual.

As were hers.

"Why not?"

She snapped her gaze from his, looking out at the ocean. Hadn't anticipated the question. Should have. "Do you?"

she verbally sidestepped. Leading them back to their long-established comfortable territory.

"I do." Scott's answer shocked her to the point of staring back at him again. Was he kidding?

Kidding himself?

Because of the wedding? The deeply felt promises they'd just witnessed Sage and Gray make?

"Seriously?" she asked him, stopping to sit on a bench facing the ocean. Keeping her gaze focused on the one thing she did count on. Those waves. Flowing in and out. Receding. But always, always coming back in again.

He sat down beside her, and she was glad. She hadn't been sure he would. And yet, she felt uncomfortable about even that much vulnerability—needing him outside their established parameters. Even for a minute.

"I do," he told her, also staring out toward ship lights bobbing in the distance. A few other hotel guests shared the beach with them. From a distance.

"You looking for it for yourself?" she asked then. And waited for his answer as though it somehow defined her.

"Nope."

Relief flooded through her. She hadn't lost her like mind. And knowing that, she was suddenly curious. Both Scott and Sage had told Iris that Scott was divorced. Sage had made a comment or two about her own interpretations of what had gone wrong. About her less-than-stellar impression of Scott's ex-wife. But the conversations hadn't gone any further than that. Iris hadn't needed or wanted them to do so.

But sitting there in her own depths, struggling to get back to an even keel, she asked, "Why not?"

She just didn't believe. But couldn't imagine believing and not reaching.

"That kind of love takes a commitment and dedication that I don't excel at," he told her. Shocking her.

"You're kidding, right?"

His glance at her was long. She didn't want him seeing things inside her, but, again, didn't stop searching his gaze for what she didn't know.

"No." One word that seemed to carry many.

She wasn't sure what he was telling her. Or himself. But had something to tell him. "Sage? Leigh?" The man was as committed as they came.

And turned his gaze back out to sea as he said, "I didn't say I don't love. I do. Which is how I know it exists. And I know that I'm good at it when I don't have someone at home counting on me to be their first and always."

First and *always*. Two words she'd heard in the promises Sage and Gray had made to each other. He'd been Sage's first love. And was her always.

But the way Scott said the words...as though he was as bereft as she'd once been...

Her hand moved, finding his, threading their fingers together.

It wasn't like they hadn't touched before. They'd walked the aisle together, arm in arm. Twice during rehearsal. Twice that night.

And had been holding each other all night on the dance floor.

So why did her fingers holding his suddenly seem like so much more than any of that?

The night was calling for more.

The night. Not life.

Looking at him, watching him study her, she said, "Just so you know, you're the first person I look for on the beach when I get home. And I'm always happy to see you." Truth.

It seemed important in that moment to offer it to him.

He watched her lips as she spoke.

And she couldn't tear her gaze from his as he said, "I'm always happy to see you, too." She watched as he leaned closer to her.

Knew the second his lips were going to touch hers.

Had to know what would happen when they did.

And didn't recognize the sensation that shot through her.

At all.

Chapter Two

For a second, the fire in his groin was all he knew. Then his mouth opened, his tongue met Iris's...

Scott jerked away. Stood up. All in the same move.

Iris must have done the same. She was on her feet. A yard away from him. Eyes wide. Staring at him.

With horror? Shock?

There was definitely no pleasure there.

Nor was he feeling any himself.

Panic consumed him. The women he kissed were separate and apart from his life. Mutually casual encounters, mostly. Except for Sheila. A widowed FBI agent who hit him up sometimes when she was in town.

Or had until he'd realized that she was beginning to look to him for more than just the friendly, enjoyable sex they'd agreed upon. He'd called her on it. She'd broken things off with him and he hadn't heard from her since.

He wasn't sorry about that.

"I'm sorry, Iris," he blurted, standing there in his tux feeling like a randy teenager who'd stolen a kiss and was about to get slapped. "I don't know why I just did that. I swear to you, I don't think of you that way..."

Shut up!

His usual talent for articulation seemed to have evaporated.

She took a step back. To the side. Seemed to be focused on his nose. "I'm sorry, too."

Wait. Why was she apologizing?

She didn't appear at all affronted, accosted or defensive. Just seemed...about as uncomfortable as he was.

"We don't do this," he said then, to be clear.

She looked him in the eye. "No, we don't," she said, her tone unequivocal.

And the prosecutor in him had to tell the story to the court. To get it officially established. "It was a strange-as-hell day. The wedding. All the kissing. We've been thrown together as a couple. Neither of us had dates. And...it's Sage. She was one of us, and now...she's not."

One of the single-for-life residents on Ocean Breeze. There weren't all that many of them. There had been three. Only two left.

"Yes, that's all it was." Iris was nodding. Vigorously. To the point that, for a second there, Scott was put out. His ego taking a hit that she found the idea of sex with him so abhorrent.

Until his brain kicked in and relief soon followed.

Iris took another step back, then, looking straight at him, said, "I value you more than just about anyone else on earth."

Mixed signals! Stepping back. But confessing...what? Iris had feelings for him?

Panic returned, in triplicate. Attacking his mind. His body. His emotions. Consuming him.

"Sex isn't something I can offer, Scott. But the thought of losing your friendship scares me even more..."

Wait. What? She didn't want sex, but she'd be willing to have it to keep his friendship? Scott's body came out of panic mode first. Appreciating the gorgeous woman with her long auburn hair loose and curling around her shoulders, those vivid green eyes and a body to die for.

His heart followed next. She didn't want sex. She did want *them*.

And his mind skidded in. "Our friendship means the world to me, too," he said. Taking a step closer to her. Meeting her eye to eye. "Seriously, Iris. You, us…as we've been these past three years…it's all I *can* do. It's the only way I can have someone to come home to." The words came out without forethought. Or even fore-realization.

And rang so true, he couldn't look away from her.

She nodded. Smiled. And as he started to breathe again, she said, "I come home to you, too."

His face split into a huge grin.

It was almost like they'd just done their version of a wedding.

"So we're good?" he asked.

She nodded toward the bench as she spoke. "As long as we don't do that again, we sure are."

"Deal." He held out his hand.

She took it.

They shook.

And headed in their own directions as they walked back inside. The bride and groom had left. Iris had end-of-the-night bridesmaid chores.

He had to take care of the final bar tab. Added a drink to it, and sat there, consuming slowly. Until he saw Iris get on the elevator.

Then, leaving his half-empty glass sitting there, Scott paid the tab.

And took the stairs.

Iris didn't sleep well. The first time she awoke, her body was thrumming with desire and her drowsy mind floated with seemingly real-time images of Scott Martin. In swim trunks. All muscles honed as he rode in on a surfboard, landed just inches from her and grabbed her up in a full-tongue kiss.

Shaking away the impossible dream—Scott had taken every surfing lesson known to man and just couldn't stay up on the board long enough to ride one wave—she rolled over, hugged the bed's second pillow to her and put herself back to sleep.

As she'd learned in rehab so long ago. Deep, even breathing. Relax one muscle at a time. Have an innocuous mental conversation that interested her and felt good.

That night she chose to talk to Leigh about spending the night at her place. Telling her what games they'd play. Seeing Leigh's sweet features, hearing her lispy replies. The little girl usually shared Iris's bed when they did slumber parties...

Iris didn't want to spend the night. The other girls were asleep. She heard someone arguing. Wanted to go home. The phone was in the hall. She'd wake everyone up. Worse, she'd bring the angry voices closer. Arms the same size as hers reached over. Pulling her close...

"Huhhhh!" With a gasp Iris shot straight up in bed. Heart pounding, she threw back the covers and stood. Walked slowly, concentrated on the benign. Got to the door leading to her hotel room's balcony. Made it outside and took her first full, deep, relaxing breath as she stared at the ocean. Sat down.

And slowly returned to herself. Thought about the day ahead. The photography session she'd booked—individual graduation photos of all the dogs completing a memory unit visitation program. Service canines who'd be out in San Diego's mostly senior living facilities as early as next week.

She was fine.

Good.

Knew the ropes.

But...damn. She'd thought herself through with it all. Hadn't had an episode in years.

Had long since stopped being swamped by waves of emotion.

Until Sage had promised Gray forever.

And even that didn't make sense. All the weddings Iris photographed...almost all of them had vows making promises neither party could realistically keep.

Not without knowing what the future held. How things changed.

So...the sun would be up soon. She was a little earlier than she'd figured but jumped in the shower. Best to get on with the day. Check out before everyone else.

Be gone from the wedding venue by the time others came downstairs.

She'd thought about attending the impromptu breakfast one of the bridesmaids had been informally planning the night before. But she hadn't confirmed her presence.

So she felt no guilt as she wheeled her bag out to her car, loaded up and drove off.

She'd had a brief relapse.

Which explained the way she'd participated in that kiss the night before, too. Leaning in. Opening her mouth.

Feeling.

Heightened emotions were a symptom of suffering a tragedy that her psyche had been unable to accept.

She'd recovered. As completely as one could.

But there'd always be a part of her that was broken.

She hadn't lost her memory.

She'd just lost her twin.

Iris wasn't at breakfast. Scott hadn't gone, either. Had, in fact, specifically chosen not to do so knowing that Iris would be there.

But as he checked out, he saw the group in the restaurant, in a back corner. Very clearly missing any sign of amber hair.

And was bothered that she'd chosen to skip the breakfast. Seeing it as a sign that things weren't right between them. That she was avoiding him.

Contradictory to the extreme, considering his own lack of attendance.

Realizing that his worrying over the nonissue of the kiss the night before could create a problem where there wasn't one, Scott went home. Collected Morgan from the dog sitter a few cottages down, took the corgi for a long run. Then pulled on a wet suit and took his surfboard out for some January practice. Managed to stay on long enough for the wave to actually catch the board before torpedoing into the water. And called it a win.

You couldn't fail at a skill you'd never learned.

And you couldn't fail to learn if you were still in the process of learning.

He'd worked that one out years before. While his father was still alive and asking him why he continued to pursue a sport that clearly wasn't suited to him.

As always, taking the board out renewed his confidence in his own inner strength, determination and endurance, and he was fully back to himself by the time he took Morgan out for her Sunday-afternoon socialization. Iris wouldn't be out yet. She had a photo shoot.

But he and Morgan saw Angel. The miniature collie was

still with the girls' sitter from the night before and Morgan greeted the smaller dog as though they'd been apart for years. Laughing, Scott offered to keep Angel with him and Morgan until Iris got home. Something he and Iris had each done many times over the years.

The three of them, him and the girls, ran a couple of miles and then stopped to have a beer with Dale, who was out with Juice. The bearded writer was one of Morgan's favorite people, and Scott's, too, outside Sage, Leigh and Iris.

Dale had helped Gray start up a water rescue course for service dogs—classes that were on hiatus only long enough for Gray to family-moon. Gray used Juice to demonstrate many of the exercises.

Everyone on the beach knew that Juice was Dale's very dedicated, personal service dog. As far as Scott was aware, no one knew why the athletic man needed one.

Scott had never asked. He didn't like questions coming at him in return. So he didn't pry.

Other than missing little Leigh, and Sage and Gray, too, the sunny, midsixties Sunday afternoon was nice. Bordering on great.

And, as Iris's auburn hair showed up in the distance, her tall, lean body distinguishable among others out enjoying the day, Scott saw the day as being exactly what he wanted out of life.

She'd come home from work and headed to the beach. Just like always.

She wasn't avoiding him.

Having finished his beer, he stood as Iris drew closer. "She doesn't know I confiscated Angel," he said as he clicked his fingers to the two dogs who'd been lying by Juice. Thanking Dale for the beer, he headed off toward the friend who, he'd just found out the night before, looked for him first on the beach every night, and who was always glad to see him.

He was even happier than usual to see her, too.

So she hadn't made it to breakfast. Hadn't been in touch all day. Neither had he been. That wasn't their usual way.

Wasn't his way with anyone except Sage. When situations called for it.

Angel saw Iris while the twenty-eight-year-old gifted photographer was still thirty yards away. Took off toward her. With Morgan right on her heels, of course.

Filled with relief, Scott continued at his own, casual pace. Reached Iris when she was still bending down, greeting the girls as though they'd been apart for weeks instead of just overnight, Scott let her voice wash over him. Appreciating the familiarity, aware of Iris's value to him, more than ever before.

Because of the near loss of what they'd had.

And not at all to do with the memory of her lips responding to his.

When she stood, he fell into step beside her. Just as he did every other night that they were both at home in time to let the dogs run on the beach. Didn't matter that Morgan and Angel had already had all the exercise they needed.

It was what they did. Walked. Talked.

Before heading home alone for dinner or whatever else the evening had to bring them separately.

"How'd the shoot go?" he asked when she failed to immediately fall into step. He was watching the dogs. Something they both did often. Checking himself to make certain that he didn't do or say anything out of the ordinary.

"Fine." One word. Where normally there'd have been paragraphs. Pages even.

"Did everyone graduate?" he asked. She'd been worried about a golden retriever who seemed a bit too shy to take on rooms of strangers in any kind of serviceable way.

Finally starting up the beach with him, after seconds of hesitation that had seemed to stretch into agonizing minutes, she said, "All but Sissy." The golden. "She didn't show up today. I'm guessing her owner realized that it's not fair to Sissy to try to make her into something she is not."

A very clear message seemed to ring there. He couldn't tell if it was her tone as she said the words. The words themselves.

Or his own hypersensitivity to doing all he could to make sure the encounter went perfectly.

Did she think he wanted more from her?

Or that he thought she wanted more from him?

Not sure how to answer, but feeling as though she'd thrown a rope that would tie them up if he couldn't grab it, he said, "That's about the cruelest thing you can do to a person. Expect them to be different than they are. Or to have talents they don't have. Rather than encouraging them in the talents they do have."

He might not be husband, or life companion, material, but he had a lot of good things to offer. She'd said so herself. The night before. He showed up whenever he could. Didn't put expectations on his friendship. Supported wherever he could.

Of course, they'd been talking about dogs, Sissy in particular, not people.

Not him.

Or her.

She'd been heading down the beach from her place to his and so he'd continued walking that way. Slowing his pace when she barely kept up. Scrambling for the right thing to say.

To draw her out.

Not sure what it was.

Was she avoiding him?

Afraid he'd already screwed things up with his people's-expectations analogy, he ended up saying nothing.

And the dogs, as though sensing that something wasn't right in the air around them, or within their owners, didn't offer any distraction, either. No chasing each other, or anything else. They just walked, Morgan beside Scott, Angel right at Iris's heel.

Scott tried to tell himself that was okay. Tried to remember if he and Iris walked in silence sometimes. Was still on the silent mental subject when she stopped in the sand.

"It's been a long weekend, and I've still got pictures to go through for a meeting in the morning so I'm going to head back," she said, bending down to ruffle Angel's ears.

She was avoiding him.

"Sounds good," Scott told her. "It was a long one. See ya later."

With a click of his finger, he headed up toward the row of cottages, glad to see that Morgan was right beside him.

No embarrassing need to turn around and coax his housemate to stick by him.

But nothing to distract him from the words he'd left in the air behind him, either.

Not his usual *enjoy your evening*, or *sleep well* or even *have a good night*.

See ya later?

What in the hell was that?

It was not good.

That's what it was.

Just not good.

Chapter Three

Iris spent Sunday night lost in her photography. Sinking into a pair of deep brown eyes, surrounded by rings of brown fur in a bed of white that segued back to brown for the ears, she could almost forget the way Scott's blue eyes had clouded just before he'd responded to her comment about Sissy. An introverted dog who was sweet, loving, loyal, eager to please and just not suited to public service.

That's about the cruelest thing you can do to a person. Expect them to be different than they are.

She hadn't been talking about people.

But he'd somehow thought she'd been referring to him. His comment had been so pointed, sounding emotionally driven, almost defensive.

Because of the damned kiss. A friendly peck he'd delivered at the end of a lovely, romantic, highly emotional and somewhat tough day. She'd responded like a lovesick schoolgirl.

Giving Scott a hugely wrong impression.

Working on the sky behind Lacey, the beautiful girl on the large monitor in front of her, Iris played with tinges of color, needing a softer tone to fully complement the warm soul of the King Cavalier. To make clear to the viewers the things Lacey had seemed to be saying to her as the canine had gazed into Iris's lens that afternoon.

Maybe she could capture a photo of her own essence. Mail it to Scott. And transport them back to reality. Prekiss.

Because nothing had changed. Would ever change. *Could* ever change. She couldn't promise to love and cherish, or to be someone's everything for always. She'd done that once. And knew that life didn't work that way. You got the present. The moment.

Nothing more. To pretend otherwise was life crushing. Permanently debilitating.

Not that she and Scott needed to get into all that. The fact that they were able to fill voids *without* getting into it was what made them work.

She'd found her own happily-ever-after. The one that was meant for her, that suited her, in walks on the beach. A friendly face and voice that was just there. Not waiting for her. Or expecting anything from her. But always welcoming her when she arrived.

And had assumed that Scott had found the same in her.

It wasn't forever. That was a given.

But why lose it, if they didn't have to yet?

They'd gone to a wedding. Been caught in some moments swirling with intense emotions. And then they'd left.

Sage's wedding was a memory. Not a life changer.

Lacey's gaze made everything so clear.

Because dogs didn't bother with the vagaries of life. They lived in the moment. The only reality. Giving their best, accepting what bounties were given to them and moving to the next minute in which they did it again. All without questioning why. Or worrying about what came next.

Iris slept better that night, and, as usual, took Angel out for her walk on the beach the next day when she got home from an afternoon wandering the streets of San Diego, catching great everyday moments, as part of a job she was doing for the city's public relations department.

And tried to tell herself that she was fine when Scott didn't show up for their after-work sojourn.

Scott saw Iris on the beach. Purposely didn't go out.

He'd had a long day in court—preliminary court hearings for a high-profile trial that was due to start the next week. He was prosecuting a woman for attempted murder after she'd sued her decorated-colonel husband for emotional distress, lost, in spite of the reams of proof of neglect that she had, was consequently sued for divorce and then hired someone to kill him before the divorce was final.

She had a team of high-priced attorneys attempting to bring in the previous civil case, with various arguments, all of which took a lot of research into former case files he could use as precedent to keep the evidence out of his trial.

He'd won some. Not all.

But the biggest loss wasn't work related. Waiting until after dark to walk the beach left him and Morgan completely alone out there.

Without…anyone.

Granted, darkness fell early in winter months. Before six. He'd barely made it home before the sunset. Dale, Harper, some of the occupants of other cottages on the beach, weren't even home yet. They'd all be out yet that night.

And it wasn't any of the others he was missing.

It was Iris. Who he'd purposely avoided.

She'd let him. *No expectations* kind of required that. There were no strings attached.

Morgan, trotting beside him, stopped to do her business as usual. In his shorts, tennis shoes and long-sleeved pull-over, he picked up after her as usual, too. Lobbed the bag into one of the disposal bins installed along the beach just for that purpose. His girl watched, looking to him for her entertainment since he'd robbed her of playtime with her best friend. She didn't seem to mind.

But then, she was a bit of a minimalist. Just happy to be. Grateful to have a human come home. To have food and water. She didn't waste a lot of time worrying about things she couldn't control.

Scott tried to learn by her example. Walked with her. Ran with her some. And didn't feel any better at all.

The emptiness inside him was his fault. His mistake to fix.

Because there was every possibility his actions had affected someone else, too. He'd made no promise to be out on the beach that night. Or any night.

Wouldn't make one.

But to deliberately stay away…that wasn't right, either. Not without some kind of understanding so that she didn't blame herself.

It was that thought, the possibility that Iris could be suffering due to his choice to let that damned kiss come between them when they'd both promised it wouldn't, that drove him to head over one more cottage after checking on his and Sage's old place.

His sister had put it up for sale. She lived half a mile down the beach now, in the cottage Gray had bought and had renovated. There'd been a showing at Sage's that day. Scott had stopped to check that all the lights had been turned off, and to grab the showing realtor's card, which had been left, as was protocol, on the kitchen counter.

Not sure whether or not he'd knock on Iris's back door—while he'd done it several times in the three years they'd been buds, it wasn't their normal way—he was at least spared that decision when Angel came running down from the cottage toward them, her paws throwing sand up behind her in her eagerness.

Bending down to greet the girl, he saw Iris's tennis shoes in the sand before standing again.

"Late day at work?" she asked.

"A hard one," he told her back, diving into a more detailed account of the day than he might ordinarily have given.

Buying himself time.

He had to fix things between them.

Knew how to do it, too. Prove motive.

He just wasn't eager to go there.

Not with her.

Not with anyone.

Ever again.

Iris hated how pubescently eager she felt, standing on the beach with Scott. She wanted to believe she hadn't been watching for him. That she'd had legitimate reason to visit her kitchen, to glance out the window, four times since she'd come in.

But she'd learned that the only way to mental and emotional health—for her at least—was self-honesty.

She wasn't looking for promises of a future with Scott Martin. Or anyone. But she hoped their moments in the sand weren't done yet.

They'd said they looked for each other first when they came out at night. And were always glad to see each other.

And to that end, she needed to do what she could to put things right between them. If that meant listening to legal technicalities with which she wasn't all that familiar—verbiage he'd never used with her before—then she'd stand there and listen.

She was an intelligent woman. Got the gist of what he was saying. Just wasn't sure why he seemed to be quoting law textbooks rather than just talking to her.

And, hoping it wasn't denoting a change in them, asked, "This case, is it bothering you more than most for some reason?"

Her job as close friend, as listening ear, was to hear what was said. And what wasn't, too.

His shrug wasn't clear to her. Was that a yes or a no?

He started to walk. As Morgan and Angel joined in, she fell in beside them. Trying to home in on the sliver of life bouncing in the moon's beam on the waves enough to distract her from the tension suddenly tightening her insides.

"She's guilty as hell." Scott's words, as lethal as they were, calmed her.

It had been a yes. It was the case bothering him.

Not her.

Or their weird sojourn at the wedding on Saturday.

"I'm going to put her away for attempted murder without the least bit of regret for doing so. She made a horrible decision, knowingly, with forethought, intricate planning. Interviewed hitmen. Jumped through hoops to pay him without a trace. The actions were clearly deliberate. And wholly wrong. Illegal on many counts."

Iris nodded.

And waited.

There was a *but* there. She could hear it.

Felt invested in it.

Because he was. And she was his friend.

"But it all comes down to motive." Scott was always

about the motive. The reason that made the crime believable to a jury. He found it. And he won his cases.

"She wanted him dead. That one's pretty clear," Iris said, putting her hands in the pockets of the leggings she'd worn that day.

"It's *why* she wanted him dead."

Invigorated by the conversation, the fact that they were *them* again, she said, "Doesn't matter. Her motive was clearly murder for hire. Those are the only charges you have to prove. You've got her dead to rights there."

"The defense is trying to prove that she wasn't in her right mind when she made those choices."

Seemed pretty cut-and-dried to her. And Iris frowned. Wondering what she'd missed. Hating that she was still allowing worry about them to interrupt their getting back to normal. "They had to come up with something. What else was there?"

When he didn't answer she said, "It's a common defense, right? I've heard you mention it many times."

He nodded but was looking down. Not at the dogs. Not out at the darkened beach lit only by cottage porch lights. The waves, or at her. Which would have been his usual. His feet seemed to be holding his interest.

"She...went through a rough patch. Ended up in counseling. On antidepressants for a while—"

"A lot of people struggle at different points in their lives," Iris shot back. Interrupting him. Suffering, being on medication to regulate emotions, was absolutely not any indication of one being out of their right mind, nor did it serve as permission to commit murder.

If it had been...

Just...no.

"She lost her job. And then a second one. Crying in class.

Having panic attacks. As an elementary schoolteacher, that pretty much tanked her career. Developed a type of waking coma where she'd stop talking in the middle of a conversation and just stare into space, sometimes for five minutes or more, not remembering what she was talking about when she came to. Her pysche's way of checking out because she couldn't cope…"

That time when he paused, Iris didn't say a word. Scott was struggling. And had come down the beach to her.

Nothing else mattered.

"Her psychiatric staff finally determined that it was all caused by her high-profile, hugely visible husband being neglectful of her. He worked ungodly hours. Didn't call. Missing appointments. Social engagements with her friends and family. Had at least one affair. But wouldn't divorce her because of his image. Due to the prenuptial agreement, if she sued him for divorce, she lost everything. So she sued him for emotional distress."

Oh, God. "And that's the case her lawyers are bringing in."

"Yes."

She had no words of wisdom. Or even of encouragement. Except, "You aren't God, Scott. You're an officer of the court. Only one part of the vast legal system. You do your job to the best of your ability, and the rest…the outcome… You have to trust the system to make the final choice."

He nodded. "I know," he said then, sounding as though he had no problem with that aspect of the situation.

So, what was his struggle?

When he stopped walking, turned to her, she had a feeling she was about to find out.

And suddenly wasn't sure she wanted to know.

"Motive is everything, Iris," he said, looking her straight

in the eye, and while he wasn't touching her, it felt as though he was. He wasn't telling her anything she didn't already know about him, though. She stayed silent until she knew where he was going with the conversation.

"I screwed things up between us the other night. Kissing you. It has to go away."

Her heart sank. But she rallied. "It already has."

"Yeah, that was über-obvious last night." His words didn't need to drip with sarcasm for her to get his point. The tone just made the hit a little sharper.

"And tonight," he said then, surprising her. She'd been out as normal. He'd been late getting home, but had come down the beach, just in case. Them. Completely.

"I saw you out. I stayed in." His words hit her like a death sentence.

"I need us to be what we were," he said then, still looking right at her.

Angel's front paws hit her legs right before the small, cold and wet nose nudged the inside of her palm. Iris petted the top of her girl's head but didn't take her gaze from Scott's. "I do, too," she told him.

"Yet...we're failing."

Death, all right.

"I think that if you understand my motive for needing to keep things platonic and unencumbered between us, then you'll be able to trust that when I say what happened the other night won't happen again. It won't."

"I do trust you."

Mostly. It was herself she was struggling with. The way she'd reacted the other night...she'd never ever have believed she'd react that way. Had never felt like that before. So, if Scott did get close to kissing her again, could she trust herself not to respond?

Or even invite the gesture?

His look, even in the darkness, was clear. They had a problem. It had to be fixed.

Motive was his solution.

Except that…she couldn't give hers. No way was she opening up the box she'd closed. Not even for Scott. She'd moved. Reinvented herself.

"Other than the affair, I was that guy."

For a second, she let the sound of the waves carry his words away. But they repeated, clearly, in her mind.

Frowning, Iris took a step back, but continued to watch Scott. "I don't understand."

"My divorce," he said as though that explained everything.

"You want me to believe that you had a prenuptial agreement that stipulated that your wife lost everything if you divorced?" She paused, and when he just watched her, she went with the thought and said, "If you brought the money into the marriage, and she agreed to the prenup…"

Iris stopped midsentence. The prenup would be no motive for Scott's unwillingness to take on a life companion— other than Morgan. Who was happy to sleep all day, without contact. To be fed by others when Scott couldn't be there.

"You neglected her," she said then, as things started to make a little bit of sense. The other night, he'd said that he wasn't good at being someone's everything.

"I'm married to my work," he told her. "I have no shut-off valve. As a matter of fact, trying to rein in would make me tense, irritable and not at all the healthy guy who stands before you."

The last was clearly tongue-in-cheek. An attempt to lighten the moment.

Iris let it pass. Studied him without a hint of a smile. Hurting for him.

And oddly, for her, too. Which made no sense.

"It's who I am, Iris. I have to give one hundred percent, which means I can only have one priority."

Unless his wife was equally committed to her job. Like, say, a photographer who could only live a healthy life through her lens?

The thought came. Scared the liver out of her. Until she realized she'd just been playing devil's advocate. For his sake.

Scott had too much to give to sign his entire future away. Unlike her, he still believed in love's happily-ever-after.

"She was unhappy and the solution you two came up with was divorce?" she asked him then. Trying to find the other side. A way to show him he could be wrong.

"I called her one night to tell her that I wouldn't be coming home again, that I was spending one more night on the couch in my office."

"And she gave you an ultimatum?" She got it. Completely. Everyone had their breaking point. But not everyone shared the same one.

"She told me that she wasn't there, either. She'd moved out the day before."

He hadn't sensed his wife's withdrawal? Hadn't noticed bank charges for a moving van? Packing? A down payment on a new place to live? Hadn't seen the millions of tears that had to have fallen before it got to that point? Or heard the desperation in conversation?

"To show you the extent of my neglect, I was completely shocked. I was served divorce papers the next day, and I'd had no idea my marriage was even in trouble."

Because he hadn't been there. Physically, or mentally, either.

Iris finally got it. Needing time alone to digest the pit in her stomach. The pain she felt for him.

She nodded, shrugged and, keeping her tone light, asked, "So, now that we've established that there's no risk of us suddenly falling madly in love, are we okay?"

Scott's smile distracted her from the darkness. Lit her up. "We are," he told her.

And she wanted to believe him.

Chapter Four

He wanted her.

Badly.

In his office on Tuesday, writing an argument that, depending on the judge's ruling, could make or break his case, Scott caught himself staring at the computer screen. Hands still on the keyboard.

Thinking about Iris's comments about the case when he'd shared it with her the night before. She'd been fully engaged. Hearing not only the facts, but the nuances, too.

Her motive was clearly murder for hire. Those are the only charges you have to prove.

Polly Ernst's emotional distress had already been litigated. She'd lost. Scott typed. If she'd won the previous case, perhaps the evidence brought by her psychiatric team could be admitted for the current case, but trying to prove that a suspect was not guilty due to a mental state that had not been deemed duress in civil court was egregious. The accused was clearly distressed. Upset. Lividly angry. That didn't give her a free pass to take another life.

That fact was a basis of the entire justice system.

You aren't God, Scott... You have to trust the system to make the final choice.

Right, but the system relied on his ability to do his job.

No matter how strongly Scott felt the sting of prosecuting a woman whose husband had committed the same moral crime as Scott, he had to stick with the prosecutable facts.

He'd married a woman, promised to be her partner and then deserted her, chaining her to an empty, lonely life. And she'd left him. No matter how angry she'd been, how hurt, how much she'd probably hated him, she hadn't tried to murder him.

And he couldn't let a personal issue interfere with his duty to provide justice.

He was staring at his screen again. Knew his argument was strong. Solid.

And the rest...

His brief was done.

Iris was still there. Taking up mental space in his office.

His way forward, to be accountable for the distress he'd caused, was to avoid future failure.

A process he'd set in motion the night before.

"So, now that we've established that there's no risk of us suddenly falling madly in love, are we okay?" she'd asked.

They were.

He'd smiled.

So had she. His mind conjured up the image of her grin the night before.

Which led his inner gaze to her lips.

And his body jumped on board.

Big-time.

There were women who could help with that. He had no shortage of date prospects.

The idea didn't appeal at the moment.

Felt sleazy.

His body concurred.

And all was well.

* * *

Driving across the bridge from San Diego to Coronado Island on Wednesday, Iris couldn't help but smile. Blue skies and sunshine above, waves beneath her for the two-mile-long stretch and memory of time on the beach with Scott the night before.

Scott as he'd always been.

Charming. Caring. Engaged. There.

And not at all weird.

He'd finished his brief. The judge had ruled in his favor. Iris had shown him the photos she'd taken that day—a series of dogs up for adoption—and he'd been so moved by the portrayal, he'd emailed one to a woman he knew in his office who'd already put in for adoption.

He'd said that she'd caught the sweet boy at just the right moment, somehow depicting his longing to be loved.

Probably because her heart lived behind her lens, not that she told him so. It wasn't *them* conversation and there was no way she was going to risk a relapse.

She'd fought too long and hard to find an acceptable level of happiness without her other half in the world.

She was still smiling as she walked out onto the beach, cameras and lighting in cases on her back, and set up for the day-long shoot of Navy SEALs in training. Photos that had been commissioned for a brochure.

Some would be staged. And she'd be doing live shots of actual training, too.

She'd done her research. Knew what to expect. Was completely professional as she homed in on taut muscle in action, on bodies in superb shape, seemingly indefatigable as they ran on the beach carrying heavy rubber boats above their heads, did sit-ups, rowing, surfing boats onto rocks, underwater training and grinned at her when they were posing for hunk shots.

But that night, as Angel bounded ahead of her out the door and down the beach toward the water, as she caught her first sight of Scott jogging up the beach toward them, all she could think about were his muscles.

The perfectly toned, tall, lithe body coming toward her.

The swelling she'd noticed in his dress pants when he'd first stood up off the bench on a different beach four nights before.

She'd looked away.

He'd covered it, quickly, buttoning the jacket of his tux.

And there the image was, in her mind's eye.

She blinked it away.

It came back.

She blinked again. And found herself in a loop where she couldn't stop thinking about it because she was thinking about not thinking about it.

While she was busy trying to escape, her body lived in the moment. Reacting to a previous hard-on from the man running toward her.

Her nipples were hard and she was wet by the time he reached her. Crossing her arms, she nodded at Scott, and then almost immediately dropped to the ground to greet Morgan. The corgi's enthusiastic greeting knocked her to her butt and Iris stayed there, loving on both dogs, letting them pounce on her, laughing.

Grateful for the distraction, she was still smiling when Scott offered a hand down to her to help her up. She took it automatically, swung up and stood there, inches from his face. Staring at him eye to eye.

For too long.

Neither of them could pretend it hadn't happened.

But they tried. He dropped her hand as though he'd been burnt. She turned down the beach. Toward his place. Which took them to Sage's old cottage next door to Iris. And she latched on. Asked if there'd been any more showings since Monday. If there'd been any offers.

He answered in a kind tone. But succinctly. As though his thoughts were elsewhere.

The dogs had raced down to see Dale's Juice.

"It's really strange, not having Sage here," Iris blurted. Needing desperately to make whatever was happening to her where Scott was concerned just go away. "And Leigh."

That was it. Most days when she and Scott were together, Leigh spent time with them, too. Not the entire time. They always had the chance for their adult conversation. But they never knew when they'd be interrupted.

And with Sage… Scott's sister had been the supreme chaperone. At least where Iris was concerned. No way she wanted her friend to think she was developing feelings for her twin brother. Because when Sage discovered that those feelings only went skin-deep, Iris could lose one of the most important females in her life.

Or both of them, if she lost Leigh, too.

"I had no idea how much seeing Leigh lightened my days," Scott said as they walked at their normal pace. With maybe a few more inches than usual between them. "The beach is too quiet without her."

The elephant was there. On the sand in between them. In front of them. Beside them. Behind them. "That's all this is," she blurted. "Our daily routines have been disrupted. It's kind of like being alone together on a desert island out here…"

No. Wrong words. The image they created had to be

crushed. Quickly. Islands. Coronado. A day behind her lens filled with testosterone overload.

"I like that." Scott's words ricocheted through her. Sharply. Leaving vibrations in all her womanly places. And then he added, "There's nothing different about the two of us. It's the lack of the rest of our immediate gang that's plaguing us. Take away the sister, the best friend, the kid…and you've got…"

He stopped.

Neither of them needed to hear what was left. They both knew.

She kicked up sand with her tennis shoe. Watching the dogs. Looking for Dale, but not finding him, she did what she'd learned to do to save her life. Faced the challenge head-on. "You're still feeling it, too, huh?"

Harper, Scott's next-door neighbor, was out with Cassie, the pediatrician who'd just gotten married to a professor from the university. They'd been jogging together lately and were a good half mile away from their places.

Most of the other cottages were still closed up, their owners not yet home from work.

There was no one to save them.

Except themselves…

Scott hadn't answered.

"It's not going to do any good to bury it," she said, irked that he wouldn't admit that he had the hots for her.

Unless…was it just her, still feeling that way?

"It's better than talking about it," he said, his tone unusually somber. Hard to hear above the sound of the waves. Better that way. To be on the edge of the words, rather than drowning in them.

Maybe he was right. Would any attraction between them suffocate if they didn't give it air to breathe?

Or would their friendship just slowly wither and die from the awkwardness?

She watched as Morgan and Juice raced Angel up to Dale's back porch in the distance. The writer must have come outside.

The hope that possibility gave her, as though rescue was just ahead, lightened her spirits some. Until she realized just how critically in trouble she and Scott were if they needed someone else around to save them.

"We're both attractive people," she said then, as though reason could provide a ladder out of the hole into which they'd fallen. "It's possible that the feelings were always available, simmering beneath the surface, but with all the distraction, just never had a chance to present themselves."

Until they'd been at the most romantic wedding of all time, maid of honor and best man, without dates.

Which didn't explain the nearly debilitating surge of emotion that had hit her right as Sage had been finishing her vows.

Could it be that something was happening within her? Her defenses weakening as she aged? Could she be having a relapse?

She'd been her normal self all day.

Other than the wedding—and the dream following it— she'd been fine for years. No point in making the issue bigger than it was.

She had the hots for her friend.

An ordinary physical irritation.

Period.

She wanted to talk about it. Fine.

"I've never been turned on by you before." There. In three years' time she hadn't done it for him once.

Then she had.

What more was there to say?

Except, "Have you…been attracted to me in the past?"

His body jumped to full alert as he waited for her reply.

"No."

Oh. Deflation had never been a pleasant experience.

But, good.

"So it's got to be just a reaction to the wedding finery," he said, his analytical mind coming up with motive for the recalcitrant, unwelcome reactions that seemed to suddenly be intent on plaguing them.

Were they really doing this? Walking on their beach, talking about his hard-on for her?

And the nipples he'd noticed tightened against her dress the other night.

She could have been cold.

He didn't think so.

Her response to his kiss certainly had not been.

It seemed as though he felt her nod as a physical brush against his chest as she said, "We *were* in completely different roles, with Sage and Gray pretty much nonexistent, as consumed as they'd been by the marriage, the rituals, all their guests…"

"And Leigh going upstairs with her babysitter…" Like a drowning man, he grabbed hold.

"And the three of them gone for so long… It's just residual. We know it's there. Acknowledge it. Have made the very mutual decision that it's not a right move for us—"

Feeling his body leap to attention with that, he jumped in, cutting her off. "As long as we do nothing, time, and Sage and Gray's return, will take care of the rest. You watch, a year from now, we'll be laughing over the whole thing."

He'd give his fortune to be able to laugh about it right then.

Instead, his only hope, at the moment, was an ice-cold shower. An hour-long one, minimum.

"Okay, good, we have a plan." Iris's words gave him a start. It was as though she'd just read his mind. Was agreeing to the cold shower.

Which had him immediately, mentally under the spray together.

"I'm sure I can keep my hands off you," she said, a slightly teasing note in her tone. One that was almost swallowed up by the near choking sound that came with it. "Can you keep yours off me?"

She'd issued a challenge.

Something she'd done many times over their years of hashing out life together. Challenging him to succeed at whatever goal he'd set out for himself in the moment.

From getting his deck stained to handling his first full weekend alone with his niece the time Sage and Iris had gone to Palm Springs for a girls' weekend of shopping and no responsibility.

She'd issued a challenge that left no room for failure.

Issued to a man who viewed failure as the kiss of death.

Which meant…she'd left him only one option.

Absolutely no kissing at all for him.

And he was good with that.

Mostly.

"I can if you can," he replied.

Because if she came on to him, all bets were off. He couldn't guarantee his ability to reject her.

Which told him he wouldn't.

And then they'd lose everything.

Chapter Five

Working from home Thursday, Iris tried to get lost in the three monitors that arced around her on her workspace. The week's output surrounded her from different angles as she edited. One photo at a time. Scrapping some attempts. And way more edits.

She couldn't seem to get anything right. Couldn't create anything that gave her the feeling she got when an image worked. Nothing was grabbing her. The internal guidance that normally led her choices was absent.

Once she'd acknowledged the anomaly, she put it down to having had an exceptionally good week, photographically speaking. Because her work had been saving her from the near relapse she'd had over the weekend. Of all the shots she'd kept, she'd managed to catch the image perfectly first time through. Nothing needed editing.

She almost believed herself for a minute or two.

No matter how good someone was at something, no one was perfect.

The photos were good enough. Likely she'd be the only one who'd see they were lacking at some point. But she couldn't turn in inferior work. Not and live with herself.

Her ability to publish pictures that spoke to viewers,

photographs that people remembered, was the one thing she counted on.

The part of her soul that had survived the ravage, speaking to the world in the only way it could.

When Angel nudged her forearm for the fourth time that morning, Iris finally got the point and left the desk. Grabbing her camera, she took Angel out to the beach. Caught the girl at every angle. Running. Sitting. Digging in the sand. Standing still as a wave came in and wet her paws. She caught sunshine on the water behind her housemate. Got a shot where Angel, with a slightly open mouth, was clearly smiling.

With every tap of her finger against the shutter button she released some of the panic that had been barreling her way.

And gained confidence from the steadiness of waves washing to shore. Backing off. And coming in once again.

Right up until Angel tore off down the beach in the direction of Scott's cottage and her stomach leaped, her heart rate picking up.

He wasn't home. Scott never came home at lunchtime. He had an arrangement with Dale to let Morgan out on weekdays.

Fact replaced reaction and she followed her girl down to say hello to Morgan. Waved to Dale, who was up on his porch with Juice. She filled with relief, while her mind reeled with implication.

Something was going on with her. More than just finding a friend attractive. It had started before that. When Sage said her vows.

Right after Iris had walked up the aisle in her formfitting dress, heels and professional makeup, with Scott's tuxed arm holding her hand against his side.

Before he'd left her at the altar to head back and walk his sister in.

Yeah, but Iris had been fine then.

Herself. For the most part. As much as she could be trussed up as she'd been.

The first time she'd ever been such.

Had that been it?

The fact that she used to dream about feeling beautiful, in fancy clothes, on the arm of a faceless handsome stranger.

Back when she was still naive enough to dream.

And suddenly found herself a part of an event, wearing them, in real life?

Made sense. Good sense.

And explained her completely out-of-character and damned weird reaction to Scott since, too.

Her psyche had been subconsciously thrust into an old fantasy.

It wasn't reality.

She really was fine.

After years of counseling, Iris knew what professionals were going to say before they said it. Had learned, from their teaching, to rely on self-analysis, and complete honesty, to keep herself mentally and emotionally healthy.

Back at home, fifteen minutes later, she grabbed her keys, and Angel, and with the sixteen-pound mini-Lassie tucked up under her arm, made her way out to the garage. She was headed north up the coast before thoughts of the past grew more prominent in her conscious mind.

She'd be turning off. There was no way she was ever going back.

But she had to take care of something.

A minute of looking deeply into herself, being truthful with what she saw there, and she knew what the problem was.

Her stepmother had moved from San Francisco to Fullerton the previous summer. Just an hour and a half away from San Diego.

Five weeks before Sage's wedding, Diane had sent a Christmas card to the post office box Iris used for her photography limited liability corporation. She'd sent Iris her new address. Telling her that it would mean very much to her if Iris would come see her.

And Iris had thrown it in the trash.

No way was Iris going to see the woman.

But she'd remembered the address.

Which meant she'd clearly been wrong to avoid the situation. To pretend the card hadn't been sent.

She'd drive by the house. See that everything looked fine in Diane's world. Know where she was so she could put the information in the mental address book that cataloged her past.

Which would free her up to get fully back into present life.

Where she didn't break down at weddings.

And where Scott Martin was a dear, wholly platonic friend. Held at arm's length. Just like everyone else in the life she'd reinvented.

For their sake, and hers.

Arm's length was all she could take.

And all she could give full out.

Scott didn't see Iris on Thursday. Her text came in just as he was heading in from the beach to get dinner for him and Morgan.

needed to drive almost to Anaheim back late not avoiding you

While the communication itself was odd—no expectations, no explanations—and hadn't ever happened before, he was glad she'd sent it.

Prevented any need to waste mental energy fighting with himself over the possibility that she'd been avoiding him.

He'd had a text from Sage, too. With pictures of the small but growing Bartholomew family at a world-renowned theme park for children in Europe. His twin's life had done a total 180 in just a few months' time. Sage was living the life she'd once dreamed she'd have.

Was making him an uncle for a second time.

He couldn't be happier for her. Would have given his life to make it happen, if that's what it had taken.

And there was a shadow side to everything.

His own life seemed a bit emptier at the moment. While his best friend and twin sister were on a family-moon with his niece, for sure. And afterward, too. He'd still be a big part of their lives. Would probably still even see them as often.

But he wasn't as…needed day to day as he'd been.

In the long run, that would be a good thing. It would give him back the freedom he'd had after his divorce. He could travel, explore, surf as much as he wanted without having to feel guilty about leaving Sage alone with Leigh.

Not that she'd ever wanted him to do so.

He just had.

Helping Sage out with Leigh had been the right thing to do.

He was glad he'd done it.

And would be glad to be unencumbered with familial

responsibility again, too. As soon as he had time to adjust to the changes.

They'd happened so rapidly, anyone would have had to take a moment to get used to the different landscape.

Case in point, the next afternoon as he left work. Fridays were always only half days in court, so it was the one day he generally left work early. The day he went down to Diego's, the fish market their housekeeper had always taken them to as kids. He didn't have to wait in line. Not only did the owners know him, but he had a standing order—a Friday-night spread for three of whatever the fresh catch of the day had been—which he'd cook up when he got home. If Sage and Leigh were home, they'd join him for dinner.

If not, he'd take theirs down to them to have for lunch the next day.

The four-year-old preferred Dungeness crab, of all things, which wasn't all that common in commercial numbers in San Diego, but when the fishermen brought it in, everyone at Diego's knew to put a good amount in his order.

That first Friday after Sage and Leigh flew off with Gray, there were three crabs in the order Scott had failed to change to feed one.

He was happy to have them. Had a few ways to cook and/or freeze the meat. But as he put the three full crabs into his big stew pot to boil, replaying the conversation he'd had with his friends at Diego's as he told them that he no longer needed a standing order for three, seeing their sympathetic looks, he felt just a tad bit sorry for himself.

Not one to wallow in self-pity—most definitely not something one of Randolph Martin's kids would do—he glanced at the rest of the spread Diego's had sent along for dinner. Some was from the successful restaurant that was now attached to the market. Including the cup of mac and cheese for Leigh.

He thought of the other person he knew who liked the stuff. He'd seen her sharing it with Leigh more than once.

Picking up his phone, he texted: Forgot to cancel Friday night seafood. You have any interest? Every capitalization and punctuation correct. Because that was how Martins did it.

is there crab

And macaroni and cheese, too.

we're on our way

We. Angel and her. Accepting an invitation to visit Morgan and him. Dogs who were inseparable friends bringing their owners along to eat.

Smiling, he got busy getting ready to put dinner on out on his porch. Starting with dog dishes hosting nibbles of fresh tuna.

Life changed, but there was good around other corners if you made the effort to find it.

Iris walked home with Angel Friday night with a smile on her face. A couple of neighbors were out, separately. One walking a dog. Another just walking. At different depths on the beach. Close enough to see, to nod. Far enough away to not require conversation.

Dale's porch light was on.

She'd seen Harper's on, too, on the far side of Scott's place.

He didn't seem to walk the beach in that direction much.

But it made sense. Until recently, he'd always been heading down the other way to see Leigh and Sage. With Iris one further than them, and the Bartholomew family's new place at that end.

Iris just happened to have been in the vicinity a lot. Especially after she and Sage had become friends the day Iris had moved in.

Scott. He'd served the crab with a sauce made from the mustard juices and even without the mac and cheese, she was stuffed.

He'd had containers of coleslaw, potato salad, broccoli salad and a cooked cauliflower medley, too. Along with Diego's delicious homemade rolls.

She should have been rolling home.

Instead, her step was light. Scott had shown her the pictures of Leigh at the amusement park. She'd shown him photos her friend had texted from the ornate lobby at the hotel where they'd stayed. Gray had been standing with Leigh, his arm around her back, as she gazed out a window at the sea.

They'd talked about work. The judge had granted his motion to quash his defendant's prior mental health case. She'd finished editing a week's worth of photographs that day. And when the food was gone, she'd left.

Just like any other night that she'd joined Sage and Scott for an impromptu dinner. The food was all takeout. Other than his crab preparation, there'd been no dishes.

And…she'd never been inside Scott's home.

Not that she couldn't be.

The occasion had just never arisen.

Angel, as though understanding that things were back to normal between her and Morgan's owner—clearly sensing the lack of tension that had been present on occasion that week—trotted alongside Iris with a happy gait.

All they'd needed was for Iris to take a drive to Fullerton. She knew better than to try to avoid her emotions. Had grown complacent after her years on Ocean Breeze.

And that complacency had almost cost her one of the most valuable aspects of her life. Her friendship with a man who knew when she wanted to talk, and when she didn't. Who made her laugh. Was able to sit in silence with her. Whose conversation always interested her. Who saw more in her photography than most, catching nuances that she wasn't always even sure were anywhere but in her imagination until he pointed them out. A man who'd sworn off commitment long before she'd come along with the same life choice.

Diane had a nice home. In a lovely neighborhood with lots of green grass, dog parks and a couple of community parks, too. The two-car garage was a sign that her stepmother had someone else living with her.

Had perhaps remarried.

It wasn't uncommon anymore for women to keep their own names after nuptials.

Not that Diane's life choices were one iota of her business.

Regardless, she'd absolved herself of any guilt in that area. All on her own. Not even Angel knew.

And she'd come home to be fire on wheels at her worktable.

Saturday was as good a day, spent on a private boat following a school of dolphins. Catching shot after shot of the marine mammal family having fun together.

Still feeling the day's energy when she got home, she had

her camera slung over her shoulder when she headed out to the beach with Angel. Anxious to show Scott her photos.

If Sage had been home, she'd have arranged for her friend to take Leigh out on the same boat the next day. The little girl loved the dolphins at the San Diego Zoo.

As it turned out, Scott was at Sage's old place. Morgan told her so when the girl came galloping in her corgi way toward her and Angel from the cottage up for sale.

Heading up the beach to the building, she was just stepping up to the porch when Scott came out.

"Hey, I'm glad you're here. I've got to hang around for a half hour or so. The realtor who showed the place today just called. The couple wants to see it a second time and write a full-price offer. They have to catch a flight back to Ohio tonight. They're about fifteen minutes out. You wouldn't happen to have a beer, would you?"

He sounded upbeat. Sage really wanted the cottage sold, and Scott had joked that getting it done while she was gone would be his wedding present to her.

But at the same time, an era was ending…

For Iris, as well.

"Two beers coming up," she said, leaving Angel with him and Morgan on the beach as she traipsed across the sand back to her place an acre away.

Inside, she quickly picked two bottles of beer off the refrigerator shelf, grabbed her bag of cut-up veggies, too, because they were there and she saw them, and was out the door. She wanted Scott to have a chance to get at least a sip in before meeting with the people who were likely going to be taking over his sister's home.

Joining the Ocean Breeze family.

Did they have a dog?

The thought hit as she saw Scott, still in dress pants,

shirt and tie, sitting on the bottom porch step petting both dogs at once. His lips were moving, but she couldn't hear what he was saying. Wanted to.

Did he keep things light with them, offer his affection in teasing ways, as he did with her and Sage and Leigh?

Or did they get more of his heart?

Stopping at the sudden longing to know, Iris watched him haul both dogs up onto his lap and hug them both at once.

And for a second there...as her heart melted...she was jealous.

Chapter Six

The realtor, Walt Wright, asked if he could sit with his clients, a young couple without pets, right there at the cottage to write the offer. Since Scott, as a lawyer, was acting agent for his twin, he granted them permission and then headed toward the back door, to the half-finished beer he'd left outside.

As many times as he'd been in and out of Sage's house without knocking, it didn't feel right, suddenly, to remain on the porch, even. In fifteen minutes' time, the feeling of ownership had transferred.

Figuring Iris would have gone home to dinner, he told Walt as he was leaving that he'd be at his place. Told the realtor to call when they were ready.

And walked outside to see Iris still there. Sitting in the sand, a dog lying on each side of her. A light in the darkness that had fallen.

Both on the day, and in his life at the moment.

His sense that the life he'd loved so much was changing was ridiculous. Sage and Leigh, and now his best friend, were all going to be right there. Underfoot. Just a few cottages farther down. He wasn't losing his family.

He'd gained a brother.

"Change sucks," he said as, beer in hand, he plopped down beside Iris.

"Even good change," she agreed, staring out at the waves, not studying or analyzing him. Something he'd always liked about her.

That had changed for a second or two there over the weekend. Thank God his friend was back, at least.

"I don't know how long they'll be," he told her. "I should get back. Morgan needs to eat."

As did he.

"I've got a large baked potato in the oven," she said. "I only eat half. And there's salad. If you'd like to eat down here rather than walking back and forth. Angel has food to share with Morgan."

He'd rather. Not because of Iris, in particular, but because she understood the melancholy that had fallen over him. More, she shared it.

With Sage's marriage, her move down the beach and a new baby on the way, life was changing for Iris, too. She was bound to see less of both Sage and Leigh.

And the new buyers, that night's activity, they'd affect Iris most as they'd be living right next door to her.

Besides, he hadn't yet had a chance to see all of Iris's dolphin photos before Walt had interrupted them.

"Morgan, you want to eat with Angel tonight?" he asked the corgi contentedly lying in the sand. Hearing the word *eat*, the girl stood up, her short little legs doing her rendition of a dance as she stared up at him.

"I take that as a yes," he said, watching as Iris stood, too. Resisting an inner nudge to offer her a hand up. He'd never even had the thought before.

Told himself not to have it again as he walked by her side to the lighted cottage he'd only been in once or twice. To help move in the new living room furniture she'd purchased a couple of years before. And once to add an electrical outlet to her workroom.

She was a friend. Just like Gray. Not a slender woman dressed in finery, dancing in his arms.

What a mistake the whole best-man, maid-of-honor thing had been. When Sage had announced the coupling, suggesting to Scott that he bring a date, telling them both that there were seats and meals for a plus one for each of them at the bridal table, Scott had politely declined. The last thing he'd wanted that night was a casual person by his side who had no idea who Sage was, or how big the day was for her.

Or him, as it had turned out.

He'd given his twin away, so to speak.

Sharing the evening with a good friend who'd get it, while expecting nothing from him, had presented itself as the perfect choice.

If anyone had told him that the night would end with a kiss that didn't seem to fade, he'd have scoffed. Clued them in on his and Iris's very solidly platonic relationship.

She'd been talking about salad dressing choices. And the turkey and ham she'd already cut up for that night's meal.

While he'd been trespassing on off-limit territories.

If not for the awkwardness he'd create, the questions he'd have to answer, he'd back out of the dinner invite.

And he comforted himself with the reminder that nothing could happen between them with a realtor next door calling him at any minute.

He was just lonely without Leigh's pudgy-legged run and boisterous laughter on the beach. Her four-year-old way of seeing straight through him and calling him on any inconsistency he might make.

Whether it was a missed *excuse me* after he burped. Or a look of sadness on his face.

Times of adjustment were hard.

For everyone.

Human beings were comfortable in their routines.

But with no change, there'd be no growth. And limits to their happiness.

None of which he wanted. For himself, or anyone else.

They'd all get through it together and be a bigger, happier family on the other side.

He'd managed to make the short walk without creating a scene but hadn't said a word.

Iris stopped in the sand in front of the first step up to her porch. "You okay?" she asked. Studying him again.

Danger! Danger! He had a flash of an old sitcom his father used to watch when he was young, one that he'd introduced to his kids, about a family living in outer space. Their robot always called out the danger to the young boy, Will, if he remembered correctly.

"Fine," he told Iris, smiling at the memory as he answered her. "It's just..."

"Sage's place," she filled in when he might have made a critical miss-turn into something more. "Having strangers in it, soon to own it, is just...weird."

With a roll of his eyes, he said, "You got that right," and, taking a sip of warm beer, followed her and the girls up the three steps and into the house.

As hungry as Iris had been, she wasn't feeling it all that much as she took her first bite.

They'd just sat down to dinner at the wooden kitchen table Iris had eaten on as a kid when Walt Wright called to let Scott know that he'd just sent over the offer. The couple, Liza and Burt, needed to get to the airport, and Walt was rushing to get them there.

Scott had read the offer as he'd consumed the other half of her baked potato and two bowls brimming with chef salad with barbecue sauce and ranch dressing mixed together.

How it could be that they'd been friends for three years and she'd never known he preferred the combined dressing she didn't know.

Didn't really like the fact.

It was just more of the way that he was changing, morphing into a guy other than the friend she'd known.

With their status quo gone, it was no wonder she'd been heading toward a bit of a relapse into the emotionally crippled young woman she'd once been.

He'd sent a text to Sage when he'd completed his read through, telling Iris that he was certain his sister would have him accept. Iris didn't ask for details. He didn't offer them.

And then he did. "They want to take possession next week. I'll need to get the rest of Sage's stuff moved out."

"I'll help," Iris said, glad to have a part in things—and something concrete to do with herself—as she stood up to clear the table.

Scott typed on his phone. And by the time she came back for the salad dressings and plates of fixings on the table, he was grinning and said, "She appreciates the offer." And then added, "I'm sure she'd rather have you packing boxes than me."

She remembered a time he'd had to move stuff out of his spare bedroom to have the floor redone due to a bathroom plumbing fiasco. She and Sage had offered to help him pack, but he'd said he'd already taken care of it.

Turned out he'd thrown everything in suitcases and random boxes, without any kind of protective wrap. And hadn't labeled anything, either. She knew that because he'd groused later about wasting an hour looking for something he'd needed.

Not that she told him so. While she and Sage had been amused, he had not been. Instead, she left him on his phone at the table and headed into the galley cooking area, happy to have had him over.

And to have dinner done, too.

"Tomorrow's Sunday," she called from around the corner. "We should probably do it then. You'll be in trial all week, and I have a wedding to shoot next Saturday." She was backing up from bending over in the refrigerator, to drop meat in the temperature-controlled drawer where she stored it, as she spoke.

And shoved her butt right into a hard male thigh.

Jerking, she moved quickly, turning, intending to step farther into the kitchen to let Scott pass, and he'd done so as well. Both of them moving forward in tandem, as they turned.

The hardness that touched her hip that time was not a thigh.

It was an unmistakable body part.

And not at all in a platonic state.

"I was just coming in to throw the napkins away," Scott blurted, holding up their used paper products. And then, backing out of the galley, he shoved them in his pants pocket saying, "I'm going to head out so I can set this up for electronic signature and get it sent to Sage tonight. Thanks for dinner, it was great. Morgan, let's go, girl."

He was still talking as he shooed the girl out her back door. Giving her no chance to make anything out of what must have been a purely instinctive bodily reaction due to a part of the body being touched.

She hadn't been going to. No need.

Guys got hard randomly.

Without conscious thought involved.

A common bodily function. Like breathing.

No way she was going to embarrass Scott, or make a problem where they didn't need one, over something completely innocuous.

She gave him time to get home, and then texted him.

what time tomorrow later in the day works for me

And breathed her first good slug of air when he texted right back.

Four?

They'd faced another, brief, potential friendship-threatening storm. But they'd done what they'd said they were going to do. They'd kept their hands off each other.

All was fine.

She slept well.

And was fully on track when she presented herself at Sage's door just before four o'clock the next afternoon. Scott had been on textile duty, packing clothes into suitcases, towels, linens and blankets in boxes, and would be taking them all down to Sage's new home, rather than putting them into storage.

Armed with the professional moving boxes Iris had picked up, along with a ream of packing paper lodged under her arm, tape over her wrist and a black marker in her jeans pocket, she called out, "I'm here!" and started in the kitchen, wrapping glasses.

Sage had taken her everyday dishes with her, but there was a set of Christmas china with matching crystal, wine-glasses and various other random pieces in the back of the first cupboard she tackled.

Gray had owned a huge, lovely home, including a kitchen with state-of-the-art everything, and a lot of what they were using had come from there.

The rest was going into storage until they got all their permits and were able to build on to the cottage at the end of the beach.

Another couple, also married since Iris and Sage and Scott had moved to Ocean Breeze, Cassie and Dennis, a pediatrician and a college professor, lived in the cottage at the other end of the beach, over a mile away from Gray's. They were planning on a major addition as well. They'd already been through paperwork and had told Sage and Gray just before their wedding that they were certain the Bartholomews' cottage renovations would be approved.

Iris was just diving into the second cupboard, a half-empty one, holding a plethora of pink depression glass, and turned to see Scott standing there, watching her.

He was in jeans and a black T-shirt. All long legs topped with solid muscle...

"You need something?" she asked, turning back around so quickly she dislodged a creamer and would have broken it if she hadn't shoved forward against the cupboard, effec-tively catching the vintage glass against her chest.

Of course he wasn't in the dress pants, or beach shorts in which she normally saw him, Iris berated herself, pray-ing he hadn't seen her giveaway gaffe.

"A beer." Scott's response sounded a tad bit desperate.

Praying it was only her ears making up the nuance. Packing wasn't his thing. And though Sage had moved out, there was a somewhat daunting amount of stuff left behind.

They had a long night ahead of them.

"There's some at my place if you want to make a run for it," she said into the cupboard. No more turning around. She'd learned her lesson.

Scott in jeans was a rare enough sight that she'd do well to avoid a second encounter for the moment.

"There's some right here." His voice came from just behind her right as she heard the refrigerator open. "I stocked it this afternoon. Help yourself when you're ready."

Right. She would. Gladly. As soon as he'd disappeared back to the other side of the cottage.

And left her to prepare herself for the next view of him. One in which she knew what was coming and therefore wouldn't feel as though shock had done her dirty, leaving her dripping with unwanted desire for a man she didn't ever want to touch.

Scott left Sage's bedroom for Iris to handle. He tackled his sister's office and Leigh's room instead. He had movers scheduled for the next day. Everything going into storage, including what furniture was left in the place—Sage's bed and dresser, a couch and the kitchen table and chairs—had to be ready to go.

Bathroom stuff he could handle himself later, if they didn't get to it.

Same for the laundry area cupboards.

Sage had figured she'd have time to pack up the place after she got back. To go through things. But she'd already taken out much of the stuff that meant the most to her.

Scott found some photos, though. On the bottom of her

file drawer, underneath the hanging files. Mostly of her and Scott, taken at various times through their early years, all when their mother was alive.

Back when failure had been a natural part of the learning process. Not a sin.

So what was his latent, persistent and momentarily intense attraction to his good friend there to teach him?

Not to fail. He answered the mental question with an immediate and strongly felt response. Put the photos in a manila envelope to take home until he could personally hand them to Sage, and moved on with the job at hand.

Rejecting thoughts right and left as he went.

Those hips.

Stop. File folders in file folder boxes. He might need more boxes. Started stacking folders along the wall so the cabinet in which they were held could be moved.

They smelled musty.

Iris smelled like lilacs, fresh sea air and… *Stop.*

The hour went on. His packing progressed. The mental workout continued.

And the office was done.

Passing Sage's door on his way to Leigh's room, Scott caught a glimpse of movement in his sister's bedroom. Thought Iris was still in the kitchen.

Figuring the shadow was from one of the dogs, he glanced in.

To see his platonic friend standing in her leggings and long-sleeved tee, with a cloth bag in one hand and what could only be described as a still-packaged sex toy in her hand. No other way to see that one.

As he paused, Iris glanced up at him. And continued to look. As she had the previous weekend.

Not staring. More like searching. Definitely crossing a line from friendly to…more.

Until she blinked.

And he looked away.

He meant to move down the hall. His feet remained in place. His gaze resting on the package in Iris's hand.

Seeing not his twin sister, at all—the package wasn't opened—but Iris…as though she'd brought the thing into the house with her.

"She got it as a gag gift from a law clerk a couple of years ago," the gorgeous woman said, her amber hair like a fire around her, over her shoulders and down her body.

The kind of flame that burned a man with pleasure. Not pain.

"I just found it on the top closet shelf, back in the corner. Looks like it fell out of that thing of plastic storage drawers she kept there…"

She seemed to be rambling.

Not at all Iris-like.

"I'm off to Leigh's room," he said.

And with a nod, he took off.

Chapter Seven

He'd seen her standing there, holding an object that had very clearly been made to take the place of a man's penis.

Other than the wrong color, lack of warmth of any kind and batteries, she figured the sex toy could do the trick. For a woman who was sexually healthy and unable to commit herself to another human being in any way that involved a belief in, or desire for, a happily-ever-after.

Dropping it back in its drawstring gift bag, she placed it in the bottom of the box she was packing without the least bit of temptation to know more.

Let alone have one of her own.

Dress her friend in blue jeans and give him a hard-on, and she became mush. But a chance for adult sexual release—no commitment, no risk of getting messy, no human unpredictability involved—and she'd rather sit alone, fully dressed, in the sand with her camera.

She never had been one to make things easy.

Too much depth, Ivy used to say. Her ability to be aware of hidden emotions, to see in moments things that others couldn't, defined her.

According to her identical twin.

That week, her definition was a curse. And on the blink. Showing her things that weren't real. Taunting her physically until, on Monday afternoon, on her way back to Sage's to help Scott with final details after the movers were gone, she actually thought about ordering one of those toys online.

Surely, there were better options than the one she'd found on Sage's shelf.

As unappealing as the thought was, she preferred a practical resolution to the condition bothering her, rather than losing one of her best friends.

Someone who could be that person because he respected, accepted and even seemed to welcome her limitations, rather than trying to analyze or change them.

He was waiting for her in the front room of Sage's cottage when she got there. Seeing him there, on the heel of the thought she'd been having, she felt a well of…gratitude… for him.

To him.

"What's that look for?" he asked, sounding as though she'd just made him uncomfortable.

In a rush to reassure him, she said, "You're the only person I've ever told that I don't believe in love or happily-ever-after and you were okay with it. You didn't challenge me. Or try to convince me otherwise. You just accept me. I was thinking how nice that was," she told him. More than she should have.

A simple *I'm grateful for our friendship* could have done it.

An easy shrug, a shake of the head, a pretense that there'd been nothing behind any look he might have seen would have been best.

The warm look in his blue eyes almost undid her. Until he said, "Ditto," and dived right into discussion about the most efficient way to finish the job they'd shown up to do.

She agreed with every suggestion he made. Added none of her own thoughts to the mix, and quickly went about completing tasks while keeping herself in rooms other than the ones Scott occupied.

She was happier when he was close.

Yet she didn't want to be directly around him.

How was that combination ever going to work?

And yet...maybe it did.

When others were sharing space with them, she and Scott weren't *directly* together.

Except...at the wedding...there'd been more others around them than would ever happen in their daily lives and none of them had been enough to keep the monster at bay.

Feeling as though she was running out of time, thoughts flew as she worked. By night's end, if she didn't find a way to rid herself of the appalling new reactions she was feeling around Scott Martin, her friendship with the lawyer could effectively be over.

Sex toys. Getting more desperate as one hour moved into two and she had her designated rooms emptied, with everything piled in the front foyer for the move down to Gray's cottage, Iris actually thought about doing a phone search.

Producing her solution at zero hour. Only to herself of course.

Saving their world.

She didn't even want to type the word *sex* into any browser associated with her name. Who knew what memory bank would store the search and throw it up on her in the future?

Adult toys were perfectly legal. Accepted in society. Much better solutions than sexual encounters that could lead to horrible things happening. They were used by couples, too, not just people without human partners.

Her mind duked it out. Back and forth.

With only one positive on the search-and-buy side.

If it would get her and Scott back to who they'd been…

She missed him.

More than she'd ever have thought possible.

You know I'm right here, in the next room, right? Her mind played his voice for her, as she imagined he'd playfully say were he to know what a tied-up little nit she was being.

But would he be there on Tuesday night? Or Wednesday?

Because…while yes, she'd been conscientiously choosing her spaces based on where he was not that evening, she hadn't really had to make an effort at all to do so. Which told her he was doing the same.

All because of some ridiculous sexual awareness that had suddenly invaded their systems?

Claws of death seemed to be closing around her, soon to imprison her forever, locking her in solitary confinement from which there'd be no time of day for fresh air or conversation, ever.

A state far worse than the one she'd invented to keep her healthy in her new life.

As she stacked her last, smallest box on top of the rest, feeling her time in Sage's home coming to an end forever, she was struck by the sudden realization that one ending could be mirroring another. Her time with Sage's brother as she knew it could be ending, too.

Desperate, she barreled around, determined to fight the devil at her door. To win this time.

And ran straight into Scott.

His arms came out, steadying her, and eyes wide, feeling frantic, she stared at him. Did he sense it, too, their time together coming to an end?

Not just that night, but forever?

His blue eyes seemed to bore into her. To be filled with the same enemy that had been slowly building in her.

His hand slid. Up her arm.

Ready to let go?

To say goodbye?

Forever?

She started to shake.

Felt the ragged breath he drew against her stomach as he swayed on his feet and their bodies touched. Leaned in for a moment. Both of them. Taking a last breath while they found the strength to break apart. Turn their backs.

Walk away.

Still looking up at him, she almost cried out with her inability to find the words, the solution that would send them back to who they were.

She opened her mouth. Willing answers to burst forth. To save them.

But his head lowered. Stifling any answers that might have come to her.

And obliterating further thought.

Scott kissed. He touched.

He was devoured. By the passion within him.

And the woman who'd brought it to that point.

Her lips, her tongue, her moans consumed him. He had no control.

Clothing ripped off.

He had no sense of anything but getting her to the floor, shoving a condom from his wallet down on himself and entering her. He'd have taken a breath then.

A moment.

But she bucked against him. Sliding up and in, and then down, once. From there, he had no idea how it went.

There was sweat. A hard floor in there somewhere. And a drive to explode out of the hell that had been taking over his sanity. His life.

When it happened, right after her inner folds started clenching around him, he could do nothing but let it take him. Ride the waves.

Until there weren't any.

Waves.

Or barriers to thought, either.

Feeling the bruises forming on his elbows and knees as he held himself above the woman he'd just had sex with, Scott pulled out, and stood.

Horrified by what he'd done.

Scrambling for a way to fix the damage.

There had to be one.

Dressing. The first step.

Iris obviously felt the same, judging by the speed with which she'd righted her leggings, getting them back on both feet and up.

She hadn't been wearing panties.

Not something he was ever going to forget.

He opened his mouth to apologize. Glanced at her. Got caught in the green-eyed gaze.

And heard himself ask, "What are you thinking?"

Did they say goodbye politely? Pretend that they'd hang out on the beach again when they both knew they wouldn't? Couldn't?

She seemed far more collected than he was as she continued to study him. "You sure you want the truth?"

No. But he said, "Yes."

"I think we just had to get the damned thing out of us."

He blinked. Reared back slightly.

"It wasn't going away," she pointed out, sounding just like…his friend Iris. "Were we really going to let our bodies ruin a three-year friendship that's valued equally by both of us?"

She valued him.

As much as he valued her.

The point was key. Stuck. He held on to it as he said, "You know how I am. No expectations. No pressure. No promises."

"Yes." She almost smiled as she said, "And you know I don't believe in the whole two-people-being-together-forever kind of thing."

There was a point there. He wanted to find it. Saw his way clearly. "We're both strong, independent, determined, successful professionals. Made so by the single-focused drive to be just that." It wasn't going to change. *He* wasn't going to change.

Wasn't willing to risk another failed marriage on the chance that he could. He still struggled to live with the man who'd so neglected his first wife that he hadn't even known she'd moved out.

"And that right there is why we're friends."

Her statement on the tail end of his thought of failure confused him for the second it took him to backtrack to the statement he'd made aloud.

Clarity started to show itself. "We're determined enough that we put an end to the physical desire raging between us," he told her. "We took it on, ended the torment. Shined a light right in the face of it. Our life choices reign." They'd killed the beast.

Without getting emotional. Or looking for more from each other.

He definitely felt more relaxed.

"Exactly," she said. Her look showing every ounce of her strength and determination.

He had to expound, just to be sure. "So...tomorrow? If we happen to get home from work in time and meet on the beach...we shoot the breeze a bit."

"Same as always."

He liked it.

Saw the logic in it.

Held on to it. Took it in with him for a long shower when he got home. Washing away any trace of Iris's scent.

And when he found a strand of her long auburn hair on his pants as he started to throw everything he'd had on in the washer, he got a trash bag instead.

Iris slept great. She was exhausted, satiated and consciously chose to slide into the place inside herself where she blocked out the world. A zone that her psyche had created to allow her once-sensitive self to venture out into the world again.

On Tuesday, rested and bursting with energy—both mental and physical—she rode a wave of relief. Just wasn't sure what fuel propelled the wave. Relief that the temptation was gone?

Relief from the godawful tense, unrequited sexual desire that had been amping up inside her?

There were some slightly uncomfortable moments in the shower, when the spray tingled against her nipples, when she washed other sensitive parts, and for a second, her mind jumped back to moments on the floor that were never to be revisited.

They'd served their purpose. And she was through with them.

So why, even when she forcefully turned her mind away,

cataloging colors in the shower to distract her train of thought, did her heart and nerves hold on to the high spirits that she might have experienced in those few seconds?

Or had it been afterward?

Either way, her mind and body were playing tricks on her. Trying to convince her the part of her that had died years before, preventing any full-out emotion, was suddenly sprouting seeds of life.

She'd lived through the accident that had killed the other half of her soul, but only on the surface. Existing on a different plane. One where she experienced life from a distance.

Iris didn't feel wants and needs personally, deep inside herself, as she once had. She felt great compassion for others. Appreciation. Most highly for Sage, Leigh and Scott Martin. Soon to be Sage and Leigh Bartholomew as soon as the legal paperwork was filed.

She was super in favor of Sage's re-found love. Rejoiced from the sidelines for her friend.

But didn't, for a second, want it for herself. No one was ever going to know her as completely or love her as fully, as unconditionally, as her identical twin had done.

And no way was she going to risk the devastation of losing even half that much again.

Period.

Thoughts firmly on board and in sync with her inner self again, Iris did what she was on earth to do. Camera to her eye, she sought out that which others didn't stop to see. Didn't know to see. Behind the lens, her spirit soared. The only place it still could do.

She had another full zoo day. Capturing the thoughts, feelings and soul of a couple of Amur leopards—a species at risk of extinction, with only eighty such leopards alive in the world. The zoo was globally committed to fighting extinction and Iris was honored to have been chosen to help them in their efforts.

Her job was to raise in others an appreciation for the nearly extinct. To show the at-risk creatures' unique contributions to the world, and to build an emotional need within human beings to help keep them alive.

She was at her best, doing what she did, on an adrenaline high, until she realized that she'd worked so long it was dinnertime and she hadn't even noticed the sun starting to set.

Sunset. Angel. Scott on the beach.

Reality hit with a force she didn't recognize. Couldn't take in stride as she always did with everything that denoted any bit of bad news, tardiness or tension.

Any other time, she'd simply call Sage, who'd let Angel out, feed her and give the girl her playtime on the beach.

It wasn't any other time. It was the day after she'd had sex on Sage's living room floor. With Sage's brother.

Who she also could not call because...

The whole sex-on-the-living-room-floor thing.

Instead, she stopped work before she was done. Cutting off her own lifeline. And drove to the beach as though death could be at her door. Angel had been out at lunchtime. The girl was fine.

But Iris wasn't. Not until, a quarter of the mile down the beach, she caught sight of Morgan about the same time Angel did.

Iris didn't take off into a gleeful run, but she smiled as she watched Angel do so, living vicariously in those four paws, the wagging tail.

Because Scott was there.

Not avoiding her.

Or them.

As he approached, every move she made was calculated. Chosen deliberately. Drawn from memory of their three years as friends. Acting as she could remember acting in the past. Forcing something that would come naturally as soon as she was certain that Scott was still in a good place with them.

The same place.

He didn't want permanence, but the man was emotionally fully alive. And what had happened the night before… well that had been…a once-in-a-lifetime combustion. For sure.

It was possible it had awoken emotions in him that wouldn't fit who they were.

"So…" he said while he was still a few feet away.

And for a second there, she panicked. Chest tight, she felt like she couldn't breathe. "So…"

What?

Was he waiting on some kind of review of the night before?

Her thoughts and opinions in the fading light of day? After having had time to process?

She had none. Hadn't processed. Wasn't planning to. Ever.

There were no words available when one didn't entertain thoughts on a topic.

"So…you going to let me see?" he asked as he reached where she'd stopped dead cold upon his first communication.

Let him see? Was he…on the beach…and…

He was looking at the camera she had slung over her shoulder. Put there, not because she planned to take it off her shoulder, but because she wore it on the beach a lot.

Usually to show Scott some photo or another.

"You had the Amur shots today, right?" Scott said then, a frown forming on his face.

"Yes!" Brain activity returned, normalizing, and Iris maybe overdid the enthusiasm in that first word, but had herself firmly back on track as she pulled the camera off her shoulder, and quickly brought the shots up on-screen.

Handing him the camera as she'd done in the past, she stepped back. Taking no chances that he'd lean in to share a shot with her as he commented. Giving herself no option to move her head closer to his chest in order to share what he was seeing.

She'd left the job so abruptly, she hadn't even had a chance to go over what she'd caught that day. Something she always did before leaving a jobsite. Making certain she had enough good shots to work with.

"These are phenomenal, Iris."

Scott's tone held a note she hadn't heard before. Scaring her.

Had emotion for her clouded his judgment?

They couldn't let that happen. She couldn't give him back the adoration he deserved. He'd get hurt.

She'd rather die, or live alone with no other souls in sight, than hurt Scott.

"Seriously, shot after shot, I feel like I know what he's thinking. Feeling. I want to comfort him. Reassure him. Praise him…"

She stared. Never…in all the time since death…in the years she'd known Sage and Scott…in her years as a photographer… Never had anyone seemed to know exactly what she'd been thinking, feeling, grasping, without her saying…

Still scrolling on her camera, his attention fully focused

on the screen, Scott didn't seem to notice that Iris was fading. Getting cold. Feeling the blood drain from her face.

Until something inside her clicked into gear. The anger. The determination not to let the drunk who'd stolen life win it all.

She was still there. Had to contribute to the world for both of them. Herself and Ivy.

She glanced over at Scott as he said, "You know..." and then held his gaze as he continued with, "All the years I've been looking at your photos, they've spoken to me. It's like I can see you in them, as well as whatever you're shooting. You know your pictures have always reached me. But today...it's like there are captions here."

She smiled. Filled with pride. Gratitude.

With a gush of emotion that overwhelmed her.

Until fear took over.

It was just like at the wedding.

And that could not be allowed.

Chapter Eight

Why in the hell was his praise of Iris's work turning her eyes cold, as though she was offended? Or in shock?

It wasn't the first time he'd found profound value in her work. It wasn't even the hundredth.

The only thing that had changed from any of those previous times and the current one was the sex.

He'd come out to the beach with determination. Optimism.

And a bit of tamped-down trepidation, too. Telling himself that if he let worry in, he'd cause the ruin he wanted to avoid.

As he watched her, Iris blinked. Seemed to focus more clearly on him. And asked, "Can you do something for me?" Even her voice sounded different.

His imagination? Or he wasn't wrong to think that they had a problem.

"Of course." His answer was a no-brainer. That night. But any other night in the past, too.

"Show me the shots, specifically, that speak to you. Talk me through them."

Eager to have such a simple task, when he'd faced the question with dread, Scott immediately clicked on the screen, and moved to stand beside Iris.

And, eventually, to sit with her, on the steps of her porch, with the outside lights on, as they munched on pita bread with fig jelly, and she brought photos up on the twelve-inch tablet she'd brought outside.

She'd noted photo numbers. He'd tell her what he saw. Sometimes she nodded. Sometimes she just wrote. And then they'd move on.

It wasn't anything they'd ever done before. And yet…it wasn't the least bit sexy, either.

It was them. Just on a deeper level.

Liking what he was feeling, seeing, between them, he continued to munch bread, rather than the baked chicken and broccoli salad he had waiting at home for dinner. And to watch Iris work.

She was so intent, to the point of not even always seeming to see him as a person, but rather, as an extension of her apps and programs, showing him a side of her that he'd never seen before.

A couple of hours later, as they reached the end of her day's shoot, she offered him a beer.

Relaxed, enjoying the new them, he nodded, and took a seat on one of the deep wicker chairs with cushions that she indicated. Uncapping a beer and handing it to her, before reaching for the other, which he opened for himself.

A move he'd have done for any date he'd been with.

After a brief glance at Iris, to make certain she hadn't caught on to the move, he took warning. Glad that he hadn't messed things up between them.

But aware that new normals didn't just appear fully formed. They had to be made. Over time. By continuous choices.

Both small and large.

Like the choice to uncap a bottle.

"This was nice, tonight. Thank you," Iris said, gazing

toward the ocean from her own chair while Morgan and Angel lay sleeping at their feet. As they'd been doing much of the evening.

"It *was* nice," he agreed. Ready to build, choice by choice, the friendship that they both wanted. Seeing a way for it to happen.

"I'm seriously thanking you," she said then, her tone serious, somewhat pensive. But still not at all a woman-to-man thing.

And so he said, "I'm not sure why you feel you need to." Yeah, she'd brought out her tablet—that had been new— but he'd perused her photo shoots more times than he could count.

Most times while sitting on Sage's porch, with his sister and Iris and a baby monitor, while Leigh slept inside.

He heard her sigh. Tensed. Waiting. "When I first started taking an interest in photography, I…knew someone…who saw what you saw tonight. Not on the same scale, maybe. I was a total amateur with a second-rate camera, but she saw what I saw behind the lens. You've always seen more than most say they do when you look at my work. I just figured it was because photography is the creative medium that speaks to you, but tonight…"

His gut warmed, spreading upward to his chest, not downward.

"You don't need to thank me for that," he told her softly. She'd said "she" when referring to the person in her past. Since he knew she identified as heterosexual, he figured she was referring to a friend. A platonic one. "It's what friends do, right? They see the person in what they do?"

She was silent, and he tensed again.

Too much? He took it too far?

She sipped. He did. Morgan snored. The waves flowed in the distance, gracing them with white noise.

"I quit work early today." Iris's words fell into the peace that was trying to encapsulate them.

Grateful that whatever had stopped her from replying to his friend question seemed to have passed, he asked the obvious, "Why?"

She'd brought up the situation for a reason.

"Because I was worried that if I didn't show up on the beach, you'd think it was because of last night and I didn't want things to get all weird again."

Last night.

Two words.

That catapulted him down to the ground, in his sister's living room, his wallet condom stretched to the limit...

All day. He'd made it through the entire day without letting himself go there.

And with two words...

"That alone kind of makes it weird, doesn't it?" he asked when he could do so without choking. He didn't look at her. Stared at waves. Sipped beer.

"Yeah."

She sure didn't sugarcoat.

He watched her beer bottle rise, looked away before the two mouths made contact—one glass, one warm, soft flesh that he'd tasted. Devoured.

"That's why I brought it up," she said. Then she continued, "I just want it clear that I don't intend to do so again, so if I'm not out tomorrow, or the next day, or any other day before Sage gets back, it doesn't mean anything more than it meant before she left." Her tone easy. Through the whole thing.

Which almost convinced him that she was as calm as

she sounded. Unless she was a very good actress, he was the only one getting hot and bothered.

Not altogether a bad thing.

Himself he could handle.

Would handle.

A man had to know how to keep it in his pants. Just part of the responsibility of being an adult. He'd been good with that one since he'd first figured out the power he had down there.

"Note taken," he told Iris, lest she think he had a problem with what she'd said. And for good measure, added, "And ditto."

She took a sip.

He did.

They'd toasted on it.

And Scott's next sip…a toast to himself.

Come hell or high water, he'd find a way to quell this sexual burning inside him for the woman he did not want to have sex with, but wanted in his life for as long as he could have her.

He was a man who put determination behind his choices.

One for whom failure was akin to death.

With one woman's emotional damage already on his soul.

There would not be another.

Iris was pretty good at engaging her shutoff valve. During the first couple of years of emotional recovery, she'd vacillated between being completely shut down, or in agony. But as she started college, took the reins of her life in hand, she'd found her permanent vibe.

One that was suddenly being challenged.

Why Sage's wedding had somehow upset her apple cart

she had no idea. But she was determined not to let the matter continue any further.

She'd had sex with her friend's brother and was struggling to wrap her mind around that one. To rationalize the bizarre behavior.

Three years of nothing in that area where Scott Martin was concerned, and then, overnight, she's hot for him?

Made no sense.

And so, as the second week after the wedding progressed, Iris made a point of shutting down every time she was out on the beach. Whether Scott was there or not. She wasn't taking any chances on herself until she had a better understanding of what was going on.

No way she was going to lose herself again.

She'd barely made her way out the first time.

One of the counselors she'd seen had helped her practice shutting off the overwhelming swells of emotion that had threatened to strangle her alive. Had given her tools.

Distraction for one.

Putting herself in a public space, rather than living in a private one, when things got to be too much. People tended to put up walls in public.

She'd gotten really good at it.

And it seemed to be working around Scott, too. By Friday, she didn't even hesitate to head out early for a long walk with Angel on the beach. Down toward Gray's new place at the end of Ocean Breeze and turning to walk over a mile toward the opposite end. She'd been at home editing all day. Had sent off final content to three different clients, including the San Diego Zoo. And had been offered a much more lucrative contract with the zoo as part of their ongoing crusade to end extinction.

As early as she was, she'd headed out for a talk with

Ivy. She'd sprinkled Ivy's ashes in the waves offshore from Ocean Breeze the day she'd moved in. And those particular waves had been a source of calm and comfort to her ever since. Of course the water wasn't the same as it had been three years before. But sediment lowered. Her heart knew there would always be pieces of her other half on that beach.

But as she got out to the sand—close enough to the water to see shells that it brought in, but far enough away that there was no risk of Angel getting swept up in it—she took one glance outward, and had to shake it off.

The intensity that had rolled up within her during that glance wasn't something she could allow. Not with the prospect of seeing people.

Of seeing Scott.

Fridays were his shorter workdays.

And so she stayed focused on being in the present. Considered what she might do for the weekend. Work, of course, but which project? Thought about getting a new comforter for her bed. Talked to Angel about a jellyfish that washed up. Looked for some of the blue blobs that had shown up on their beach—as well as many others in Southern California—the previous spring. Hydrozoans. They'd been all over the news. A sea creature from the ocean floor. She'd donated a plethora of photographs of them to local scientists studying them.

And when, almost an hour after she'd left her cottage, Angel gave the high-pitched bark that was reserved for her hello to Morgan, Iris's heart didn't even skip a beat.

Continuing her casual pace as her girl ran full speed up the beach for the lavish greeting the girls always bestowed on each other, Iris had a nonchalant, regular smile on her face as she watched Scott approach.

He was talking to the dogs. She couldn't make out his

words, but his voice carried in the slight breeze straight at her.

A voice that was familiar to her. Resonated within her.

As though a part of her.

Of her *life*, she quickly amended the thought. Just like Sage's and Leigh's voices were ones she'd know and identify with as belonging to her personal circle.

Almost as though he'd read her mind, his first words to her were, "I talked to Sage a little bit ago. She sounded happier than I've heard her since we were kids."

Hearing Scott's affection, Iris's mind immediately switched to the mundane.

Who actually remembered the sound of a sibling's happiness from childhood?

Anyone?

Everyone?

Or just multiples who'd been connected since conception?

"She asked me to look in on you. Said you hadn't texted since Monday."

Sex on the floor.

Sage's house.

Beige sand. Glistening. Angel's front paws on Morgan's back. "I'm assuming you told her that we've seen each other on the beach every night, as usual, and I'm fine?"

"I did." Good. Breathe.

"I also told her that I'm not your keeper."

Uh-oh. "And she wanted to know what was going on, right? Because why else would you have said something like that?" Had he told Sage what they'd done?

Heat rose up her neck, tendrils sliding toward her cheeks.

"She asked me why I was tense. Didn't automatically relate it to you. Or her question. She knows when I'm off, which is why I've been texting with her all week, instead of talking to her. It's a twin thing."

A twin thing.

His words slammed her in the gut. With recognition. Loss. Agony.

Maybe some jealousy.

She shoved her mind to the words he'd said before the last ones. He'd been texting his twin all week, rather than calling, so that she wouldn't know he was off.

Because he *was* off. Just as Iris had been. Fighting not to think about his body on top of hers. Entering hers.

Refusing to allow her mind to dwell any time the fire hit.

Taking a middle-of-the-night shower when she woke up sweating from a far too realistic dream of being with him again.

Apparently, they were both good at pretending, were determined to manifest the future they wanted, but neither of them were being honest with the other.

They were pretending.

Which made their relationship little more than a lie.

When she remained silent, unwilling to voice any of her current thoughts, Scott continued, "I told her about the case."

He'd rested the prosecution's case the day before and the judge had called a recess until Monday when the defense would present their side.

Of course Scott was tense.

His career meant far more to him than any sex he'd ever had. It was his life. His words, not hers. But she'd certainly seen truth in them during her three years of knowing him.

And if she was even half the friend to him she wanted to be, she'd have sought harder to talk to him about the nuances in the week's testimony from his witnesses, rather than being all about shutting herself down.

"How do you think the jury reacted to your witnesses? Especially the wife's sister? You think they found her credible?"

Hands in the pockets of the pants he'd worn to work, Scott said, "I do," and spent the next twenty minutes talking to her about expressions on jurors' faces during key parts of testimony, and also laying out areas where the defense could still sway them. Seeming to find her replies astute, if nothing else.

It was good conversation. Interesting. Stimulating.

If you didn't have the possibility of losing a friendship on the table.

Because, while she wasn't giving up yet, the stiffness between them was getting worse, not better. Scott hadn't taken his hands out of his pockets during the entire walk.

As though he was afraid that he might touch her. Even accidentally.

And she'd kept her distance, too. All week.

Because while they could easily have sex until the intense attraction waned, such a choice would be messy and ultimately, people would be hurt. Sage would figure things out. Make more of the sex than was there. Or she or Scott would. Chances were, they wouldn't both reach that point at the same time. Emotions would get involved. Sides taken.

Or, discomfort would mandate that they not all hang together.

Iris figured, no matter how it all played out, it was only a matter of time before she and Scott quit accessing the beach at the same time.

Determining, too, that it was probably for the best.

Chapter Nine

He was not going to lose her friendship. Scott had known a lot of women. Enjoyed being with them. He'd never, ever known a woman who he just plain wanted to spend time with on a long-term basis.

He and Gray had been best buds since high school. Even after Gray had left Sage just two days before they were due at the altar.

Iris's friendship meant as much or more to him.

He couldn't explain it. He just knew that he had to get as drastic as it took to save them.

No holds barred.

And he had to do it fast. The four days of excruciating discomfort on the beach had shown him that much. Every day Iris slipped away from him a little more.

The night before, the way she'd shut herself off from him even during conversation regarding their mutual love—Sage—had brought home to him how critically in danger their friendship had become.

Short of disabling his member, which wasn't an option, he could only think of one other way to keep himself firmly on the friendship track, and off the sexual one. Cram failure down his throat as hard and as often as he could.

Which meant…surfing.

The one activity he'd tried but never mastered but didn't fail at because as long as he didn't quit he was still in the learning stage. Since high school, his drive to get up on a surfboard had defined him. Didn't matter that he was too tall to have a good shot at success. Or that he didn't feel the waves in the way he should. Didn't matter that he couldn't balance on the board long enough to ride a wave even if he managed to get on top of one.

What mattered was that he didn't give up.

That he pushed himself to do more. Try harder. Face waves that no beginner should ever be on. He wasn't a beginner. He just wasn't what the world considered to be good at surfing.

For his purposes, he was all-star.

Because surfing reminded him that if he quit trying, he failed.

And every time the board slid out from under him and he went under, he experienced the feeling of failure, without having failed. And those seconds underwater, that feeling of not succeeding, were enough to spur him on to not let the sensation become reality in his everyday life.

No one, not even Sage, understood why he kept purchasing the latest and greatest in the surfing world, why he signed up for master classes, and spent so many hours trying to perfect a sport he hadn't mastered in over fifteen years.

But it made complete sense to him.

He did it because surfing made him the best at everything else he did. Helped him excel in law school. Spurred him on to passing the bar exam first time out.

It would also light the fire under him to lose his attraction for Iris. To get his ass back to the place it had been in her world before Sage's wedding. It was a case of mind over matter, and surfing beat into him the best and worst there, too.

The best because he kept going back and giving it his all.

And the worst because he hadn't yet ridden one wave into shore.

Surfing without mastering the skill was dangerous. For Scott, failure was more so.

And because if he didn't get himself in line soon, he was coming up on a failure of a magnitude he'd never before faced, he got up before dawn on Saturday morning, intent on surfing waves that were larger, more dangerous, than any he'd taken on previously. He drove up the coast. Joined a couple of master surfers for an early-morning, wet-suited display of...pure humility.

Forced himself to stay there, trying again and again, until he was the only one left trying. And, bruised, but not showing it, attended the private black tie gala he'd been invited to Saturday night. Celebrating a well-known prosecutor from the attorney general's office who'd recently been elected to a superior court judgeship.

Sunday was a Saturday repeat. Different beach. Different waves. Same flying board and underwater forays into fight or flight. Strengthening his determination to choose fight every time.

He took on the waves again and again. Fought his way up to the surface, swam to collect his board, and cold, even in his wet suit, would call up a mental image of Iris, and get hard.

Which sent him back out again. As though he could beat the damned thing out of himself.

With the board in position, every part of his body at the ready as he'd been trained, he waited for the swell that would challenge a good surfer to stay on board, and when it hit, gave his all to it. Thinking that he was going to stay up. To ride…

The wave slammed against his board. A hard punch hit his lower back, something sharp stabbed his left knee and Scott went under.

Iris was just getting out of the shower after a morning of lounging on Sunday when her phone rang.

Dripping wet, she held a towel to herself while she read the screen lying on her counter. *Sage.*

Sage? Calling in the middle of her family-moon?

She grabbed the phone with one hand, running the towel over herself as best she could with the other. "Hello," she said, tension gripping her. Barely holding back the *What's wrong?* that was on the tip of her tongue.

"Iris?" One word and fear struck Iris, forcing her to lean against the counter, towel clutched to her chest, just from Sage's tone. "I just got a call from the hospital," Sage continued before Iris even had a chance to confirm that she was on the line. "Scott's been in an accident…"

No!

No. No. No.

"…he's insisting on leaving and they can't make him stay, and I need you to go get him, Iris. Please. You're the only one he'll listen to…"

Leaving? Insisting?

He was alive.

"How badly is he hurt?" she asked, not caring if Sage had already said so. She'd missed some things. Had to be on top of them.

"He has a torn MCL and a lower lumbar sprain. They've already taken him into surgery for the knee, but when I talked to him, he said he'd be home tonight."

Pulling on underwear, with the phone held to her ear by her shoulder, Iris reached for the closest jeans, pulled a button-down shirt off a hanger. "I'll need permission to get to him," she said.

"I've got his medical power of attorney and it's already done," Sage said. "The staff knows that all reports are to go to you."

Good. "Does Scott know?" Putting the phone on speaker, she dropped it to the bed. Donned her bra and shirt in record time.

"He will when he comes out of surgery."

She slid into tennis shoes without untying them. "I'm on my way," she said, picking up the phone to take it with her.

If Scott balked she'd deal with him.

No way in hell was the day going to end with his life on the line.

Keeping her mind focused, Iris made a call over her vehicle's hands-free system as soon as she was on the way. Dale picked up right away and agreed to take care of Morgan and Angel until she got back. She had no idea how long that would be. Maybe even overnight. Told Dale where she'd left spare keys, to her place and Scott's. And disconnected the call.

The man had asked no questions. She'd offered nothing.

She concentrated on traffic. Being in the right lane at the right time. Watching lights and turning to avoid them.

Prior to going into surgery, Scott had spoken to Sage. She'd said he'd insisted on doing so after the hospital had called her. Just as he'd insisted he'd be home that night.

His sister had said something about how he'd sounded. The memory was vague.

Iris couldn't bring the rest of it back to mind.

Except that Sage was waiting to hear from Iris. Not catching the next flight home.

And that Scott had spoken.

Both key things she focused on as she drove. Parked.

Walked briskly into the emergency room.

And, after a brief wait, was shown into a small office where a nurse filled her in on Scott's situation.

He was already out of surgery. In the recovery room. Not yet fully awake. They'd take her to him shortly. His MCL tear had been a level three. The worst.

The surgery was normally performed as an outpatient procedure, but under the circumstances, the doctor would like to keep Scott overnight, but wasn't insisting on it. He'd left the choice up to Scott.

"What would you be watching for tonight if he stays?" Iris asked. And listened to various indications of medical distress.

All things she recognized from her months in and out of the hospital.

"He's not going to stay," she said then. "I'm assuming I can get everything at the pharmacy I'm going to need?"

Including bed restraints if she could figure out a way to tie them to a king-size bed.

The thought came with determination, not humor.

Or even a hint of sexual connotation.

Scott was in no condition to pee by himself, let alone perform any other physical feats.

Sage was out of town.

And Iris was up.

By the time she was shown into the curtained-off cubicle where they'd brought Scott from recovery, Iris had a bag filled with supplies and written instructions. And a head filled with everything the pharmacist, RN, neurologist and surgeon had told her, too.

RICE was foremost for the knee. Rest. Ice. Compression. Elevation.

And wound care. Warm water. Soap. Waterproof bandage. Stitches out in ten days. Antibiotics. Pain reliever. No weight-bearing. Some immobility.

For the back it was RICH. Rest. Ice. Compression. Heat.

Armed for whatever fight Scott might give her, she stepped behind the curtain quietly, not sure he was awake.

"You look better than my sister would right about now." His words were a little slow. Sleepy sounding. But still Scott.

And relief hit so hard, so fast, she dropped down to the chair beside his bed. Setting her bag on the floor with her purse. "How would Sage look?" she asked, simply because she wanted to know.

"So serious you'd feel like you were at a funeral."

She tried to smile. Couldn't. He had no idea how close he came to how she'd felt when she'd first picked up the phone earlier that day.

And he wasn't going to know, either.

The man didn't need a confessor.

He needed a keeper.

And she was it.

That face. The green eyes, oval cheeks. What guy wouldn't like to see them appear in his drug-induced haze?

"They gave me something for pain," he said, fighting sleep so that he could take charge, get up, get out, get home. "No more."

"Did you tell them?"

He wasn't sure. He'd meant to. "I think so. Could you check on that?"

She'd looked like she needed something to do.

And he didn't want anyone witnessing his first attempt to take back his autonomy. Not until he had an idea what it was going to cost him.

And knew for sure what he did or did not have on under the sheet covering him.

"I've, um, already talked to everyone."

What in the hell did that mean? "Who's everyone?" He struggled to find his beach voice. The one where he was relaxed, confident, taking on the world.

Hoping once he got the voice, the rest would follow.

"Sage, the nurse in charge, your surgeon."

They were ganging up on him. Had sent her in to do their dirty work.

Because they thought she was the one who'd be able to convince him to stay.

Sorry to disappoint them all. "I'm not staying," he said.

"I know." She held up the bag she'd carried in with her. He was pretty sure she had, at any rate. He'd been looking at her face.

Glad to see her.

"I've got everything you need right here, including pain meds. You'll have them if you decide to take them."

Wow. She was good.

He'd known that.

"And Sage is on board?" Didn't matter, he was leaving anyway. Just had expected her to have put up a fight.

"She'd rather you spent the night, but she knew you wouldn't. And the doctor says that while he'd like to have you stay, you're fine to go home as long as you follow all instructions."

He would. "I don't have them yet."

"I do."

Okay. "I'm going to need them."

She nodded. Just that. Nothing more.

He needed some privacy. Had to get on with the exploration of his current circumstances. Moved his hand under the sheet to find out that he was in a hospital gown.

And nothing more.

"Where are my clothes?"

"You were in a wet suit. They had to cut it off."

He'd opted to go nude underneath. Had left his neoprene swim trunks wadded in the laundry sink the day before and they'd stunk.

"I have pants and a shirt in my car."

She nodded again. He didn't like it much. But before he could tell her, she said, "It's still parked in South Beach."

Where he'd been surfing that morning.

Fine. He was getting somewhere. Had his first hurdle to tackle.

"I bought you some sweats and a long-sleeved T-shirt in the pharmacy gift shop," Iris said, nodding toward the bag she'd set back down on the floor. "Nurse Windsor said that you'll probably prefer shorts at home, but for now, we can cut the one leg of the sweats to prevent any friction against your bandage."

We? As in, her and him?

Made sense since he was currently immobile, and she was in the room.

Something else occurred to his slowly wakening brain, too. "Would you mind giving me a ride home?"

He didn't have his car. Could call a cab, but since she'd be going where he needed to go…unless…

What time of day was it? He'd been surfing early, just after dawn. "That is if you're going home from here," he added. Cab would be second choice. And…

"My phone's in my car."

That time when Iris nodded, her chin was puckered. He tensed. Sensing some kind of barrier coming his way. When all she said was, "I can take you home. And get someone to take me to get your car, too," he was confused.

She was there at his twin's behest. Seemingly ready to make sure he got just what he wanted. So why her sudden chin dimple?

"What's the catch?"

"You leave here, you get me as a roommate for the next week or so."

They were all plotting against him. Led by Sage, he was sure. She'd know how he'd be feeling. Know that he'd be climbing the walls caged up when his health didn't ultimately require him to be trapped in a hospital bed. The two of them had spent enough hours within hospital walls, visiting their ailing mother as kids.

And she'd called Iris.

Who'd talked to the medical staff while he'd still been out.

He froze all thought. For the second it took him to realize that once he got home, *they* were no longer in charge.

"Fine," he said.

And started his own counterplotting.

Chapter Ten

F_{ine?}

Iris had been prepared for opposition. A lot of it. Sage had warned her. Her own three years of friendship with Scott Martin had informed her. And she got *fine*?

Because of the drugs?

Or the sex? Did he think close proximity when he was at his worst would end any attraction between them once and for all?

The idea had merit. Enough that she was willing to explore the possibility. To hope for it, even. Feeling better about the hours and days ahead, energized to get on with them, she said, "Dr. Abbot will be in shortly. Once he signs your discharge papers we can go."

"There will be ground rules."

With her sudden new lease on life, she nodded, and said, "Probably a good idea."

"I'm the boss in my home."

"Understood." Unless he thought he was going to go against medical protocol. Iris wasn't the least bit averse to calling in the troops if need be. Sage had already insisted on that one. It was the only reason she wasn't flying home immediately. If Scott didn't comply with doctor's orders, Sage, Gray and Leigh would be on the next plane to San Diego.

"Fine. Then, if you could please lay the clothes you brought on the bed, I'll get dressed so we can be ready to go as soon as the paperwork is done."

No could do. "You're supposed to wait for a final check, first." She told him what she'd been told. "Something about wound seepage." And vitals.

"So no clothes. I'd still like some privacy."

He was going to get up. She just knew it. The look on his face. The way he was still holding the edge of his covers as though ready to throw them off. Without being privy to his postsurgical instructions, he could seriously hurt himself.

Perhaps she'd been a bit premature in her celebration of their future together.

They weren't even home yet, and the battle had started.

"You can't get up yet, Scott," she said, her tone firm because it had to be. "You had a completely torn MCL, stage three, the worst. There can't be any weight-bearing right now and your crutches aren't here yet."

She used logic because it was his go-to language.

The glare coming at her from his blue eyes, beneath the tousled strands of his blond hair, almost amused her.

But not quite.

He was not going to be an easy patient.

And while she was still on board with the idea that being together over the next week would kill any attraction between them, she started to have serious doubts about their friendship surviving.

Holding her gaze with his steely stare, making her feel a little bit like a losing defendant on his witness stand, he said, "I have to pee."

Maybe he did. Maybe he was just trying to unnerve her.

She'd seen a plastic, turquoise, distinctively shaped container on the bottom shelf of the stand beside his bed when she'd come in. Reached for it.

Handed it to him.

And left the room.

He was not leaving a filled urinal for Iris, or anyone, to empty. Sitting up fully, with no support at his back, Scott lost his breath, winced, but, with his hands clutching mattress and sheet, he didn't lie back again.

As the first wave of pain passed, he slowly released the grip of one hand and pulled back the covers. Getting his first look at his left leg. Though he couldn't remember the fall, he'd been aware of the bandage running from his calf up his thigh on his left side since he'd regained consciousness.

Had another moment of acute nausea as he bent to get a look and his back shocked him again. He hadn't been prepared for the discoloration on his shin, either.

Didn't matter. He was getting out of there.

Which he couldn't do if he reinjured himself. Perhaps waiting to hear doctor's orders, to know what he'd done to himself, and what the doctor had done to fix him, was the wisest choice.

Along with waiting for crutches.

For his back, not his knee. Other than a dull throb, he couldn't feel the knee at the moment. The back most definitely did not want to bear weight.

Or movement.

He'd deal with it. Grin and bear it.

Just needed a sec to prepare.

With his hands behind him, he started to lean back against the mattress. Slowly. As imperceptively as he could manage while still making progress toward the goal.

"Scott?" Iris's voice came from just the other side of the door. "You okay?"

He didn't want to use the muscles, or energy, required by talking. Didn't want a slew of medical personnel to come running.

And so, gritting his teeth, let go with his hands and fell back against the mattress. Feeling the sweat roll down between his shoulder blades. Lying back for a brief second, he closed his eyes, and said, "Fine. It's safe to come in."

And when the door opened, he found the wherewithal to clear his expression, meet her gaze fully with eyes wide open. The pain had receded.

He wasn't moving again until he'd been told how to do so without killing himself.

And when Iris reached toward the urinal he'd set on the table beside his head so it would be in easy reach once he was standing, his tone was filled with plenty of aggression when he said, "You touch that and I'm getting up right now to stop you and walk out of here."

He meant it, too.

She didn't need to know that, in that moment, intention and capability were at odds.

As soon as his talk with the doc, they wouldn't be.

Luckly, Iris took him at his word. Sitting back in her chair, she didn't glance toward the plastic container again.

And Scott felt a little better about the hours ahead.

He'd established his boundaries.

No matter what, Scott was in charge.

The man was going to be a royal pain in her ass.

And as long as they managed to still be friends when it was all over, Iris was fully okay with that. She'd been dreading the idea of sleeping under the same roof as him.

Until she'd seen his condition.

Then she'd been determined that she'd stay whether he wanted her to or not. In a head-to-head battle on that one, she had the physical ability to win, not him.

At least that first night.

No way he could shove her body out the door. Or even off the couch where she intended to sleep.

As she watched the orderly help him from the wheel-chair to the front seat of her car, lowering the back of the seat so that he was half reclining, and shoving a couple of pillows on the floor to support his knee, she noticed the wince that never left his face. The bead of sweat on his lip.

And her heart hurt for a second.

She'd been in the kind of pain that did that to you.

Knew how utterly helpless it made you feel.

And before even leaving the parking lot, she'd called Dale to ask the writer to meet them at Scott's place to help her get him inside.

A night of RICE and RICH would, according to the doc-tor, alleviate some of his current discomfort. As would the therapy that he was to start, minimally, in the morning. They'd already arranged for someone to come to the cot-tage—Scott's orders and at his expense.

He didn't speak on the way home. Just laid his head back and closed his eyes, and for the first time since she'd seen him that day, she was truly worried.

Telling herself the doctor wouldn't have released him if he didn't think Scott would be safe, no matter how deter-mined the prosecutor might be, she promised herself she'd take his blood pressure as soon as they got home, and call for help if there was even a hint of something being amiss.

"You missed a turn." His voice didn't sound like him. And when she glanced over, his eyes were closed.

"How would you know?"

"My eyes work just fine." He didn't quite snap, but the grouchy tone was there.

"The light was red around the corner. The movie is just getting out. I preferred to go straight and make the next turn as there is no business there that will be letting out a throng of people who will slow our progress." And leave him there in agony with each even slight nudge of the car.

"Smart woman," he said then.

"At least one of us has some brains in the situation," she mumbled, showing him she had a grouch in her, too. "You need to take some pain medication. Even if just for tonight."

The doctor had strongly recommended that he take one more dose before he left the hospital. Just to get home.

Super Prosecutor had firmly refused.

She couldn't tell whether his grunt was a disregard for her opinion, or his own reluctant concession. And didn't want to waste his energy trying to find out.

They'd reached their final turn and she was knotted with tension, worrying about getting him inside without him passing out. Was thinking about driving down for her office chair, which was on wheels, to get him inside as she took the steep, single-lane road down to Ocean Breeze and the cottages that were all that occupied the private lane.

Wishing, for a second, that Sage and Gray *had* flown home. She was a strong woman, but Scott, at over six feet tall, still had a lot of poundage on her. No matter how determined her conviction, there were some things she wouldn't be able to do.

What if she hurt him?

The fear was cut off at the knees as soon as she turned onto Ocean Breeze. Not only was Dale standing in Scott's driveway, but half a dozen other residents were there, too. All waiting to offer a hand if needed.

She almost cried at the sight. And to snuff out the unwanted well of emotion, said, "Wake up, Martin, you've got a welcoming committee," in a dry tone.

His eyes opened fully, and he lifted his head. Only to groan and then, turn white as he moved the seat into a more upright position.

"Just for tonight, can you please graciously accept the help being offered?" she asked, dreading the possibility that he'd send everyone away and she'd have to get him settled in bed by herself. She'd do it. She had her plan. Her desk chair. And bed could be the couch for the night if it had to be. It was lower. No lifting on her part.

"I had every intention of doing so," he told her. "I'm independent and determined but I am not lacking in intelligence." He took a deep breath. And then said, "I also have no intention of going back to that hospital tonight."

That made her smile. And to touch his shoulder as she said, "I know this is hard, but you'll be through it before you know it." She was speaking from experience.

Not that he was ever going to know that.

Scott might not admit it to anyone except himself, but he was inordinately relieved to see the turnout of Ocean Breeze residents in his driveway. Machismo was great, but it hadn't gotten him out to Iris's car at the hospital, and he'd been dreading the trip into his cottage.

Once there, he'd be fine. Figure things out.

As it was, he did pretty damned good. With a man on each side of him, supporting his back and his weight, he managed to use them as crutches and get his one-legged walk to propel him slowly inside. The trip didn't do his back any good. He was sweating by the time he was propped with his leg elevated on his couch.

Which was when he noticed Harper, the accomplished choreographer who lived next door to him, entering the cottage behind Iris, carrying his crutches. Iris's hands were filled with the rest of the stuff they'd brought home from the hospital.

Including a pad for his bed so the mattress didn't get soiled.

From wound seepage, he'd told himself the nurse had meant as she'd rambled on in her no-nonsense tone about things he'd rather not be topics of conversation with Iris Shiprock present.

He was to report if he had any change in bowel movements. Great. He'd be sure to run that one up the flagpole.

"Seriously, Iris, I can stay tonight, if you'd like. I don't have rehearsal until noon tomorrow, and that way you wouldn't have to miss your early-morning shoot."

Iris had been commissioned to do a series of photographs of the sun rising over various parts of the city for a tourist site. He'd forgotten.

Felt like a fool. And knew a moment of near panic, too. He'd been counting on her being with him that night.

Just for the night.

Hadn't thought about her needing to be home to shower and get to work.

"Like I said, I've already got it covered," Iris was saying, in a tone that got Scott's full attention. "I called and put the photo shoot back a couple of weeks. And I've got all the instructions from the hospital." She sounded…proprietary.

And he liked it.

Which sent all kinds of warning signals along his very sore spine. Whether he was better or not in the morning, he was going to have to fake it well enough to get Iris out of his home.

When he'd been accepting her presence under duress, he'd been okay with it. For the one night, of course.

But no way could he have her there if either of them took ownership of her right to be the one helping him.

"Besides," Iris said, pulling things out of her bag and setting them up on the bar he'd built between the kitchen and living room, "I gave Sage my word…"

Ahh… Scott relaxed back as well as he could under the circumstances. Feeling better as the wave of disappointment passed through him.

Iris wasn't getting all possessive over him.

She was keeping the promise she'd made to her best friend.

Who was his twin sister.

Not him.

He was free once again to resent the hell out of her occupancy of his private space.

And would get around to it.

As soon as he got the excruciating pain shooting through his back and shocking his left knee under control.

Pain was a state of mind.

And apparently he was going to need every ounce of his mental control to get his in line.

If his choice was to deal with out-of-line meanderings where Iris was concerned, or become a master of pain management, he'd take the pain challenge every time.

Chapter Eleven

They iced. And heated. Everyone but Dale had left. Dennis Mitchell, the professor married to his pediatrician wife, Cassie Miles—owners of the first cottage on the beach—had taken Harper to get Scott's car. And Harper was bringing dinner back with her. Scott had requested supreme pizza. Until Iris had pointed out a paragraph in his discharge instructions. He'd ordered lightly seasoned pasta soup and salad instead.

And while Dale and Scott worked to figure out the best process for getting Scott to the bathroom, working on Scott's crutch skills in combination with the back injury, Iris took the girls and drove down to her place to pack what she'd need for the next few days. Including a set of sheets and a comforter for the bare mattress in Scott's spare bedroom.

The room Gray had used for a while the previous fall.

Chances were Scott had bedding. She'd opted for her own. Using his just seemed too…personal. Which was why she packed towels, too. Her own stuff, touching her own body, just not in her own house.

She didn't take long, wanting to be back before dinner arrived, and walked in just as Scott was wheeling himself in his office chair, sitting on a long board upon which his left leg rested, keeping it straight. Dale was right beside him.

Other than a few gatherings on the beach, the bearded writer kept to himself, mostly. No one knew much about him. But all the dogs on Ocean Breeze loved him, which was enough for Iris to like him, too.

"We can rent a wheelchair for you," she offered as the girls ran in and sniffed at Scott's one bare foot on the floor.

He shook his head. "No need. This is only until I see the physical therapist tomorrow and find out what pain I just tolerate, and what indicates that I'm doing further damage."

And so it went.

Harper didn't stay for dinner. But she offered, once again, to take over for Iris anytime. Being neighborly. Kind. With absolutely no challenge attached. So no reason for Iris to get defensive about the offer. Or respond with the "no need" she blithely offered.

Dale, she thanked more profusely as he left. And hoped she didn't have to take the man up on his offer to come down during the night, if necessary. But left that one open-ended.

And then it was just the two of them. With at least a couple of hours before the administration of his next round of medications. The pain meds he might or might not take, as the doctor had issued them as needed, but the antibiotics and anti-inflammatories were a must.

She could go to her room for a few. Had her laptop, tablet, SD cards and a camera, too. Could do some editing. Wasn't at all moved by the idea.

Felt no creative fire.

They'd have to ice again soon. The back ten minutes per hour for the first seventy-two hours.

The knee, twenty to thirty minutes every two hours. One hour would be one ice pack. Every other hour would be two. She had the schedule set. And had come home with enough ice packs to get the job done consistently.

It was going to be a long night.

She'd had them before. A multitude of them.

Propped up on the couch, Scott had Morgan on his stomach and chest, with Angel curled around the nonelevated foot.

His bandaged leg, the discoloration around it, was visible to her now that he was wearing basketball shorts and a T-shirt. The bulge of the compression bandage wrapped around his lower torso wasn't as obvious, but she knew it was there.

And the whole day, the call from Sage, her initial fear, the manic drive to the hospital, seeing him laid up...it all rained down on her. Tightening her chest. A sense of doom sliding over her.

Until she stopped it with the anger and determination she'd learned to use. A silent, mental action meant to take back control of her psyche from the fear that always loomed, ready to pounce.

Except that she didn't stay silent. "What in the hell were you thinking? Taking on South Beach? It's where the professional surfers go, Scott! Even I know that much. And you...you can't stay up on a board on Ocean Breeze, which—" Shocked at herself, she stopped abruptly. Bit her lip for a second, but then, chin up, stared at her patient.

Her friend.

Opening her mouth with an apology ready to spill out, she closed it again as Scott looked her in the eye and said, "You don't want to know."

He had that wrong. "Actually, I do." More than just about anything in that moment. If the man had a death wish, he needed more than physical help. And she wasn't going to sit around and watch him dwindle without at least trying to get him what he needed.

"Trust me, you don't."

He had no idea. "Trust *me*. I do."

His lower lip jutted as his chin tightened and he said, "Fine. You want it? I surf when I'm fighting the possibility of failure. The higher the possibility, the bigger the waves."

She frowned. "But…you…can't surf…"

She and Sage had talked about Scott's continual pursuit of a sport he'd never mastered. Sometimes his twin worried about Scott's refusal to give up. Sometimes she teased him about it. Everyone on Ocean Breeze knew of his quest to ride a wave. For all she knew, everyone in his office knew about it, too.

"I surf," he told her. "I just don't stay up on the board."

Which was the whole point of surfing.

Sending her a sharp-eyed glance, he said, "As long as I keep trying, I haven't failed."

Ahh. Her stomach flip-flopped. Tightened. They weren't talking about surfing anymore. The waters she'd pushed them into were murky. Suddenly seeming far more dangerous than a fancy board taking on the waves of South Beach.

The man was deep. More so than anyone she'd known in her adult life. Except maybe Sage. Not because the people in her life didn't have depth. But because she wasn't open to experiencing it with them.

So how had Scott managed to slide inside?

More importantly, what did she do about it? While part of her went into immediate defensive mode, sending out orders to build walls, to distract, another part of her asked, "So what possible looming failure were you fighting this morning?"

His didn't even blink as he continued to eye her and said, "Sexual attraction."

Right. Somewhere, in her convoluted psyche, she'd known. Had needed to hear him say it for some unforsaken reason she wasn't ready to pursue.

There was a much more pressing issue. "You could have been killed."

His shrug left room for the possibility to exist. Which made her angry all over again. "That's ludicrous, Scott! Better that we do it every day, twice a day, that we lose our friendship, end up unable to be in the same space together, to breathe the same air, than for you to..."

No longer be on earth.

What did it say about Scott that he was feeling better, more energized, more like himself, arguing with Iris than he'd felt all day? Even before he'd gone surfing.

She was pissed at him. Sage was, too. He got that. Even understood why. And regretted that he'd worried them.

And was putting Iris out for the night.

A situation he'd put an end to in the morning after the physical therapist gave him the information he needed to figure out how to tend to himself. *By* himself.

At which time he'd do what it took to forget the warmth he was feeling right then, with Iris's concern bleeding all over him.

If he'd needed proof that she valued their friendship as much as he did, he was getting it.

Which was all the more reason for him to make certain that his desire for her, returned or not, did not ruin what they had.

Because there was no other road for him to take.

Platonic friends. Or nothing.

In spite of the fact that her *do it every day* comment had his crotch tightening amid the pain he was in from the waist down.

If she saw it, she did. Nothing he could about it in his current state. Nor was he sure he wanted to try. Pretending it wasn't there didn't work. They had to acknowledge the situation. Fight it together.

Which was something that had occurred to him as he'd been beaten up by waves that morning. And was only just then coming back.

"I oftentimes get insights when I'm out battling waves," he said to her then. "The mental space I'm in out there… it's unlike any other. The clarity, but also the way whatever is on my mind becomes the only thing there." He sounded like a drunkard in his head. Stood by what he'd said as he told Iris something he'd never put into words before. Not even for Sage.

Her expression softened, which did nothing good for his midsection. But eased the tension in his heart some. More when she said, "Strangely enough, I get that."

The way she said it, as though she'd been there, left him in no doubt that she had been.

And called to him, too.

When? Where? Why?

He couldn't ask. Not without knowing what dangerous territory it could lead to.

But wished he'd said something, anything, to keep the conversation going, when, instead, she asked, "What clarity did you get this morning?"

He wasn't ready to talk about it. Didn't have anything concrete. "We're going to have to tackle the sex thing head-on."

"Have it, you mean? We already tried that."

And it hadn't worked. Or rather, had worked far too well for his body's sake. And maybe for hers, too. He couldn't help but notice that she hadn't proclaimed being over it. Which would be half the battle right there.

He shook his head, her *have it, you mean* still ringing through him. "No," he told her unequivocally. "Just… acknowledge it. Fight it together." Peace settled as he heard the words aloud.

And when he saw her features relax, too.

They didn't have to fight each other. They had to join forces, allow their friendship to work for them and, as a team, battle that which was threatening to ruin them.

A new regime. One that could actually work.

His body might be a little the worse for wear, but surfing had been a success once again.

She'd iced him several times already that evening. Somehow, doing so at midnight, with the lights so low, and both of them having been asleep, felt entirely new.

Cozy.

And probably far too intimate. At the moment, she didn't care. She could see pain on his face even while he slept.

"How you feeling?" she asked as she woke him with ready ice pack in hand.

He groaned. Helped bear the weight of his leg some as she slid the pack in place. Adding another pillow to the elevation. And then went for the pack for his back. The leg was ten minutes longer. Came first. She had it down to a science.

So did he.

Hadn't even opened his eyes.

"Turn your head." He did, confirming that he was still awake, and she put the fancy digital thermometer in his ear.

And when the reading was normal, reached for his arm, applying the blood pressure cuff.

As long as vitals stayed good for twenty-four hours, they were in the clear in terms of invisible enemies creeping up on him. At least enough to not need to monitor blood pressure and body temperature. There were still symptoms to watch for.

And dangers to prevent.

At least his penis wasn't hard. She wasn't proud that she'd looked. But they were fighting together. She had to take an active role to ensure success.

And for honesty's sake, too. Both self and otherwise.

When she saw his chin tighten, she asked softly, "You ready for a pain pill?"

"No."

"You'd sleep better. Which would help you heal better."

"No."

Irritated, but resigned, too, Iris collected used ice packs as timing required. Put them back in the freezer and went back to the chair she'd decided to use as her bed just for that first night. The only way she'd seen herself being able to nod off was to know that she was close enough to hear Scott if he needed her, to reach him instantly if necessary.

And the chair, a recliner, with her own pillow and blanket, let her keep guard over a man who would try to fend for himself rather than call out to her, too.

Three in the morning and Scott had to pee. So bad he couldn't keep holding it. Pain throbbed and shot whether he was lying still or moving, so he sat up, keeping a watch on the woman sleeping a few yards away. She looked beautiful. So much younger with her features relaxed in sleep. Oddly so. As though, awake, she carried a heavy burden.

He'd never have known the lifelines in her expressions weren't just effects of years lived, and constant exposure to the California sun, if he wasn't looking at the evidence.

His need to pee reared. A reminder to him. And he pulled the chair he and Dale had devised the foot or so necessary to bring it to the edge of the couch. Where he could use his arms to lift and slide, leaving his bad leg on the couch until last. Using his arms to help lift the leg to the chair.

The back pain would be intense for a few.

Less upsetting to him than peeing his pants would be.

"Tell me you aren't actually planning to tackle that on your own." The voice shot through him. Almost as painfully as the jerk her sudden conversation caused him to sustain in his lower back.

He didn't bother responding. The truth was clearly obvious, right there, in front of them. Continuing with his plan, he raised his weight off the couch with his arms. And felt Iris's hands slide beneath his pits, helping to glide him smoothly to the chair without wrenching his back. And before he could reach for his left leg, she was there, too.

Handling it completely by herself.

As much as he hated the helpless feeling she'd just injected into him, he was relieved, too. And without a word, used his good leg to wheel himself to the hall bath and, once inside, shut the door behind him.

Wise woman that she was, she let him.

Iris waited right outside the bathroom door. The nurse had told her to be sure not to leave him alone that first night. Most particularly during bathroom runs, if he refused to use the urinal. According to Nurse Windsor's experience, falls, tears, further injuries, happened most often during the night in the bathroom.

She heard something pour into the toilet. Heard it flush. Heard water run.

Heard him swear.

And her eyes filled with tears. Crazy, uncalled-for, foreign tears.

What the hell?

The doorknob turned and she blinked quickly. Rapidly. Giving her psyche a sharp reminder that she was in charge of her own life, and was herself, ready for Scott, when the door opened.

Or thought she was. Until she saw him somewhat balanced, half on the desk chair, and half off, hanging on to the sink to keep himself from falling to the floor.

The beads of sweat on his upper lip were a hint to how much pain he was in. The steely look in the glare he gave her kept her mouth shut.

At least while she swept in, slid her forearms beneath his armpits and lifted his weight until he could get his good leg firmly underneath himself.

Then gently lifted his bad leg back to the board that would support it for the journey back.

"I had a muscle spasm in my back," he bit out as he wheeled himself slowly back to the couch.

She wasn't surprised. Didn't bother expressing her *I told you so* that she was forcing herself to call up to distract from the sympathy threatening to overwhelm her. But calmly asked, "You ready for a pain pill?"

"No." The word was as much growl as English.

Saying nothing more, she assisted as he got himself back on the couch. Handed him the blanket he'd tossed at the end of the couch sometime before she'd woken up.

And as he settled back, asked one more time, "Pain pill?"

He closed his eyes. Turned his head away.

And Iris shook her head.

The man was as stubborn as they came.

Determined to walk the course he'd set for himself. Because he'd set it for good reason.

And, as much as she prayed he'd put a buffer on his suffering, she kind of admired him for his steadfastness to his convictions, too.

Chapter Twelve

Turned out, day two was not better than day one. It was worse. Scott hurt in places he'd never felt before. Inside his toes. What felt like under the skin, but on top of his left pectoral muscle. He'd discovered a bruise in the general vicinity and was guessing the board had hit him there, too. He had a headache, the nagging kind. His knee pain was off the charts, which made the back thing diminish a tad. More of a major distraction than a full-blown problem.

If he lay very still, totally relaxed, moved nothing, his pain went, on a scale of one to ten, from a twenty to a fifteen. He welcomed the proof that relief was possible. Held on to it, as he bore the icings. The heat.

Just as he clung to the sound of Iris's voice through the seemingly bone-splitting stab after sharp stab up and down his left side during any process that required him to move.

He managed some scrambled eggs for breakfast.

Gritted his teeth and sweated through the blessedly very short physical therapy session. Just some basic movement. A bend that almost sent him through the roof. Couldn't remember the name of the guy who'd been sent out. Nor any of the questions he'd previously thought so pertinent to ask during that first session.

He grunted. Gave almost imperceptible nods and shakes

of his head. He barely spoke. Slept as much as he could. Gave a thumbs-up for music. Down for television. Couldn't take on someone else's story at the moment. Just had to get through his own.

To breathe through the pain.

He insisted on getting to the bathroom when absolutely necessary but allowed anyone present to help him. Iris. The PT guy. Dale. Then Iris again.

What he did not do was take a single pain pill.

He'd said no. Would not take a chance on needing them to the point of thinking he couldn't make it without them.

He'd gotten himself into the mess. Was proving something to himself. And would not let himself down again.

He could succeed.

He would succeed.

He didn't want dinner. Drank broth, but only because he needed something on his stomach before he took his antibiotics. Puking was not an option at the moment.

The way he was feeling, he figured even a small regurgitation would kill him.

He'd drifted off after the broth and pills. Came to with an awareness of electrifying pain in his knee, and a new scent in the room.

Scott focused on the lavender smell so he didn't give in to the mind-killing pain. His nostrils weren't complaining about whatever was touching them. Something Iris must have brought in with her. He took a second deep breath of it. Didn't hate it.

Opened his eyes to tell her so, and Iris wasn't there. Harper was. Sitting on the edge of the chair he was pretty sure had been Iris's bed the entire previous night.

Alarm rent through him. So acutely that he felt it through

the rest of his mammoth discomfort. He'd sucked as a patient. Iris had had enough of him. Had left him.

He had to apologize. "Where's Iris?"

Harper stood. Smiled as she came toward him. And the not-horrible scent came with her. "She's just outside the back door, on the beach with the dogs. Your sister called. She didn't want to wake you with the conversation."

He gave his almost-nothing nod. Feeling better enough that he wanted to drift back to sleep. Iris hadn't left him.

"Can I get you anything?"

He didn't open his eyes. Just breathed deeply again. Concentrating on the scent. Picturing a field of purple flowers. Did lavender plants bloom?

Maybe it wasn't lavender. Lilac. They had blooms.

Didn't have to be an *L* word.

Scott drifted. Came fully conscious again as his own gasp woke him. He'd inadvertently tried to move his left leg to ease the stiffness. Nausea hit for a second. He was hot. On fire.

As he breathed, catching the scent again, both negative sensations receded. Not because of the smell. But because the initial shock of pain was dulling.

Still…

He opened his eyes. Saw Iris's frown as she stood over him. "You okay?"

Iris was back. Seeing her, he nodded. "Tried to move the damned leg." No. Wait. He needed to be a better patient. "What's that smell?"

She grabbed a small unit with an electrical cord sitting on the table at the end of the couch at his feet. "I'm sorry," she said, reaching down to unplug the bamboo-looking thing. "Is it bothering you?"

"No." Bamboo? Not lilac, lavender or anything else *L*.

"I like it." His voice was thick. Throat dry. She looked so good to him. So damned good. Had he seen those clothes before?

Jeans. Didn't wear them on the beach.

She'd put her hair in a ponytail. Or had it been that way all night?

No. A strand had fallen on his chest at some point. He'd been on his back and...

She was gone. Had left the room. Because he'd had an inappropriate thought. She was being such a good friend. And he'd...

There she was again. Holding what had become his worst enemy of all time. The ice pack. Knee one. The worst.

Her hand on his thigh was nice, though. So he forced himself to lift the leg himself.

"What is it?" He half stumbled over the words. But had to get them out there. To get back on track.

"What is what?"

"The smell?" He took another long whiff.

"It's aromatherapy," she said "It's called calm waters. Combination of lavender, cedarwood and rose oil." She'd settled the ice pack, put his leg down. Was loosening the compression on his back to ready it for the same frozen torture. "Rose oil is a cicatrizant, good for wound healing. Cedarwood eases tensions. And lavender is calming and will help you sleep."

His eyes shot open. Glared at her. She was drugging him? Through his nose?

"I'm happy to take it away if you'd rather," she said, not looking at him, therefore missing his silent communication. "I just found it helped me one time when I was in a car accident. I've continued to use it through the years. Mostly when I can't sleep."

Ice hit his back. He wanted to swear. To grab the damned pack and throw it at the wall. To hear the thunk of it hitting. He took a deep breath instead. And let Iris's oils invade his system.

Better that than lose any of the many battles he was waging with himself.

Iris spent a second night in the chair. The doctor hadn't prepared her for how hard Monday would be on Scott. And, in a much less brutal fashion, on her as well. Watching him hurt, seeing his face creased in pain even in his sleep, worrying about his lack of appetite, missing his repartee even...all hit unexpectedly hard.

Sage had suggested that her brother should see how his obstinate refusal to medicate properly, or to stay in the hospital, was making it hard on those around him. Had been ready to tell him so herself, but Iris had let her know that she wished she wouldn't.

In the first place, after calling someone from his office from the hospital to let them know what was going on, Scott had turned his phone off until he could speak coherently. Sage's calls weren't going through.

And in the second, Iris was bearing the brunt of the burden of caring for Scott, and she was not going to be the reason he failed in his own eyes.

Besides, it wasn't like she couldn't leave if she wanted to. Harper was right there, perched on the edge of Scott's porch it seemed like to Iris, ready to jump in and help. The woman was kind. Genuinely helpful.

And seemed to gravitate more toward the men on the beach than the women.

Not that that should matter to Iris. It wasn't like she had her eye on any of them. Still...

Not worth thinking about.

In the kitchen Tuesday morning, scrambling eggs before Scott woke up and grunted enough to tell her he didn't want any, Iris was glad for the quick shower she'd grabbed as soon as Scott had fallen asleep after the postdawn icing. She felt better. More like herself. Had left her hair loose just to dry. Was in her favorite beige cotton pants and black-and-beige leopard-pattern sweater. Ready to take on anything in her path.

And caught herself smiling.

Because of the clothes. Because Scott should be feeling better.

Both thoughts rang true, but there was more. Standing there, helping her friend, immersing herself in the task, she felt…happy.

Not behind-the-camera alive and well, but…really happy.

In a way the sense of lightness inside her felt foreign. Almost unrecognizable, but not totally. There was distant recognition. Certainly a sense that she'd known the sensation before.

"Iris!" The call shocked her so much she dropped the spatula she'd been using, spattering egg on the floor.

As Morgan and Angel gleefully cleaned up the mess, she ran around the corner to the living room. Scott, half on the office chair, which appeared to have scooted away from him, did not look happy.

She was there in seconds, helping him onto the chair. And, wearing a full-out frown, too. "You should have called out to me."

"I could smell the eggs cooking. I'm starving." Full, gruntless sentences.

"The girls are enjoying them," she grouched, but handled his left leg gently as she got it propped up on the chair.

"You're supposed to be moving to crutches today, assuming your back allows it," she continued, all business as she walked behind him to the bathroom door, and helped him stand while leaning on the counter, and then quickly let herself out, pulling the door closed behind her.

Arms crossed, leaning against the wall, she waited outside for him, heard the toilet flush. Heard him brush his teeth, too, took the move as a sign that he was getting better, and figured him for washing his face based on the sounds she heard next. They were succeeding. The two of them, as friends, were working together and he was getting better.

As he called out to her, asking for a change of clothes, letting her know where to find them, and then, telling her to leave them just inside the door on the counter, Iris collected, deposited. Waited. And when he let her know he was ready for her help getting back, experienced that oddly happy sensation from the kitchen again.

She'd never yearned to be a nursemaid. Which was all she'd been doing both times the curious blast from the past had hit.

But she'd been wearing her attitude sweater, both times.

Maybe clothes really did have a lot to do with how a person felt.

She had to go. Standing on one leg, with Iris's arms beneath his armpits as he lowered himself to his desk chair, Scott remembered exactly what he'd been planning to ask the physical therapist. And would do so.

Just as soon as he got the guy's name again.

You couldn't connect with a person enough to get the answers you needed out of them if you didn't put forth some effort.

Like remembering a name.

And then he'd get every trick the trade had ever known. How a guy dealt with crutches and a lower back sprain at the same time. How to lift a leg that was partially dead-weight with a back that was on a no-lifting order.

If the therapist wasn't privy to the answers, he'd invent some. Period. No way was he going to have Iris helping him into his chair like that again.

Bad enough that the bathroom had been involved. The discomfort of that alone was enough to drive a guy to desperate measures. But if he had to stand there one more time with Iris's arms looped under his, sliding against his body, holding him, there'd be a lot more embarrassing happenings than someone listening to him pee.

Like hearing him cry out in pain at the beginning of his physical therapy session later that morning. Definitely worse than pee. The way Iris had come running in from the kitchen, mouth open, her eyes wide, filled with fear... she had to go.

Let him be miserable in peace.

PT, while sweat inducing and painful, actually turned out to be a good thing. He managed to stay alert, to eventually conquer every one of the basic exercises he'd been given to start with. And to ask Joel—he'd managed to get the name of his in-home therapist for the duration by reading his name tag—the questions that had been on his mind on Sunday. Namely, any and all that would give him the tricks of the trade that would allow him to be immediately self-sufficient.

And while he and Joel were still alone, he had the younger man order him up the wheelchair with a brake on it that was what he was going to need. While his left side and back would continue to be tender, he had enough upper-body strength to get himself from chair to toilet. And they discovered that the bed in his spare room, a queen that was lower to the ground than his king, was better for him to get himself on and off from than the couch.

The freezer door—a top, not side, model—could be accessed with a reacher-grabber tool, ordered online for same-day delivery. And he could access the ice packs, and return them for cooling, with the same apparatus.

For good measure, he had Joel order him up a shower chair, too. Just in case. He was certain he could stand on one leg long enough to get the business done, but he knew others wouldn't approve of that course of action. And since no one would be around to witness his use of the chair, or a one-legged stance, ordering the chair was clearly the obvious choice. Just because he had it didn't mean he had to use it.

By the time Iris returned from a trip home, via a walk on the beach with Morgan and Angel, Scott was in another fresh pair of shorts and T-shirt, and was sitting up on the couch. With pillows supporting his back and another set of them under his left leg. Iris had picked up a tray with little legs that straddled him side to side and he had his computer open on it and had just hung up from the office. The call had been brief. Just a check-in. He'd answered a couple of critical questions, though, without once having to grit his teeth against the pain running up and down his left side.

Joel had made it clear that he thought Scott was lacking in mental acuity for not taking the pain medication. The therapist didn't know about Scott's greater hurdles, nor the bigger-picture course he'd set for himself.

The dogs bounded into the living room first. Followed closely by Iris. The first thing he noticed was the leopard print. Again. Accompanied by an immediate, inappropriate and not even justified jump to thoughts of wild activities.

"You're working?" Her lighter tone, the possible approval he heard in her voice, drew his gaze to her face.

And the smile she was wearing along with the leopard print.

"I am and we need to talk." Another jolt of sexual desire pushed the words right out of him. He'd meant to finesse. To use his professional skills to convince her that she agreed with the plan of action ready to be put into motion.

It was going to happen, either way. Had to happen. He'd just feel better with her support. He didn't want her mad at him.

A new thing in their friendship—the idea that she *would* get mad. Prior to his injury, their easygoing friendship had never entered those waters.

The realization required a bit of his energy for the second it took him to process the fact that things were changing in spite of their resolve. Sexual attraction, and the possibility of anger...

"What you need to do is eat lunch," Iris said, pulling a grocery bag out of the large black satchel she'd carried in and opened. A satchel he'd been eyeing as a threat and needing it to go right back out. She had the lid off a container she'd pulled out of the grocery bag before he found a refusal, and the sight of the sub...all the protein she'd piled on it... Well...he did need to eat.

He needed all the protein he could get. Protein repaired cells.

She had to go. But the food. There was a lot of it. Way more than just a sub. Chicken salad with grapes. Broccoli salad. Potato salad. Coleslaw. Some green gelatin. And a fork.

"I asked Dale to stop at the deli on his way home last night and pick up some salad. He brought two pounds of each of these. I know you aren't fond of pineapple, but I don't think any of these contain it. I tasted them all."

Suddenly starving, Scott dug in. Praised the food. The deli. Dale.

He didn't praise Iris.

He couldn't even begin to list all of things she'd done for him in the past two days. All without being asked.

Had no words to express his gratitude.

Instead, as he handed her the empty paper plate and used fork, he said again, "We need to talk."

He'd have kicked himself if he'd been able, as she turned her back and, without a word, left the room.

He'd meant to express his undying appreciation. To let her know just how much her being there during the past two hellish days had kept him going.

Admitting that he couldn't have done it without her.

Instead, he'd talked to her like she was some space age robotic servant with no feelings. Maybe a way to kill off any latent attraction that she might, somehow, if the moon fell to the earth, still be harboring for him after the past days of awkward physical TMI.

But not at all the way to preserve a friendship that meant more to him than ever.

"We're already an hour late for your pills." She was back. Handing him the medication before taking a seat in the chair that had somehow become a bedroom to her. "I kept watching for Joel's van to leave. He must have worked you hard."

Yes, well, Scott did feel as though he'd been run through an assembly line complete with paper presses. But Joel's lengthy stay had been caused by the after-workout, "provide for Scott's autonomy" business.

As soon as he'd swallowed the last pill, took a breath to dive into his charge, argument, summary and verdict.

Before he got started, Iris said, "What was it you wanted to talk to me about?"

"I'm a hundred percent better today," he started in, stopping when his words garnered him a very clearly raised eyebrow in his direction. She was all confident-looking in her leopard-patterned top.

"As opposed to yesterday," he conceded.

Had she put on the tiger that day for him?

He wouldn't blame her.

"I just want you to know how much it means to me... what you've done these past two days." He stopped right where he'd planned. And then said, "I'm never going to forget..." His voice dropped off midsentence as his ears heard his words, and something inside him rescued him from himself.

"You might want to wait until the end of the week to be saying things like that," Iris said, and pushed herself back until the footrest came out on the chair. She sat there, looking him right in the eyes. Appearing as though she had every intention to remain there. Take a nap even.

Not that he begrudged her one. She most definitely deserved some catch-up sleep after all he'd deprived her of with his heat and ice and pill requirements. But not there.

Still, he'd started the conversation. He couldn't just completely bail. "I could wait until the end of time, and I'd still be grateful."

With her lips turned, her chin jutting, her brows raised, all as though she'd suddenly decided there was merit in his words, she nodded. But didn't lower her footrest. Instead, she pulled out her phone.

Confusion replaced the huge amounts of gratitude he'd

been feeling. Panic took over for confusion. With a little anger bobbing in and out.

"I no longer need twenty-four-hour care." He told her about the wheelchair, the grabber thing, the shower chair, postulating that they were tools meant to make one independent and ending with Joel's proclamation regarding Scott's upper-body strength. Punctuating the finale with a good chest and upper arm muscle clench.

Emulating any of the action figures of his youth, if he did think so himself.

Iris appeared to be listening. She was watching him, not her phone. Seemed attentive. He couldn't read her, though. Which did not please him. Used to reading juries made up of total strangers, and doing so accurately more often than not, Scott was vexed by her ability to stump him.

Because he was already on his last nerve due to the constant pain in his left leg. Not just the knee. No, his injury had to make itself felt up and down the entire damned limb.

That was it. He'd almost lost Iris the day before by being cantankerous. He'd needed her then. Now he didn't. All he had to do was be a difficult patient. A grouch.

Something he could offer with very little provocation at the moment.

"I'm serious, Iris. I want to do this alone from here on out. I need my place to myself."

"I know. You've made up your mind. You have a right to make your own choices."

And there she sat. With the silence drawing out between them. Until she asked, "You done?"

Her question played right into his plan. Bringing out the grump in him. "Yes, as a matter of fact I am," he snipped. Then thought of something else to say, pursuant to the black weekend bag she'd erroneously brought into his home but couldn't give voice to it lest he prove himself wrong. He'd said he was done.

"Good, then here's your choice. You put up with me in your space until your back allows you to be up on crutches full-time—no need for a wheelchair..."

His gut clenched. He gritted his teeth. He waited for whatever other cockamamie option she was about to deliver with such sassy confidence so that he could hand down his third and final option—she had to go.

"...oorrr..." She drew out the word, turning her phone around, to show him a call screen. With his sister's name on top in big bold letters. Big enough, bold enough for him to read from several feet away. "Or she's catching the next flight home, cutting her family-moon short by two weeks. Your choice. I gave her my word."

Scott's mouth opened.

But no winning argument came forth.

Sage had clearly issued a threat she fully meant to keep.

And Iris was there because of the very same threat. She was there for Sage. To preserve the Bartholomews' very special bonding time as a new family.

Not for him.

Chapter Thirteen

She had to stay. She'd given Sage her word. So why when she heard the truth come out of her mouth did she feel… happy? As though she'd been given permission to do something she'd wanted to do but wasn't allowed to do?

Allowed by who?

While the quickly presenting impressions could be worth pursuing, Iris didn't have a chance to do so. Watching the expressions rapidly crossing Scott's face—reading nothing that even remotely resembled her level of well-being under the circumstances—she rushed to minimize any negative effects on the friendship she and Scott were working to preserve.

"However…"

The one word got his immediate attention. Holding his gaze, she leaned forward slowly to buy herself time to come up with the rest of that sentence.

"I understand where you're coming from in terms of reclaiming your personal autonomy." Good. She liked it.

Most particularly when, chin jutting, he nodded. And waited.

She had a few seconds to solve the problem. Put herself in his shoes. And found it…not all that much of a challenge to do. She knew him.

Suddenly, words started flowing.

"And I understand Sage's need to be here." She went with what she was getting. Trusting something more than her mind to guide her.

Something she hadn't done in a very long time.

"You can say you're just fine with the pain, but Sage senses how much you're suffering." His twin had told her so. Saying it was a twin thing.

What neither of them knew was that she totally got it.

"Sage has never had a high enough tolerance for pain to deal with me."

"I think it's more that she feels your pain with a soft tender heart, while you process in a completely different lobe." The words came from deep inside. With a knowledge that couldn't be denied. Ivy had been the more right-brained of the two of them. Living almost entirely by her heart. Iris had had her deep-heart moments but had done most of her initial processing with a more left-brained approach. Together, they'd been the perfect pair to face the seemingly devastating challenges life had handed them. Together. Until they hadn't been.

Her stream of consciousness ended abruptly. Returning her to current life. And the man who was looking at her oddly. As though she knew things others didn't get.

The twin vow, made in the womb, before thought existed.

She'd said too much. Too much. Too much. Panic hit. Her gaze couldn't seem to break away from Scott's. *Too much.*

He wasn't saying anything. She took a breath. And it was like some kind of special knowledge emanated from those blue eyes of his. Without seeing her secret. Somehow those eyes went from posing a threat, to calming her.

"Regardless…" she continued, as though she hadn't lost all train of thought. Was miraculously able to jump back, to be where she was. A nudge from Ivy. "Your sister has one foot on the plane already. Which means we have to do what we can to tame your pain as much as possible. The way I see it, we have two challenges there. The physical pain, and the more personal sense of emotional discomfort."

His lips pursed, jutted forward. Acknowledgment of her point?

Or an attempt to stifle an order for her to get out?

Before he lost that possible battle, she rushed forward. "So I stay. I continue to oversee the tasks that are critical to your fastest physical healing. Icing. Compression. Meds. And cooking." She paused. And when he didn't grunt or bark out a refusal, she said, "You take over all the personal hygiene needs. As soon as your chairs arrive."

Wheel and shower. He'd already taken over. She got that. Understood why, too.

And waited to see how badly he was taking her proposal. She wasn't going to back down. And knew that, ultimately, he'd find a way to compromise enough that she didn't call his sister. Didn't mean she was looking forward to the mental battle that was likely coming to get them there.

"I have to sleep in the spare room." The words were unequivocal. "Bed's lower. Joel and I did the dry run."

The two men had already started on Scott's excruciating physical therapy before she'd left. Which meant the rest had come after. When his pain would be at its worst. He'd been that determined to get rid of her.

For their friendship's sake.

The idea came to her. Didn't leave.

She accepted its presence.

"You'll have to sleep in my bed." His tone was unequivocal.

No. Uh-uh. Just not a good plan. Everything in her stood

strong on that one. The strong shaking of her head was testament to that fact.

"I can't take looking at the chair and seeing it as your bedroom."

So she'd sleep on the floor, if she had to. She had a blow-up mattress.

"Nor can I have you in a space that isn't behind a closed door."

Iris saw the loss coming her way. Saw the sense, heard the raw honesty, in his words.

Had to take back the upper hand enough to have her own control in the situation. "That's settled then," she said, abruptly ending his opportunity for discussion. "I'm staying."

She was standing by the time the words were out. Slinging her satchel over her shoulder, she said, "Works out fine. The master bath will give me more privacy." And left him sitting there.

Scott was about bursting with a need to pee by the time his chair arrived. But with his senses returning, there'd been no way he'd been going to have Iris standing outside the door while he took care of his business. He cringed every time he thought about the things she'd already witnessed.

Placated himself with the idea that he hadn't been himself. He'd been patient number one. Not Scott Martin.

Iris oversaw the chair's unloading, delivery into the house and making it to the couch. And then, true to her word, left the room to head back to the kitchen, where she was working on dinner. Baking some of his salmon. Putting together a salad that used broccoli and cranberries, based on her questions to him regarding his current preferences. After three years of conversation and a plethora of shared meals on the beach, she pretty much knew his likes and dislikes.

She'd left the brake on for him. And gritting his teeth against the pain, he actually took a mite of pleasure in doing for himself. Most particularly after he made it back to the couch without losing the contents of his stomach due to pain.

The mind-numbing shards of electric shock shooting through him weren't quite as unbearable as they had been the day before. That was what he focused on. What mattered. He'd made it through the worst of it. With success.

Thoughts of his victory over failure enshrined him with strength.

So much so that when he awoke from an hour's nap, and heard Iris speaking softly to Morgan and Angel, ushering them outside to the beach, he lifted himself into his chair for a second go-round. Heading to his own bathroom. To go again. But also to collect the personal items he was going to need over the next few days. A razor for one. He just wasn't a few-days'-growth type of guy. No matter how fashionable the look.

The task posed some hardships. Requiring him to stand on one leg with only the support of the counter. But that wasn't what almost did him in.

It was the sight of Iris's toiletries laid out neatly on his granite countertop, as though she was sharing his most intimate space with him, that hit him with the jolt that had him falling back into his chair.

A jolt to the groin so powerful he went from nothing to everything in a split second.

Morgan's sudden bark rent through him. Her looking-for-him tone. The one she used whenever he came home.

The three females sharing his space were back. Sweeping his things into his lap, to cover evidence that Iris absolutely could not see, Scott swung his chair around so quickly his left foot caught on the door. And he cried out.

"Ahh..." He cut off the sound of his agony abruptly, but not soon enough.

"Scott?" Iris was right behind the sound of her voice. Her expression as worried as she'd sounded.

He scowled. "I'm fine," he told her. And then glared at her. "Collecting my things, which definitely falls under personal business."

After giving him a careful once-over, she turned her back and walked out.

Without another word.

A smart woman.

True to her word.

And he was no longer even a tiny bit hard.

Giving him a very welcome revelation.

The surfing had worked. Even if he still harbored some very temporary hots for his friend, his injuries were most definitely going to prevent him from acting on them.

Which would give Sage and Gray time to get home. Built-in chaperones. Reminders to Scott and Iris of who they were and what they did and did not want. To return them to the roles they'd always played in each other's life.

He'd most definitely done the right thing, taking on South Beach.

Thanks to the father who'd been so hard on him, instilling in him the abhorrence of failure.

A sense that he had to pull from within himself, give all he had to that which he was best at, and accept nothing less than success from himself.

Turned out, the old man had been right.

Where there was a will, there was a way.

And he most definitely had the will to be Iris's friend for life.

Which meant, the hots had to go.

He was everywhere. Beneath her. On top of her. Inside her.

Even up her nose.

All she had to do was breathe to be enveloped by his essence. So she did. Long deep breaths. And it worked every time.

Iris moved, wanting to slide her arms around him…and rose to full consciousness instead. On the softest sheets. Her own sheets. She'd brought them with her. Had purchased her own king-size bed after Scott had raved about his one day on the beach. He'd said he slept better because no matter how much he moved, there was space to accommodate him.

Having been a restless sleeper ever since the accident, Iris had been willing to give his theory a try.

It hadn't worked. She'd felt more alone than ever on the massive mattress. But she'd spent the money, so she'd kept the bed. Had adopted Angel to help her sleep, at Dale's suggestion. And had solved both of her problems. Having the little collie around really did settle some of the demons that raged inside her in the blackness of night, but the girl helped fill up the spare mattress space, too.

As her thoughts traveled further from the nonsense she'd awoken to, Iris reached outside the covers for Angel. To get back in sync with herself.

And caught another whiff. Scott.

From the comforter. She'd exchanged his sheets for hers, but had failed to consider the icing on the cake.

Forbidden icing, no matter how strong the temptation

was to let her relaxed, half-asleep self slide back into a place where she could make love to Scott one more time.

In a bed. With enough time to touch every inch of him. To feel his hands on parts of her no one ever touched.

Just to get it done and him out of her system.

An idea that sounded plausible, and almost smart, as she lay in the quiet dark of three in the morning, filled with his presence. Right until Angel, probably sensing Iris's imminent slide into a bad place, woke, and climbed up on Iris's belly, flattening herself out, wagging her tail and jamming her nose into Iris's chin.

The mistress was awake, so the dog thought it appropriate to communicate her need to go out. Their regular morning routine. After which, Angel got to eat, which was what she really wanted. The bathroom-going thing was just the way to get breakfast.

Any other night, Iris would have told Angel it was too early. To lie down.

Scott was on the other side of the wall. Would he hear her?

A man who lived alone wouldn't be used to hearing a voice in his home. The anomaly could wake him.

She'd iced him an hour before.

Which was probably what had brought on the whole adverse-to-her-ultimate-happiness thought process to begin with. It had been her first care visit with him in bed.

He'd been in pain. In the moment, she'd made it worse. And skedaddled as soon as it was done. His discomfort and her concern for him far overshadowing more shallow thoughts.

Until her psyche knew she was out and had run away from home. Getting her into trouble.

Throwing off her covers as that last thought made her

groan over its melodrama, Iris picked up Angel. Probably best that she take a trip outside with Angel. Recalibrate her emotional equilibrium.

With the miniature collie resting half on her arm and half against her body, Iris tiptoed barefoot toward the bedroom door. Maybe the cool air outside would wake her fully enough that she could find peaceful rest when she went back to bed, rather than active sleep. If she got a little chilled outside in just her pajama pants and T-shirt, all the better.

She turned the knob slowly, swung the wood open inches at a time. Making certain that she didn't wake Scott. Lord knew he didn't need any more awareness of her disruptive presence in his home.

Making it to the living room without a sound, she glanced back once, toward the spare bedroom door. Scott had asked that she leave it open to make it easier for him to wheel to the bathroom in the hall. And there was clearly no light coming from the room.

Breathing a sigh of relief, hoping the man was getting some real rest, she made a quick beeline for the kitchen before Morgan got a whiff of them up and about.

She didn't dare turn on any lights. Wouldn't need them once she got out back and her eyes adjusted to the darkness.

With help from the moon's beaconing glow.

Keeping her eyes pinned on her goal, the back door, she rounded the half wall separating the dining area from the kitchen, and…pain shot through her foot.

"Ouch!" she let out before she could stop herself. Followed by an immediate, harshly whispered "Damn" as Angel moved against her, licking her nose.

Her toe hurt like hell. She'd stubbed it against…

"Scott?"

She'd walked into the wheel of his chair.

"My leg," he said, his tone threadbare. Barely there.

Filled with instant alarm, Iris flipped on the overhead light, set Angel down and was kneeling at the raised foot-rest on the left side of his chair, ready to pull up the leg of his pajama pants when he said, "I forgot Morgan's bed."

Her gaze flew to his face. Noticed the whiteness. Fearing he was incoherent, she searched his gaze. Saw pain there. A ton of it. But full lucidity, too.

Before he swallowed hard and closed his eyes. As he had most of day two. When the pain had been almost more than he could bear...

She remembered the dog bed in the corner of Scott's room. She'd thought it extraneous. Figured it for something Morgan used when Scott was gone all day.

"She sleeps in it at night," she guessed. Hoping he'd open up his eyes.

His one bob nod felt like a victory, but not enough to quell the fresh wave of worry sluicing through her. Nor did it tell her what he was doing in the kitchen. There were no other dog beds there. Just the one. In the room she was using.

She had to figure out what they were dealing with. Using both hands to gently fold up the loose-fitting cotton cover-ing Scott's leg, she took one roll up at a time.

"She can't jump...up and down...from the bed."

"I know," she said, halfway to his knee.

"She was pacing...whining... I lifted her up..."

She started in on what would be the last roll. Could feel the bandage against the backs of her fingers.

Wet. *Oh God.* Moving more quickly, she got the material out of the way, exposing the bandage that Joel had changed for Scott earlier in the day.

"She was trying to get to me…" She barely heard the words, didn't even try to make sense of him lifting the short-legged corgi and Morgan trying to get to him at the same time, as a fresh wave of fear swept over her.

Wet and bright red.

Heart pounding, Iris grabbed a compression bandage from the medical supplies on the kitchen table. "This is probably going to hurt like hell," she said but didn't pause as she swiftly and tightly wrapped from below the blood-soaked bandage to inches above it.

Then, grabbing her purse and keys from the same table, she pulled a quilted vest off the coat hooks inside the laundry room door and shrugged into it one arm at a time while she pushed the chair with the other. Taking heart from the fact that Scott was able to walk his hanging, healthy right foot along with it.

He'd lost a lot of blood. Beyond that, she had no idea what they were facing. She just knew that she could get him to the hospital more rapidly herself than calling for an ambulance and waiting for it to get down to Ocean Breeze.

Her mind pumping with clear, immediate action items, she left the chair for the seconds it took her to grab a blanket off the couch and throw it over Scott's lap. Almost cried when she saw his hand close over it, holding it in place.

And telling the girls to stay, she lowered the chair down the step to Scott's garage and headed for her car.

Parked right next to his.

And prayed.

Chapter Fourteen

Fully cognizant, fighting pain-induced nausea, Scott did what he could. He'd been going for ice. The bandage had been a better option to slow the immediate flow of blood. He'd hoped the situation wasn't serious, figured himself for an uncomfortable night fighting fresh pain.

He'd made it through the worst. Knew he'd get through the night the same way.

Then he'd heard Iris gasp when she'd gotten a look at his dressing.

And knew.

If the sight of the dressing caused that much distress, he was in far worse shape than he'd thought. Was doing everything he could to stay conscious so he could assist her in getting him help as efficiently, as urgently as possible.

Approving of her choice to drive him the ten or so minutes to the hospital herself, rather than waiting for an emergency vehicle—the call for and arrival of which would take about equal time—he wanted to offer his praise. To thank her.

But needed all his lung capacity focused on controlling his breathing. Which helped ease the threat of stomach revolt.

And, he wanted to believe, helped relax the pain a bit, too.

He held his head up, and kept his eyes opened as Iris

wheeled him into the emergency room. And while he let her do the talking, when the nurse said, "I'll take him from here," and moved to grab the push handles of his chair from Iris, Scott spoke up.

"She comes with me." His words were firm. Clear. "If I have to sign to that effect, I will."

The effort cost him. Nausea was pushing at his esophagus again. He closed his eyes. Breathed. In through the nose, out through the mouth.

Steady.

He didn't even try to open his eyes as he was lifted onto a bed. Didn't know who was lifting him. He heard Iris, talking to everyone who was there, answering questions, talking as they unwound first the compression wrap and then his bandage. While he breathed.

That was his job.

To stay the course. Endure the hard work it took to be a success.

Right up until he heard the doctor, who'd introduced himself when he'd come in, say something about needing to put in a couple of stiches to repair the tear in his wound. Just as soon as he was under.

"No." Only one word. But filled with the strength of his conviction. "Local anesthetic only."

The doctor argued. Clearly speaking to Iris. Scott was there. Waited.

"No." Iris's tone seemed to Scott to mimic his. In a very good way. "Unless his life is in immediate danger, like the pain is causing his blood pressure to soar, no pain medication."

He heard more. The doctor, in a very convincing tone. Iris's "I know" replies. Four of them.

And then she was touching his forehead. Rubbing her

hand up it, brushing the short strands of his hair. And returned to start again. Slowly. Over and over.

He breathed with the touch. Like keeping time with a soft slow melody.

Even as the pain in his lower leg went from excruciating to off the charts.

His vitals were steady. His life was in no immediate danger from the pain.

And Iris's tender hand against his skin was a constant.

Scott figured life could be one hell of a lot worse.

Dawn was breaking by the time they got back to Ocean Breeze. Scott allowed her to help him from the car to the house, but then wheeled himself off to bed. The man was stubborn as hell.

Her heart ached for him, reaching toward him even as he rejected any hint of sympathy. She had to let him go. To fend for himself per their agreement. To respect his choice. Doing what was right didn't take away the sting.

What was up with that? With the over-the-top emotions she was feeling around him since the wedding?

If she didn't care so much about Sage, and treasure her friendships with the twins, she'd head home right that minute, just to get herself back in sync again. But if experiencing vicarious emotion was the price she had to pay to have them in her life, she'd do so.

It was a whole lot less than Scott was paying for his own personal choices, that was for sure.

He'd left his door open, per protocol, and once she saw him settled in bed, she took the girls and went out to the beach. He had his phone within reach. And her number on speed dial. Only for the moment.

She didn't go anywhere. Joel would be arriving in a

few hours and that would be her chance to head home. To get back into her real life for an hour or so to get herself on track.

To rid herself of the shards of fear that were still reverberating through her—the replay of that first second she'd seen the blood soaking Scott's bandage, her frantic drive to the hospital—and get back into the peace that defined the new life she'd invented for herself.

She walked down to the water with Morgan and Angel. Talking to them. Conversation between her and Angel was a norm in their home, and Morgan had been with them often enough over the years that the corgi showed no surprise when Iris started in with "The good news is—well, first, that aside from two ripped stitches, there was no other damage." Morgan seemed to glance her way at that.

"I don't know yet what happened," she told the girl. "He was too busy getting himself through everything to talk much, but I know for certain that if you had anything to do with what happened, it wasn't intentional."

The girls, side by side, on her right, kept on walking. They might not understand her exact words. Or even what had happened. But they knew that things weren't right. That Scott was down. That she was bothered. They weren't running and playing. Or even exploring the sand with their noses as they usually did. They weren't watching the water.

They were keeping their eyes on her. Staying beside her.

"And the other good news…" She took a breath. Sighed. Then finished with "The sex thing, it's not a *thing* thing. Not a real thing. Or even a thing at all. It's just a symptom of whatever has me off-kilter, because it's not just attraction, it's all my emotions."

Right. The words rang completely true. Even aloud.

Talking to beings who didn't hear lies, but knew the truth behind them. She was on the right track.

She wasn't suddenly desiring Scott Martin. She was just suffering an influx of all emotion, which would include sexual emotions, and Scott was just the guy who happened to have been there before she'd figured out what was going on and could do something to stop it.

It explained the almost debilitating fear for Scott's life. The bouts of anger.

And his bouts? Well, those were easy to explain, too, since she understood the source. He'd merely been reacting to things she'd been inadvertently sending out.

Angel glanced up at her. Iris felt like her girl had just sent a frown her way. Knew that the possibility didn't exist. But felt it anyway.

She knew the problem. What was the solution?

First, she was going to call the psychologist who'd been her sounding board through the worst days of her life. Just to hear the good doctor tell her that a sudden flare-up of intense emotions was not an uncommon response to an emotional trigger.

Which Sage's wedding had most definitely been.

As the maid of honor, and hearing Sage whisper that she was like a sister to her...the trigger was about as obvious as it could get.

She'd grown up expecting to stand up with her own twin at Ivy's wedding someday. To have to accept that her sister would be sharing everything in her life with the partner she'd chosen and that while Iris would always be a big part of her life, Iris would no longer come first.

Instead, she'd stood up with Scott's twin—with much the same change coming as a result. Iris and Scott were no longer going to be the adults that came first in Sage's life.

Their threesome had irrevocably changed with Sage's vows to Gray.

All good stuff. Great stuff.

And, as with all change, there was a subconscious leaning toward wanting to hold on to what was. Simply because it was familiar. Normal.

Easy, even.

Finally, she had everything worked out.

"It all makes sense," she said aloud to the girls as she started back up to Scott's cottage with them right beside her. "My psyche is acting out. That's all. As soon as Sage, Leigh and Gray get back, everything will return to normal."

In the meantime, she had a very dear friend who posed no sexual concern in his current state, who needed her whether he liked it or not.

And she felt right about being there for him.

Scott heard Iris come in. He'd heard her leave before, too. Had spent the entire time she'd been on the beach with the girls figuring out a way to get her to go home.

It was either that or lose the battle of his life.

He couldn't have her around. Not when he was physically at a low point. And man, was his point low. He'd savored the touch of Iris's hand on his brow as though she was his own personal angel.

Or…someone to whom he was heart connected.

He knew the feeling. His heart wasn't dead. It just didn't get to involve other hearts. Because his need to succeed, his self-respect, his sense of right and wrong, all beat it out every time.

He wasn't kidding himself that he was falling for Iris. If that had been going to happen, it would have. Three years before when Angel and Morgan had introduced them on the beach. Iris had just adopted the miniature collie and had apologized for the fact that the little one hadn't yet learned beach manners.

Or even that it was necessary to pee outside.

No, he wasn't falling *for* her, but he was definitely falling *into* her. Wanting to be with her. To have her in his daily life. To be in hers.

On more than just a casual level.

The casual thing had gone out the window the moment she'd handed him the urinal in the hospital.

With the local anesthetic still easing some of the pain in his knee, giving the rest of his leg some peace from the shooting electrical currents of shock, he figured there was no time like the present to take care of the situation.

Where there was a will, there was a way.

Getting himself off the bed and into his chair, he noticed the leg of his pajama pant, cut up almost to his groin. Saw his dark hairy thigh sitting there far too naked for the confrontation he knew was coming.

But had to get out to Iris before Sage reached her.

He'd tried to go the twin route while Iris was out on the beach. Hadn't worked.

It was like the two women were ganging up on him. The time had come to put an end to it.

Wheeling himself out to the living room, bare leg and all, he thought, too late, about a stop at the bathroom first. Peeing could wait.

He had other more pressing business.

Iris was giving the girls their treats and stood when she saw him coming. "You feeling better?"

She'd changed into jeans and a button-down blouse. Before she went out to the beach? Or after she'd come in?

He'd thought he'd lain in bed, fully conscious, ever since they'd been home. Maybe he'd drifted some.

No matter.

Irrelevant.

"Fine," he told her, coming to a stop a few feet from her. He looked up, met her gaze. "I called Sage."

"I know."

His slight nod was acknowledgment to himself. Not meant for her. He'd drifted off. Her coming in with the dogs…they'd obviously been on a different trip outside. He was too late for the offense route. "What time is it?"

"Two."

"Two? In the afternoon?" He was putting a clock in the spare bedroom. And needed his phone and smartwatch back on and glued to him nonstop. As was his norm.

"Mmm-hmm. Joel called to say PT was cancelled for today." She sat in the damned chair-morphed-into-bedroom that she'd ruined for life. He was going to have to donate the thing and get another. Shame, too. It had been his father's.

She'd ruined his father's chair. Was changing Scott into some sort of emotional being he didn't recognize. She had to go.

And was sitting there watching him as though she hadn't a care in the world. Sage had called her. She knew he'd called in his twin card, preying on his connection with Sage to get her to feel how important it was that she change her stipulation to remain on her honeymoon. In an attempt to get her to take down her threat to return home, he'd offered to agree to hired help for injury-related physical items, but he could not have anyone staying in his house with him.

Of course, *anyone* meant Iris. Which Sage had immediately pointed out. By suggesting that maybe he ask Dale.

Or Harper. Or any number of other casual friends he had in his life.

He was pretty sure he'd hung up with Sage pointing out that Iris was the only one he could even halfway tolerate.

That she was better than anyone else.

His twin knew he wouldn't tolerate anyone else. If push came to absolute shove, he'd put up with Iris.

Sage probably also figured that no one else would put up with him.

She'd gotten the best of him.

Which only proved her point that he shouldn't be staying alone. Something the doctor had apparently reiterated when Sage, who had his medical power of attorney, had called after Iris had texted about the night's drama.

The whole thing was making him tired. Irritable.

Slowing down his ability to process as efficiently as possible.

He suddenly remembered what he'd come out of his room to say. "Sage is missing one key piece of information," he told her. "The one that would convince her that I'm thinking clearly. And am right."

Iris didn't grin, but she sure looked to him as though she was holding one back.

Spurred on by a healthy dose of irritation-laced frustration, he said, "I haven't told her that we had sex. That if you stay, one of us is bound to get hurt and she'll come home to a hole in the family she left behind."

He was standing before the judge unprepared. But had won cases with spitballing, too. Because he was that good at what he did.

Morgan, finished with her treat, came bounding toward him. Scott jerked his leg away instinctively. And winced as he bent his damned left knee and then twisted it in his attempt to ease the pain, all while watching Morgan ready to launch and preparing himself to catch her.

Preparing for the next wrench of pain.

But before the girl landed, Iris was there, catching Morgan, crooning to her, calming her and then placing her on Scott's lap.

She'd seen him shy away from his own dog. How humiliating was that?

And how in the hell was he ever going to succeed at getting them back on an even keel if she didn't get the hell out?

"She ripped your stitches, didn't she?" Sage's voice reached him, even though he was refusing to look in her direction. Giving his attention, instead, to the faithful friend who only had expectations he could meet.

Even if it meant a couple of extra stitches.

"She doesn't sleep on the bed," he said, hearing his sullen tone and not giving a damn. Or trying not to. "But I'm out of whack. Our house is out of whack. She was whining. I lifted her up. She was nervous, wanted back down. I put her on my stomach. Fell asleep. And the next thing I knew, I was waking up on my side and she was launching herself off the bed, pushing off from my bandage. I jerked away so hard, I tore the stitches."

There. Apparently, he couldn't even be trusted to sleep without supervision.

"I'm guessing she wasn't trying to get off the bed, but get at your wound," Iris said softly. "Her instinct would be to lick it. To heal you."

Maybe. That made more sense than his own take on what had happened. All he knew was he'd woken up with Morgan's paw at his leg and he'd jerked so hard he'd felt the searing wrench to his wound.

He was tired. And tired of being tired.

Even without pain medication he was somewhat foggy headed.

But he remained adamantly clear on one point. Iris had to go. And there was no way he was going to hurt her by having anyone else in, taking her place. Or something to that effect.

Lucidity came and went. Determination, the one staple he could count on, did not.

"And the other...you worrying about our friendship... it's a moot point."

His gaze shot over to her, alarm wrenching through him. She was done with him? With them? "What?"

"It's not you, Scott. Which is why you're struggling so much with it. You can't make sense of your actions/reactions because they don't have a basis in you. I figured it out this morning."

She'd lost him. As in, them being from two different planets. "What?" he asked again, for want of anything more intelligent to say.

"I...had some struggles...a traumatic time...more than a decade ago. It took me a while to be okay again. To get over the emotional overload and get on with my life. Sage's wedding triggered a blast to the past. You know, kind of PTSD. I see it all so clearly now. The sex...it was all just part of an uncontrollable surge from my emotional cortex. When that happens, all emotions are over-the-top. It first hit up at the altar, that I was aware of, but I know now that it had been building that whole week. Then, the whole weird thing of us being forced into a date-like situation at the most romantic event ever... But the sex...my overly heightened emotions...sent out an overload of pheromones, to which, biologically, you couldn't help but react. The sex was only a symptom of my relapse. Along with the surges of fear I've felt that are so unlike me…"

He had to blow by most of what she was saying. Hearing her. Not analyzing as was his usual way. Or even fully comprehending at the moment. But that last… "You're afraid? Of what?" He wanted to help.

The way she threw up her hand, as though she was on stage, struck him hard. Iris wasn't into bold demonstrations of any kind. She was always the one who melded into the background. They'd be on the beach, in the midst of a group of residents, and she was the one on the outer edge of the gathering.

"Well…" she finally started when he kept staring at her. He didn't know what to do until he knew who or what was scaring her. "First when Sage called to tell me you'd been in an accident."

Her face went white, but she licked her lips and continued, "And then this morning, when I saw your soaked bandage, and on the way to the hospital, too. That's what opened my eyes to the truth." Her face cleared as her tone gained momentum. "So, anyway, you can relax. I've already put in a call to Dr. Livingston, but I know I'm on track."

Dr. Livingston? He had another doctor other than the ones who saw him at his two hospital visits? For follow-up? He had no memory of being told.

"Who's Dr. Livingston?"

"The psychologist who helped me in the past." She said the words as though they were supposed to give him confidence.

She'd suffered some kind of serious incident more than a decade ago. And she and her counselor were still in touch? Must have been some trauma. And…more than a decade ago? Iris was only twenty-eight. She had to have been a teenager.

None of which added up. At all. As close as they all were, he and Sage would know about a tragic history. He sat still, seeming to watch her, he hoped. Feeling completely unprepared for the conversation he'd somehow launched himself into.

As it dawned on him that he couldn't think of anything he'd heard about Iris's past. No, wait, she'd taken photography in high school. And her mom had died. He remembered Sage mentioning that she and Iris had that in common.

But what about siblings? A father? Aunts, uncles, grandparents? For the past three years she'd spent Christmas with him and Sage, as the three of them spoiled Leigh with tales of Santa and surprises.

"Anyway—" she stood, startling him "—the only thing that matters here is that you can relax, okay? Accept my help, because we all know you need it…"

"We all?" He interrupted because he couldn't just sit there and listen to her spout things that were counterproductive to his mission.

"You, me, Sage, Gray, Joel, the medical professionals at the hospital tending to you…"

Damn! That was a lot of opinion stacking up against him.

"And now you have no reason to worry about us. We aren't changing at all. It was just my subconscious reaction to Sage getting married."

He didn't follow that part. But, maybe if he knew what she was talking about…

She looked so…happy, standing there, meeting his gaze head-on. Smiling. That grin…it looked good on her. Great. Why hadn't he noticed it before?

"So…we're good?" Her tone pushed him to agree.

Tired of questions that came with no answers, and certain

that he didn't want to be the one to wipe that look off from Iris's face, Scott did the only thing he could do. He nodded.

But he didn't believe himself.

Or her.

Unless she could find a way to convince him that the touch of her hand on his forehead had somehow transfused her "surge" of emotions into him.

Because he was feeling a whole lot more than sexual desire for the woman.

He might be foggy, but even in his current state, he knew that pheromones didn't pour compassion through skin.

Stuff like that came from the heart.

And matters of the heart—his twin and her daughter withstanding—were off-limits to him.

Other than the twin thing that had been formed at conception and permanently solidified in the womb, the heart was where he faltered.

And there would not be another failure.

Chapter Fifteen

Reestablishing status quo was a difficult thing when one was in the aftermath of an emotional hurricane. Iris had had to do major cleanup before. She knew it didn't happen in a day. That she'd be in a state of surrealism until she was back in her routine.

But Scott… For him she had to pretend for all she was worth. She'd gotten really good at that, too. She had to, to be okay.

Still, she couldn't get the prelunch call from Sage out of her mind. Or rather, couldn't rid herself of the concern the call had instilled in her. It had taken everything she had to keep her dear friend off a plane home. Sage had said she'd never heard her brother sounding as off as he'd sounded when he'd called her that morning. Not only had he been mentally a bit out of sync, but he'd sounded…needy. In a way she'd never heard before.

Like he was in crisis.

Iris hoped to God it wasn't because of her. And then, considering other options—that the board had maybe hit Scott's head, too, causing damage that no one knew about—she hoped his less than stellar state *was* because of her.

For that problem, she had the solution. She'd focus on distancing herself from her emotional cortex long enough to let it get back into sync with the rest of her. And the intensity between her and Scott would dissipate. She just had to convince him to buy into the solution and let it work.

By pretending she was already in sync.

Nothing she hadn't done many times before.

And to start, that meant not hovering. She had her instructions. Knew what to watch for. And beyond that, she needed to leave Scott to his own counsel. Worry accomplished nothing.

If something did go wrong again, she'd handle it just as she'd handled their early-morning issue. With calm and clear thought.

She'd watch for signs of head trauma, too. He'd shown no signs of concussion or other cranial disturbance at the hospital. Nor in the twenty-four hours post accident. She'd been told what to watch for. Hadn't seen a single sign. But she'd start monitoring again.

Just in case.

And for the rest, her own authentic healing, she needed to get back behind her camera. Do the work that allowed the part of her soul that still lived to breathe. To be heard.

To that end, after lunch, icing and bandage check, she left Scott alone long enough to get to her place and collect more camera equipment, including the electronics she used for editing. Taking the dogs with her, because until she got herself under better control, she was still seeing him that morning, nearly passing out in the kitchen while his wound bled out.

Had she not come out…

But she had. End of that story.

However, until Scott was more mobile, she was acutely aware of the chance that Morgan could inadvertently hurt him again.

And…she checked that he had his phone nearby.

Not overcompensating out of fear on that one, she assured herself. Just being a reliable caregiver.

All went smoothly until she got back to Scott's cottage, had her equipment set up and ready to go, only to turn a complete circle and stand there.

What was she going to photograph? Wall hangings? He had two or three. Furniture. She could, but for what purpose?

She'd already been out of the house too long. Couldn't spend an hour or two on the beach.

The girls were both out in their beds in the kitchen. Worn out from the day's adventures on the beach.

Her charge was asleep, dressed in basketball shorts and a T-shirt, with his leg elevated, on top of the spare bed. She noted that his face was smoothed out. He wasn't moaning, groaning or exhibiting any of the inadvertent movements that had populated his attempts to rest the first couple of days.

Her camera rose as if of its own volition and before she caught an outside-in glimpse of herself, she'd already taken dozens of shots. Close-ups. Zoomed out. His bandaged leg. His face. A hand on the bedspread. The portfolio would be a study.

In pain?

Recovery?

Resilience?

The strength of the human spirit?

Maybe, sometime in the future, when he was off living his carefree bachelor life again, she'd show him the portfolio as a reminder of how far he'd come. Give him proof of his ability to keep his word to himself. No matter how much he'd suffered, he hadn't broken down and taken pain medication.

The story would be better if she'd taken shots during the first two days. But even the thought of having done so made her cringe in fear for what had been such a close call.

That memory needed to fade as far and as fast as possible. Not be preserved for all eternity.

And…what in the hell was she doing? Taking photos of a sleeping man without his knowledge or any kind of permission?

Her entire body tightened with tension. With chills and a sense of horror. How could she possibly have thought she had the right to just…?

Turning abruptly, she left the room. Clicked off the camera. Stashed it in the bottom of her largest camera bag. There would be no touching the thing again until she could make herself dump the photo shoot.

No one, absolutely no other being on earth—including the girls—could be witness to what she'd done.

Food.

Grabbing another camera, she headed to the kitchen. Almost stumbling over her feet in her rush to get there. Before Scott's accident—on and off since before Sage's wedding actually—she'd been thinking about ways to show what food said to her.

In scarcity.

In abundance.

In a color study.

To entice appetite.

Suddenly—almost desperately—energized, she pulled things out of Scott's refrigerator. Out of his cupboards, and let her soul speak from behind her lens.

Snapping shot after shot—hundreds of them in an hour.

Colors. Shapes. Telling stories. Even engaging the dogs in them.

The high she felt when she was doing good work slowly trickled through her.

Then consumed her.

And she welcomed herself home.

He needed her gone. Still. Just as badly as ever. But as Scott awoke from the first good sleep he'd had since the accident, he came into full consciousness with a clear head and a new, two-point strategy.

First, accept the help being given. Experts and nonexperts, friends and even family knew he needed assistance in order to heal most expediently. And his number-one goal was to get back on his feet. Both of them. And regain full control.

Only then could he direct his full attention to more-pressing matters.

His prior plan, to do it on his own, would have given him a semblance of control, but it had lacked clarity. He'd faced tough cases in court, creating case law that could reverberate nationally, and had always sought others' thoughts, and research, and assistance at the table in the courtroom, too. More eyes, ears, thoughts and hands on deck made him better.

Same went for recovery.

Doing it alone was going to slow him down.

And the second prong in the plan—be the friend to Iris that she was being to him. By accepting her spin on the sudden flare of awareness between them, he allowed her to pretend that it wasn't happening, while at the same time taking the onus fully on himself to ensure that nothing more *did* happen.

Once he was well, Sage and Gray and Leigh were home, and Iris and he were back in their normal routines, they'd be fine.

Feeling more like himself than he had since his sister's wedding, Scott called out to Iris. Waiting for her to spot him as he slid from the bed to his chair, admitting when a hand from her would make the job safer. Just until he could put some weight on the ripped wound.

He glided through knee icing and antibiotics in good spirits, joking with Iris, rather than grousing or grunting as he sat propped up on the couch, accepting her ministrations. He did all the exercises Joel had given him, as often as he'd been told to repeat the relatively small, but very painful movements.

And managed not to tense up when Iris suggested that he was overdue for application of the compression bandage on his back. He'd been aware of the lateness. Almost an hour. Had been bothered by it.

But not as much as he was by the idea of her touching his bare skin. He'd been working up to it. Getting into a professional mindset. While trying to figure out if there was a way he could twist and wrap his own torso as effectively as someone else could do it for him.

Segueing into looking for excuses to call Dale over— and, *Hey, while you're here...*getting the writer to wrap him.

His mind came up with various levels of inventiveness. Just nothing that wouldn't make it look obvious to Iris that he didn't want her fingers grazing his back, his sides, his stomach...

And the more he tried to find another option, the more his mind was locked on those fingers and his skin. Sending him in the direction of turned on before they'd even gotten to the deed.

No matter what, he had to let her float undisturbed in pretend mode. He'd taken on the responsibility to keep all hint of something more happening between them off the table. And he would not fail.

And there she was, fresh bandage in hand, approaching him from the hallway entrance to the living room. His mind spun. His body, hidden by his T-shirt, was already starting to grow.

She had to lift the shirt to complete her task.

She was two steps away.

With roaring in his ears, Scott tried to think of something gross.

It wasn't working.

Work. It came first.

And...just as Iris told him to lean forward, and reached for the hem of his shirt, Scott's gaze fell on his laptop.

Work.

Grabbing the opened electronic device from the table, he flipped it to tablet mode, opened his email and, just in time, dropped the thing on his lap.

A good attorney—which he most definitely was—did not cover up evidence. Ever. For any reason.

But a good man trying to be a friend did.

Iris was fixing dinner—spaghetti with her mother's homemade sauce recipe—when she finally received her return call from Dr. Sandra Livingston. Her stomach tightened, filled with butterflies, as she saw the name on her screen.

Though the two hadn't spoken in the three years Iris had lived on Ocean Breeze, she got a birthday card from the psychologist every year. With a reminder that she was always there for her. The doctor had never said so, but Iris knew that she was one of Sandra's most memorable patients. One who, though their relationship had always been nothing but professional, had become personal to her.

The job she took home with her at night.

Putting her sauce on low, she was calm as she stepped outside and then down toward the beach as she took the call, assuring the psychologist that she was fine.

"I wouldn't have called except that someone else is involved and I need confirmation of what I know is going on," she said, confident again as she heard herself speak.

The name on her phone…another flashback of angst-driven anxiety…had triggered her stomach for a second. All part of the surge.

"Tell me what's going on," Sandra said, her tone as calming and authoritative as always.

"Nothing really," Iris said, taking a deep breath of ocean air. Then glanced back at the cottage. She'd left the dogs inside with Scott. Should have brought them out with her. Had to get the call done.

"It's just a trigger," she said quickly. "I'm good with it. But, unfortunately, the episode happened when someone else was around. I really just need to confirm that these flashbacks to experiencing over-the-top emotions apply, not just to the original types of feelings or source of feelings, but to any emotion I might be experiencing at the time." She was still down by the water but couldn't take her gaze off the back door. Willing the girls to show themselves, stand there, asking to be let out with her.

"In theory, that's certainly possible." The doctor's voice shut out all other thought, sound, for the moment as Iris sank into it. And relief came, making her weak for the second it took Sandra to continue. "However, that's not the only possibility. Tell me what's going on."

No.

She was no longer under Dr. Livingston's care.

Didn't need a counselor anymore.

Her life was good. Great. More than she'd ever hoped it could be following the accident.

"Iris? You called me."

Right. "I'm sorry. I shouldn't have bothered you."

"Please don't hang up." The words came quickly. Loudly enough that she could hear them even as she was lowering her phone to see the button to end the call.

Dr. Livingston had known. Which sent another wave of alarm shooting through her. "I'm still here," she said, forcing calm into her words. And, with steps on the beach, into her demeanor, too.

She could pretend with the world. She'd promised herself, and Ivy, who always watched over her, that she would never pretend with Sandra Livingston. The woman was the sounding board that had helped her find a healthy life again. She was Iris's checkpoint.

And so she told her, in just a few sentences, about her friendship with Scott and Sage, about the wedding, and the way she'd leaned into Scott as they were dancing, tempting him in a way that had introduced a sexual component neither of them wanted.

"Are you sure about that?"

"Sure that my surge inadvertently tempted him?" she asked. Needing to hear the diagnosis so she could get on with the cure.

"Sure that neither of you want your friendship to be more?"

"Positive." She didn't have to pretend on that one at all.

"On both sides." With another two sentences, she told Sandra about Scott. A workaholic confirmed bachelor. And then, facing the door again, as mentioning the man brought back her worry about him alone with the dogs, she said, "I swear, I'm not wrong about this," she finished. "I'm panicked about the thought of losing what we had. I miss him. And I'm already on the way to being back to my healthy self," she said, when she'd meant to be done talking. "I had a great afternoon. Doing what you taught me to do. And found the peace and clarity that have seen me through."

"I'm glad to hear that." The voice over the phone sounded truly pleased. A familiar sound, even if not heard in a while.

"I just need to know that I'm not missing something," she said then. "That I'm on the right track here. I don't want Scott to get hurt."

Truth rang so loudly she felt like everyone in every cottage on the beach must have heard it.

"I can't tell you that," Sandra said. Then, while fear surged through Iris again—ripping her breath out of her lungs as it went—the woman continued, "I know that you might be. What you're saying is most definitely feasible. Believable even."

Then what was the problem? She didn't ask. And felt as though she should have when Sandra left a long pause before saying, "It's also possible that your psyche is not only ready for more, but that you've healed to the point of yearning for more."

Shaking her head, Iris let that one go even before the psychologist had finished the last word. There was no way anyone would ever know her as completely, love her as unconditionally as Ivy had, and she couldn't settle for less. Nor could she let someone else give her their all when she knew she'd be settling. And, on another, more selfish level, she couldn't risk loving and losing again.

"Picture it as your emotions having been in a deep sleep." Sandra said what Iris already knew. A part of her had gone permanently to sleep along with Ivy. They'd died together.

Waiting to be able to end the conversation without being rude but needing to get back up to the house—to check on the dogs—Iris headed in that direction as she listened to Dr. Livingston saying, "It's possible that they've woken up."

They hadn't. It wasn't like she was surging all over the place. Or even for more than random moments in a whole day's worth of hours filled with hundreds of normal minutes.

"But it's just as likely, if not more, that Sage's wedding, a twin sister, though not mine, and me being maid of honor, triggered an emotional setback," she said, halfway to the door of Scott's cottage.

"I can't tell you that, Iris. The mind isn't that cut-and-dried. What you say is feasible. A valid possibility. One that I would not push aside." Thank God.

She took a couple of more steps to the door, feeling her smile come back.

And Sandra said, "Just as I wouldn't discount a resurgence of life."

Reaching for the door handle, Iris saw both girls in the kitchen, lying by the stove, right where she'd left them. And her smile grew as she thanked Dr. Livingston, promised to keep in touch and hung up.

Surge. Resurgence. The psychologist would be remiss not to point out both sides of the equation. She was, after all, a scientist. One of the mind. It was her job to make sure everything was on the table.

Just as it was Iris's task—the task of any healthy, one-time patient—to be able to discern which applied to her.

And she knew for certain, could feel in her core, that she was most definitely experiencing only a surge.

Resurgence hadn't been an option on her table since the day she'd woken up in a hospital bed without her twin.

But having a friend, being a friend, was something she wanted with all that was left of her.

And that realization was new.

Chapter Sixteen

"Ehhhhh!"

Scott woke, his mind hearing the scream, not remembering a dream attached to it. Looked for the clock on his nightstand. Saw a smaller one, on a shorter night table, and realized where he was.

The spare bedroom. Two in the morning.

Leg throbbing. Still resting on the pillow he'd placed underneath it after an eleven p.m. icing and bandage change.

"Hehhhhh…aaahhh!" The sound ripped through the air, hitting him hard. Without thought he threw the sheet away from him and swung his leg toward the side of the bed. Remembering in that split second, that his second leg couldn't follow. The problem didn't slow him down.

Iris was in trouble.

Morgan stood at attention, watching him as, with both hands lifting and supporting his bad leg, Scott ignored the pull in his back and had himself in his chair in record time. Grabbing his phone off the nightstand, he ordered the girl to stay and wheeled himself through the spare room door, down the hall they were keeping lit at night, only pausing long enough to open his own door, before wheeling himself inside. Wide-awake, and with the help of the hall light and the moon's brightness through the window, he swept the room with a quick gaze, ready to act...

He wasn't sure if he noticed the body shape beneath his comforter first or heard the sound of weeping. Didn't much matter. Angel lay on top of the covers, against Iris's back, her head at attention, facing Iris, but otherwise not moving.

"Iris?" he spoke in a near whisper. No response. From either of the females in the room. Human or canine.

Angel knew he was there. Wasn't even bothering to look at him, to ask him why. To see if he had food. Or be curious about what he was doing. Her attention was on her person.

The intensity in the dog's response seemed to demand that Scott give the situation the same attention. It was as though she was expecting him to do what needed to be done.

"Aahmmm." The almost nonhuman sound sent a sense of despair through Scott. "Garohohohn." A strangely guttural lashing out.

Followed by more weeping. But in spurts. A dry sob. Then silence.

And still Angel lay, watching. Not moving. Pointing out the source of need to Scott? If she stared long enough, he'd get that he was supposed to take care of the situation?

Not sure why the dog didn't wake Iris herself, Scott listened for nearly a minute, eavesdropping on a moment he hadn't been invited to join. Not sure what to do. Iris was clearly in the throes of a nightmare. But not in immediate physical danger. She wouldn't want him there.

But he couldn't go. Couldn't turn his back on her.

Her breathing slowed. Steadied. Hands poised on the wheels of his chair, Scott started to propel himself backward, until he heard the anguished moan come from deep inside his friend. Just a dream or not, no way was he leaving her inside that private hell.

Wheeling his chair right up to the bed, he pushed with both hands, standing on his good leg, and then, with a hand on the nightstand and one on the headboard, he hoisted himself, held his body weight enough to get his right hip up on the mattress, then, with a hand still on the stand, he pushed off to roll himself fully onto the king-size bed. Feet away from where she lay on the edge of the opposite side.

"It's just me. Scott," he said softly, sitting there, with his left leg propped fully on his right. And his back warning him to change positions.

Angel was the only one who responded. Glancing at Scott, as if to say, *It took you long enough*, the girl jumped down off the bed.

"Iris?" He called her name softly. Repeated his. Trying to wake her without instilling more alarm. Holding himself awkwardly so he was as far away from her as he could get, with no chance of touching her, he continued to talk softly to her, calling out to her. Letting her know she was safe.

"Scott?" Her voice, groggy sounding, shocked him at first. Mostly because he hadn't realized she'd woken up. There'd been no sudden jerk back to consciousness. No change of position. No sign of shock that someone else was on her bed.

No reclamation of her independence with the confidence and inner strength that defined her.

He didn't move but was prepared to slide back down to his chair. "Yeah."

When nothing else happened, no words, no movement, Scott was at a loss. "You want me to go?"

He'd consider her silence as an affirmative. Leave without taking offense. He had no right to invade her space.

But didn't regret what he'd done, either...

When no response came, he braced his hands to scoot himself toward his chair.

"Don't go."

The words froze him in place. Braced. But not moving.

She hadn't moved, either. Not a muscle that he could see. And he thought of Sage. Of the nights he'd sat with her through heartbreak after Gray had broken their engagement the week of their big society wedding.

Which led him to remember Iris's recent revelations. The surge she'd mentioned. Residual from a past trauma.

"You want to talk about it?" he asked Iris. "According to my sister, I'm a good listener."

Her back remained toward him as she stayed hunched in the fetal position he'd found her in. "She told me you saved her life when Gray walked out on her."

"I just sat there," he told her, stating the truth.

"You knew she needed to not be alone. But to be left alone."

He was willing to continue the conversation about himself and his twin if it helped her get through the moment. "She told you that?" With an affectionate shake of his head, he could hear his sister saying exactly that. He'd always been able to sense when Sage was struggling. He'd just never been all that good with the words.

"No."

One word. That seemed to freeze the moment. In his mind. But deeper, too. Like Iris was telling him something. Talking about more than the relationship between him and his sister.

Or needing to do so.

She knew him well enough to have guessed what he'd done for his twin during her darkest nights.

Wanted him to do for her what he'd done back then. Be there. But shut up.

He could do that. Just needed to adjust his body a little, to ease the stress on his back. And prop his left leg differently.

And then he'd sit there all night, silently watching over her, if that's what she wanted him to do.

Because he could.

Sitting quietly through the dark moments was what friends did.

The night, her need had nothing to do with sex. And with his body in its current state, it wasn't like he could be more than brotherly, even if she turned over naked and asked him to make love to her.

At the moment, he didn't even want to try.

He'd made a commitment to be the friend to Iris that she was to him.

And he was not going to fail her.

She was being selfish. And a crappy caregiver, too. Scott needed to be in his bed, leg propped. Iris just needed a couple of minutes. Time to cross over from the darkness that had been, to the life she'd found on the other side.

To turn her mind away from the horrible truth she couldn't change, to things that came after, which was the only way to get the sense of anguish to dissipate. It was up to her. Let depression rob her of the good she had left. Or choose to focus on the good even when she couldn't feel it. To trust that it was there. Give up. Or fight for herself.

"Where's Angel?" The second canine angel in her life. Adopted after the first one, the service dog that Sandra Livingston had gifted to her at eighteen, had died of old age.

"She jumped down when I came up."

Scott's voice. Normal. Reassuring. Nothing dramatic. Still there. A small wave of relief passed through her. Easing a bit of the strong hold the past had gained on her while she was unconscious and therefore unable to fight it.

She was going to have to tell him something.

Wasn't sure what he'd heard. Or for how long. Living alone, she had no way of knowing if episodes were seconds, minutes or hours long. There were no witnesses other than Angel.

And hadn't been anything to witness a long time.

What in the hell was going on with her?

And how bad was the situation with Scott? How big did her cover-up have to be?

On the bright side, sex wasn't the problem. She almost wished it was. There was a plan in place to handle that.

The thought brought another wave of fear-engulfed hopelessness. She refused to lie within it, even while the feelings continued to linger.

She had to move her thoughts elsewhere. Focus on the present. She wasn't alone. "Did I wake you?" she asked.

"Yes."

He was there. A voice. A friendly one. One she trusted.

Witnessing more than she could easily explain.

The episode had been severe enough to wake him from behind a closed door and down a hallway.

Heaviness hit again. She couldn't have everything she wanted. Couldn't go back to who she'd thought she'd be when she was growing up. Still huddled into herself—afraid to let go until she could trust herself not to cry—Iris fought her mental battle. Refused to wallow. To give in to the moment. To let grief win.

The damned surge was a huge one.

On her own, she'd get up. Take a walk on the beach. But there, with Scott…

She hadn't seen it coming.

People lost family members to car accidents all the time. She was one in millions. Billions even.

What if Dr. Livingston was right? What if she wasn't in a surge? But was dealing with a psyche that had loosened its reins and had let her deep emotions decide not to be dead after all?

How in the hell did one fight that?

Didn't she get a say in the matter?

Of course she did.

Mind over matter. She knew how it all worked.

And was letting an injured man sit there with her anyway. Definitely a low moment.

That had to end. Disgusted with herself, she rolled over, glanced up at him. Figuring her tangled hair, lack of makeup and the T-shirt and sweats she was sleeping in— in case she had to get up in the night to tend to him—were enough to make sure she wasn't emitting any unwanted come-on signals.

His glance was worried. Kind.

All Scott. The man she'd known for years. Her friend.

And nothing more.

"I'm sorry." For the nightmare. Of course.

Any sense of loss over what had happened between them on the floor of Sage's cottage, or emptiness due to the ending of all possibility that there could be more someday, was just a product of the nightmare. They were all about loss. Every time. And seemed to put a shadow on every other incident in life. Until she came fully out of them.

He frowned, seeming truly perplexed. "For what?"

"Waking you" seemed to be the obvious answer. "You

shouldn't have come in here, climbed up. If you'd hurt your-self—"

"I didn't," he interrupted, his gaze not going away. As though he knew she was hiding from him.

The effect of that look was eerie. Confusing. Throwing her back. Holding her captive in the moment.

And Dr. Livingston's words came to her again. With a stab of fear. She didn't want to go back to who she'd been. Had been happy to be half-alive. Or fully alive, but half emotionally engaged. No way was she going to risk being all in, trusting in a lifetime relationship. She couldn't go through that loss again. It had nearly killed her the first time.

Well, that, and the accident itself…

Scott was watching her. Her gaze met his a time or two, as she checked in to measure his mood. Get a sense of what, given the circumstances, she could get away with. *Thank you for coming, you can go now* didn't seem appropriate.

But she had to say something. The silence was getting way too weird. Both of them waiting for something that wasn't going to happen. There was just no casual way to get out of such a moment. "You want me to help you back to your room?"

He didn't flinch. Just kept watching her. "Is that what you want?"

No. Yes. She didn't know what she wanted. Or wasn't sure it even mattered. What she wanted was to be the woman she'd been on Ocean Breeze from the day she'd moved in until Sage's wedding day.

"What do you want?" she threw back at him.

"I want to know if I can help. And if so, how."

Because they both knew more was going on. A lot more.

No one, other than medical professionals when she was in the hospital, had witnessed one of her nightmares.

Back then, she'd been told they were pretty intense. Loud. Severe. All she ever remembered was the darkness. The fear. The loss she couldn't prevent, no matter how hard she tried.

Iris sat up straight, ready to get off the bed. "There's nothing to help," she said. Looked at him. And couldn't look away. His gaze seemed to hold her secrets. Which was ridiculous.

"Talking makes things easier sometimes," he said, as though he'd suddenly become a guru of emotional wisdom.

The thought was beneath her. Unkind. Pure defense.

Because...she actually wanted him to know.

For the first time since the accident, she wanted someone to know who she'd been.

Truth sliced through her. Leaving her...weak. Defenseless. Unsure.

Until he said, "Maybe this...surge...you talked about earlier...is happening with me because you know I'm safe. Maybe sharing it will set you free."

Free. That's what she wanted to be. Free.

The word sounded so good. She'd always imagined that free would be the best feeling ever.

"Or you could blow me off, I'll go back to my room and we'll both pretend that I don't know that something's going on with you."

Yeah. That was the easier choice. The wise one.

"I'd just hope that when Sage gets back, you'll talk to her about it."

Her gaze darted back to him. "No one should go through life alone, Iris. Unattached, hell, yeah. For certain people. But not *alone*."

She wasn't alone. She had him and Sage. Little Leigh. Angel. The residents on the beach.

None of whom really knew her. They only knew who she'd wanted to become.

Which had been fine with her. Enough.

Until she'd stood beside the man's twin, had seen the look in his eyes across from her. And started to cry.

Chapter Seventeen

Scott didn't know what in the hell he was doing. Why he was still sitting on his bed when he was clearly free to go.

Iris would be better off with Sage, not him.

But Sage wasn't there. And she'd want him to step up. Because Iris was his friend, too. He didn't need his twin in the country to know that much. He could hear her voice in his head all the way from Europe. Even with the time difference.

"I didn't think I'd ever *be* in life alone." The words brought his gaze from the doorway he'd been studying back to Iris in a flash. Head down, she was pulling at a string on the hem of her oversize T-shirt. And it hit him, like a rock on the head...she'd been in love.

Like Sage, she'd been hurt young.

The trauma she'd mentioned...a decade or so ago. It must have been more than just a normal teenage romance and breakup.

He didn't know who the guy was, but sitting there, right then, Scott hated the guy. Wanted to give him a serious piece of his mind.

"What happened?" He was a gifted interrogator. Knew that it was easier to get to the emotional meat if he entered through the back door. What, not who.

"A car accident."

He blinked. Frowned. Stared at the bent head just out of his reach. Felt the strongest urge to get close enough to put his fingers under that chin. Lift it. So he could see into her eyes. Maybe stroke her forehead as she'd touched his when he'd been hurting...

Had she been in the car? "Where?"

"The neighborhood where I grew up."

She still wasn't looking up. Had started on a second thread. Best to stay at the back door. Where Iris was concerned, it would always be best.

Yet, looking at her, he needed more. Felt raw with the not knowing.

The way she'd helped him when he was at his worst, he wasn't sure he'd ever be content on the outside looking in again.

She'd helped him to the bathroom. Rushed him to the hospital. Had sex with him on the floor of a vacant house.

"When?" He finally got the right word out. Holding back for all he was worth.

"Almost eleven years ago. I was seventeen."

Younger than he'd figured. With an older man?

Or a sweetheart she'd grown up with?

She'd given him a personal fact. Brought herself to the page. "Did you see it happen?" He approached the apex slowly. Told himself he was only doing what he knew to do well. Interrogate.

He'd never before had to hold his breath while awaiting a response.

A breath that seemed lodged forever in his throat when Iris looked up at him. Those green eyes, usually so cool and calm, seemed to be melting pots surrounded by a nest of flames—her messy amber hair.

He was cooking, that was for sure. His heart melting more by the second, he couldn't tear his gaze away.

And felt an almost physical blow as she held his gaze and said, "I was in the car, Scott."

She'd survived. Clearly her love had not.

Knowing what Sage went through when Gray left all those years ago...his sister hadn't been all that much older than Iris when it had happened...the way it had sucked the life out of her. And Gray had still been alive and well. Out of Sage's life, but not gone forever. He'd still loved her.

And Sage had never stopped loving him. She'd adopted the child she'd always wanted to have, built the family she'd wanted, had dated a lot, but had never been in another serious relationship. Until Gray had needed her help. A more mature Gray, who'd had the courage to believe that his love would be enough...

Had Iris's love survived? Maybe with a permanent disability? Rejected her, as Gray had rejected Iris? Was he out there?

Could there be a happy ending for her?

The jolt of jealousy the idea gave Scott was unwelcome. Beneath him.

And wholly unfair as he had no intention, ever, of being a part of any happy ending for anyone, most particularly not Iris. No way he'd risk hurting her...

She'd resumed her head-down position. Had found a third string to work.

"Did he live?" The words hurt his throat.

But got her to look at him again. The frown she was sending him made him regret the question he hadn't wanted to ask in the first place.

"She. And no."

She.

The look in Iris's eyes, intent, filled with a pain he seemed to understand…

And he knew. Even while his mind told him he had no basis in the thought, that he was being ridiculous…things fell into place. The way Iris understood him and Sage—knowing that he'd known when Sage had been hurting that she'd needed to not be alone, but to be left alone—along with so many other little nuances he'd picked up on…

"What was her name?"

Tears filled her eyes. She blinked them away. "Ivy." Her lower lip trembled. She bit it. Let it go. Gave him a weak smile.

Iris and Ivy.

Twins.

Identical?

He'd been told that the bond was sometimes stronger than fraternal. "What did she look like?"

"Me." Iris faced him straight on, crossed her legs, let go of her shirt and looked right at him. "She looked exactly like me."

His sweet strong friend.

She blinked back tears. Her chin trembled, but she got the smile out, too.

Raised her eyebrows at him.

Nodded.

And Scott knew his life had just been forever changed.

He'd been right. Iris had thought even hearing the words aloud would be so gut-wrenching, that having her previous life known in her current one would ruin everything. But as she sat there in Scott's bedroom, seeing the unspoken understanding in his gaze, she felt…better. More complete.

Known.

Honest. Real.

His lack of words were a gift. He wasn't trying to fix her. To make her better. She wasn't broken. Not anymore. Not for years.

Nor did he attempt to ease her pain. That miracle had not yet been invented or discovered.

With nothing more to say, she sat there, waiting for him to quietly go. When he was ready. Or thought she was.

He'd said himself, he'd sat with Sage, with nothing to say.

She got that.

Was still very glad he was there.

That they were friends.

Needing each other in very different ways.

And both being able to walk away, too.

"What was she like?"

His question disarmed her. In the first second, she rejected it. Until an answer sprang to her lips. Along with a smile. "Fun. Artistic. A bleeding heart, sometimes. But as strong as they come. She always said that I had the knowledge, and she had the knowing." Her smile grew. "She didn't think I was as great at discerning as she was."

"Did you agree with her?"

The question engaged her. Thinking back, she said, "I don't think so. But she was definitely the more artistic of the two of us. Although I was a better cook. Probably because I was more into nutrition…"

She stopped as the words took her places she hadn't been in a long, long time. "Our mother was sick." She couldn't believe she'd said the words. Hearing them aloud startled her. But didn't stop her. "She'd been diagnosed when we were thirteen, but for a few years, we all thought she'd beat it. But either way, she had us prepared. Telling us that mothers weren't meant to be in their children's lives forever. But that we were luckier than most because we were one of the few with a special bond given only to chosen, special people. As twins, we'd always be close, no matter how far apart our lives might take us on the planet. That we'd always feel each other. Telling us that neither of us would ever be alone."

She paused as a surge hit. Darkness. But looked at Scott, took a breath, and said, "I know now that she was preparing us for her death. I will revere her forever. Because while we both grieved when she died, and missed her hugely, we were all right, too. We had each other…"

Until they hadn't. The room darkened. Or her mind did. Fear slid down through her.

And then a hand touched hers. Physically. Warm fingers, wrapping around her palm.

Iris looked up. Saw the look in Scott's eyes. Knowing he understood.

And she smiled again. A smile loaded with sadness. With grief.

But with gladness, too.

As the night slowly moved on, Scott and Iris ended up on opposite sides of his big king-size bed, sitting with pillows at their backs against the headboard, his leg propped up with more fluff. The light from the hallway, and moon through the window, encapsulating them in a soft glow.

The girls were both in the room with them. Lying together on the floor sharing a pillow Iris had given them.

He'd had questions. She'd seemed to want to answer them. She'd apparently seen signs of his discomfort on his face and had insisted that they get him in a better position.

He'd heard about her parents' divorce due to her father's drinking. A defense attorney, Calvin Shiprock had been fine at work, but after hours, out with other attorneys, he'd succumbed to an addiction that eventually followed him home. He'd sobered after losing his family. Eventually marrying his sobriety sponsor. But after Iris's mother died, and he and his wife moved into the family home so the girls' lives didn't have to be further disrupted, he'd started drinking again. His wife, who stood by him in spite of the relapse, also stepped up for Ivy and Iris, helping them in their quest to emancipate so that they didn't have to live with the man who'd never been around much for them anyway.

He'd died of liver disease shortly before Iris moved to San Diego.

"My father was always around," Scott said. "I'm not sure that was such a great thing, either." And wanted to immediately take back the words. Regretting the thought as much as having expressed it.

"Sage said he was pretty strict on you."

For his own good. Scott had misled her. Had to correct the image of the man who'd made him the success he was. And who'd always loved him. "He had high standards but lived by example."

Iris nodded, glanced toward her toes as she said, "And failure wasn't an option."

Had he told her that? Had Sage?

"The man was a self-made millionaire. Started investing small amounts while he was still in high school. He had a gift. Just knew what would work and what wouldn't. Growing up, I witnessed these powerful people coming into our home to ask him for advice. He could have made millions at consulting, but he did it for free. For people who he knew would use his help to better the world. That's what it was all about for him. Using the life you'd been given to make the world a better place, not to litter it. So, yeah, failure wasn't an option. Except as a lesson to do better. Be better."

"Failure is a part of life." Iris's words fell softly into the dimly lit night. "If children aren't allowed to fail, they're at risk for developing an inability to try. Think about learning to walk. If a toddler had to fear failure, they'd never try again after the first time or two they took a step and dropped to their butt. You have any idea how many tries it takes to learn to walk?"

He didn't. But the passion in her words drew his gaze to her face. "For some, maybe as many as it's taking me to master surfing?"

Her eyes widened, as though something was dawning on her. He wanted to know what. Didn't feel free to pursue the knowledge. They were talking, sharing in ways they never had before, but there were still boundaries. To him, it seemed like very clear ones. He went where he was welcome. Stayed silent where he was not.

How he knew the difference, he couldn't say.

Maybe because he'd spent so many years reading juries, he'd developed decent people-reading skills.

He liked the thought.

"You surf because you'd rather risk killing yourself than to accept that failure is a part of life. Fear of failure drives you."

His shrug was easy. "I'm good with that. As long as what I'm driven to do helps make the world a better place." He was Randolph Martin's son. The legacy he strove to live up to was a great one.

"Right, but if you don't learn to fail, if you can't be okay with not succeeding at everything you do, you don't allow yourself to try things that you think you aren't good at."

The words, so quietly delivered, hit him hard. He had an argument to them. He could always argue another side.

Iris kept talking before he got there. "It's like the child learning to walk. You don't remember being that child, but imagine him, pulling himself up to a couch, and immediately falling back down hard to his butt. He's too young to understand failure, so he tries again. He sees something he wants and strives to take a step toward it but falls again. Maybe even so hard he hurts himself. He cries. Hard. He's coddled. Because failure is a valid possibility. One that doesn't define the child in any way. And when he's ready to try again, he's encouraged to do so. And if he falls, if he fails again, he's loved, not berated. Not met with disappointment. He's met with pride because he tried..."

They weren't talking about him. The passion in Iris's voice...

"And if it turns out he just doesn't have that physical capability, or that particular talent, he's not a failure, Scott. He just failed at an attempt at something. He learns from it. And, if he has the learning, he becomes a better person for it. At least he tried. And tried again."

Exactly. His surfing was that. Trying and trying again. Not that he failed at it. He just wasn't the best.

"But you...you have one failure and sentence yourself for life."

What the hell...?

His face getting hot, Scott was ready to call it a night. The conversation was no longer friendly.

"All I'm saying is that failure, in and of itself, isn't a negative thing. Sometimes it's a stepping stone toward success. But if you're unable to accept an initial failure, you'll never take a second step."

Yep. He was done. Looked toward his chair, bracing his hand on the mattress for a push off.

"It's a lesson I learned the hard way."

Iris's tone hadn't changed, in volume or timbre. But the words stopped Scott's exit trajectory long enough for him to turn and look at her. To get out of his own space and back into the shared one where he'd sensed that Iris was speaking from experience.

"How so?" he asked.

Nodding toward her feet, she said, "I was hospitalized for six months after the car accident that killed my sister. Among other things, I had a spinal cord injury, and I was told I might never walk again…"

The child, learning to walk, hadn't been him. Nor had it been a child.

"Seeing you with that back injury, and the leg, seeing that chair… I lived in one, Scott. Thinking I'd be in it for the rest of my life. Sometimes it's okay not to master a skill. You tried. You've spent years trying. Spent money trying. You aren't good at it. And it's okay. You indicated that as long as you're surfing, you haven't failed. So the only way to prevent the failure is to just keep surfing. But quitting doesn't make you a failure at life. Or litter in the world. It just means you aren't meant to be a champion surfer."

Relief flooded him. She hadn't been referring to his failed marriage in terms of letting a fear of failure stop him from trying. As in trying to get him to try again. She, like Sage, maybe with Sage's instigation, just wanted him to quit surfing. To be okay with failing so he'd let surfing go.

Why his mind had jumped to the other—the idea that it could be wrong to let one failure stop him from trying something, a committed relationship, a second time—he put down to the rest of the weirdness of the past couple of weeks.

To experiencing such high levels of pain that he'd had moments that lacked complete lucidity.

To sharing his home with a woman who was important to him.

Not to any desire on his part to change his life.

Chapter Eighteen

Iris woke up Thursday morning eager to get on with her day, in spite of a lack of sleep. An hour or so before dawn, she'd helped Scott back into his chair and watched him wheel himself off down the hall.

There'd been no big ending moment. No hug. No acknowledgment that their conversation had been anything but ordinary for them. Just a yawn. A suggestion that they should get some sleep and get him off the bed. All very practical.

And very them.

She woke up with the sense that she and Scott were back to normal. Thinking of him as the valued friend he'd become over the years, not a sex mate.

And she felt free.

To the point of wondering why she thought she'd had to reinvent herself, move hundreds of miles south, to be able to live a somewhat-normal-to-her life.

Maybe Dr. Livingston and she had both been right. She'd come full circle and her psyche had had a bit of a resurgence. Allowing her to bring her past into her present. To quit pretending that she hadn't suffered. And she was right, too. The emotional overload—a surge as the result of the melding of her two selves.

Not a psychological choice to reignite an emotional way

of life that had died when a drunk driver hit her and Ivy head-on.

She was accepting her past. She couldn't ever bring it back to life.

As she walked the beach with the dogs midmorning, she wondered if maybe she'd needed the distance from what had been, in the beginning, but that time had healed her more than she'd ever thought it would.

And at the same time—even with new perspective, with the ability to accept what had been, to be able to welcome some good memories back—she was in full approval of her current life. She liked herself. Her choices. Her world.

So while she felt as though she'd undergone major change—nothing in her daily life, or life plan, was changing. Or needed change.

The same couldn't be said for Scott. Maybe because of being so in tune with his sister, or because of his awareness of what made others tick, the man was far too giving to spend the rest of his life alone.

He'd failed once. By the sounds of things, in a big way. But as she talked to Sage on Thursday afternoon—a daily check-in to let her know that Scott was fully cooperative and doing well in all aspects of his treatment—she couldn't help but mention that which had been bothering her so much she'd had to bring it up the night before.

"He's actually really easy to share space with," she reported to his worried sister. "Respectful, but also aware… like preserving hot water for a second shower, considering my needs into the timeline, giving me space to work, physically, but by not interrupting, too."

"Gray said he was a great roommate," Sage offered. But Scott with a boarder hadn't been where she was going.

"I was thinking more in terms of his failed marriage,"

Iris said, glancing at the dogs as they trotted beside her for their afternoon trek by the water. "Scott takes full responsibility, but it seems to me that if he was even half as attentive to his wife's autonomy and comfort, there'd at least have been some indication to her that he was present in the relationship. That he cared."

She heard the words. Shivered as fear sluiced through her for the second it took her to catch her breath. Yes, Scott was present in their friendship. Of course he cared, as did she. Both qualities were basic to any good relationship. She wasn't seeing herself in his ex-wife's role.

She was seeing Scott blaming himself for a failure that might not have been all his to claim. Or for which to take the blame.

"I think he did care," Sage said. "As did she. Just maybe not enough."

"On both their parts."

"That's how I saw it. Why?"

Afraid that Sage was reading her wrong, Iris wished she hadn't started the conversation. But she had. Was in. "He takes full responsibility. As though the failure was one hundred percent his."

"I know. I've tried to talk to him about it, but he won't listen."

Iris rolled her eyes. Back to herself. Talking to her friend about her twin brother. As they'd done many times over the years. "I tried last night, too."

"Same result?"

"Pretty much." They were two people who cared platonically for a mutual someone. Of like minds. The same as they'd been for years. Unchanged by Sage's marriage.

The relief was palpable. Had her smiling as Morgan and Angel glanced up at her.

"So what brought up the conversation?" Sage's question stopped Iris's celebration midstream.

Not because it was all that unusual to delve further when they were discussing Sage's sometimes recalcitrant twin. But because Iris's immediate reaction was to not want to answer.

And she didn't have a good reason why not.

"Talking about his surfing." The response came to her in the nick of time. A good one. And totally honest. Which made her hesitation even more off-putting.

"He needs to be able to fail," she continued, brushing aside the tinges of uneasiness that kept trying to rear up and darken her day. "To see failure as a way to learn. A natural and necessary part of life. Not some kind of egregious wrongdoing."

"You told him that?" Sage sounded like she wished she'd been there.

"Yes."

"What did he say?"

"Nothing."

He'd yawned. She'd taken the hint and sent him on his way.

"Sounds like that hardheaded brother of mine," Sage said, just as Leigh's voice came from a distance, calling for her mommy.

In normal life, on the beach, the child would be running for Iris, too. She missed the little tyke. A ton. Felt lonely just hearing the lispy young voice sounding so far away.

But as she hung up, and headed back up the beach toward the house, figuring Joel—who'd had to do an afternoon appointment that day—would be done, Iris's thoughts weren't on Sage or Leigh. On the wave of loneliness that was so unlike her. Residue to be disregarded.

Her mind was fully occupied with the girls.

Talking to them.

"Obviously Scott was negligent," she told them. "He hadn't even been around enough to know that his wife had moved out. But some of the fault was hers, too. Because if she'd told him how lonely and neglected she felt, he'd have done something about it. That's his way. He'd never just let a problem lie there and not try to fix it. That's a recipe for failure, and he would never use one of those."

Angel barked. Morgan ran a few steps forward and turned around to look at them.

Iris upped her pace, jogging with them.

Satisfied that she finally had life fully under control.

Scott wasn't sure if it was because he'd quit fighting Iris's presence in his home, the talk they had, that he was just feeling better or a combination of the three, but over the next couple of days, he and Iris shared the same friendship in his home that they'd both grown to value so much on the beach over the past few years.

She was there when he needed her. Absent when he was about his own personal business or working. He was watching out for her, making himself available if she wanted to talk, giving her her space without question when she didn't. Appreciating her help. Teasing with her. Helping with the chores as much as he was physically allowed to do.

Keeping his distance. As she kept hers.

And the other side of those days—because life, his job, had taught him that there was always another side—was learning how critically he needed that distance.

Because ever since he'd sat on his bed with Iris, talking about things they'd never spoken of before, he was struggling not to reach for more.

That one night had shown him more of Iris than he'd gleaned in three years' time. The twin thing—the two of them didn't share it with each other, but their shared knowledge of the connection, of the silent understandings, gave them a bond of their own. At least for him, it did.

As to the rest of her confidences…it was like the woman had been a figure in a black-and-white video to him before, and had now appeared in three-dimensional, full-color, concrete form.

And boy did he want to touch that form.

To hold it while she slept. To tickle it and make it laugh, just to hear the sound.

To raise it to heights of ecstasy that made it emit other sounds he yearned to hear. Carnal ones.

It. Not her.

With Iris, he could only live on the friend side. To cross over would obliterate that which he most cherished. Knowing her. The beautiful person she was.

Not just because he didn't trust himself not to start taking her presence for granted and getting wrapped up in the daily life that he knew consumed him. But because he'd come to realize that if he pushed her for anything more, she'd have to back away.

He had no idea what he'd do if he lost Sage. But he could make some pretty accurate assumptions. It would literally be like losing his legs. Or a portion of his thought processes. The way Iris had described her mother's handling of her own terminal illness—teaching her daughters to rely on each other, instilling in them that because they had their special bond, they'd never be alone—explained why she didn't want another committed relationship in her life.

Chances were good she'd never be able to trust her heart

that completely again. She'd lost faith in forever with any-one, for sure.

Along with an ability to trust that there'd be years in between finding love and losing it. Ivy dying at seventeen had shown Iris an awareness of death's toll, of its ability to come at any time for anyone.

He could only imagine the pain she associated with lov-ing someone deeply. But his awareness of the pain's exis-tence told him what he needed to know.

Unfortunately, none of his new awarenesses, his under-standings, shut down his attraction to her. The more he knew, the more he wanted to know. The more he had of her, the more he wanted to have.

Period.

Had nothing to do with any pheromones or other hor-monal nuances she might be sending out. Nothing to do with her having been hit by an emotional tornado.

He looked at her, he got hard. He heard her voice, he got hard. He thought about her, he got hard.

A small price to pay for knowing her.

And not nearly as painful as the leg and back injury he'd been dealing with all week.

The bigger worry was that she'd figure him out. See the evidence he'd been managing to hide. Which was why, on Saturday afternoon, when Joel went out to his van after their session and came back to hand him a pair of crutches, telling him he'd graduated from phase one of his recovery journey, Scott let out a whoop loud enough for the dogs to hear from the beach. And very studiously and carefully fol-lowed all the instructions the therapist had already given him to prepare for crutch use.

The crutches were the key to his freedom. To having his

house to himself again. Where he could walk around hard all damned day if that's what happened.

More likely, with the woman and her scent out of his home, his libido would settle back to that of a healthy, thirty-one-year-old male. He'd get hard. He'd deal with it. And move on.

He'd never been short of women open to having casual sex with him. Had never had to go looking for them, either. The invitations came on an embarrassingly regular basis.

And although bringing to mind a few of the most recent women who'd hit on him raised no current reaction in him at all—there wasn't one of them he'd want to have see him in his current state—he knew himself well enough to know that as soon as he was healed enough to please a woman, he'd feel all the right things in all the right places.

But he was getting ahead of himself. First step back to normal life was getting Iris home to her own place. And meeting up with her on the beach, rather than in his bedroom.

Filled with victory, with determination and a rush of energy, he thanked his physical therapist, waved him off and, positioning the crutches under his arms, headed off toward the back door, planning to meet Iris and the girls on the back porch.

He was halfway through the kitchen when the door flew open. "Scott!" Iris called before she'd stepped inside, her voice kind of frantic sounding.

"Yeah?" He hurried forward, wincing as his back took on the unfamiliar work.

She rounded the door, saw him and stopped. "Oh!"

Frowning, he watched for the girls to follow her in. "What's wrong?"

"I heard you yell..." Her tone brought his gaze to her face. Her eyes were wide.

He grinned. Couldn't help himself. Didn't even try. "A victory cry," he told her, holding up one crutch. "Sorry if it startled you."

Iris blinked. Stared.

She didn't smile.

He'd dropped his gaze to her mouth. Of its own accord, it went lower. Saw the pointed circles of clearly hard nipples pushing against the long-sleeved T-shirt she was wearing.

I'll be damned. His only coherent thought.

Seeing him on crutches had turned her on?

He'd figure himself for being out of his right mind, for being so horny he was seeing sex everywhere, if not for the fact that Iris's cheeks reddened and, blurting that she had to pee, she quickly brushed by him.

Apparently, they both needed her to get the hell out.

She had to go. The past couple of days had shown Scott's body gaining in strength and endurance. She just hadn't realized how big his arm muscles really were, until she'd seen them flexed and bulging on the outside of those crutches.

She'd seen him shirtless countless times on the beach. How could she have missed such an obvious portion of his physique?

How could she honestly be salivating over an injured man's arms?

The size of a guy's biceps had never turned her on before. More surge residue.

It had to be. Any other option was out.

If Scott knew that she was standing in the bathroom with her belly on fire, getting wet for him, he'd become a control freak and insist on staying away from her until they both regained their usual footing.

Which meant until Sage and Gray got home, at the very least.

That was another full week away.

And he needed bandage changes and compression wraps.

He was the patient. The one in need. It was up to her to control the situation for the good of his care.

Decision made, she pulled her satchel up onto the king-size bed she'd spent those soul-freeing late-night hours on with him, and as efficiently as possible, loaded her things inside. Her camera equipment was next.

Their agreement had been that she'd remain in house until he was on crutches.

For the sake of their friendship, now that he was mobile and capable of tending to most things himself, now that he was strong enough to do everything he needed to do, she couldn't stay.

He was in the kitchen, at the table with his laptop in front of him, when she rolled her bigger bag out—her smaller satchel over her shoulder and on her back. Whistling for Angel, who appeared from under the table immediately to stand beside her, she didn't meet the man's gaze as she said, "There's plenty of stuff in the fridge for dinner. I'll be back at eight for compression," and reached for the door handle. He knew where his antibiotics were. Knew when to take them.

Even if he didn't, he could read the bottle.

She was pushing through the screen door when she heard, "Iris?"

Glancing behind her, she saw him standing, those damned muscles hugging his crutches again. "You don't need to come back if you'd rather not. You've gone over and above this week. I can call Dale over…"

It was probably for the best. On the verge of nodding, she assessed him instead. Afraid suddenly that if she didn't come back, that's how the future would be for them. One or the other turning to someone else, walking on the beach with someone else after work, as a way to avoid what they both feared.

Ending up with the result neither of them wanted. Losing each other.

But the choice wasn't just hers. "Is that what you'd prefer?" she asked him, point-blank, her eyes daring him to look away from her.

"No, of course not. I just—"

"Then I'll be here at eight." She cut him off. Didn't want to hear what he just…when it referred to her possibly being cut out. Cut off.

She recognized that the emotions were over-the-top. Gave herself some slack for them until she had time to reacclimate to her regular routine back in her own space.

"Hey…"

She had to turn back. Couldn't ignore the disappointment in his voice.

He looked her in the eye. Warmly. Friend to friend. With a knowing that comforted her. "Thank you" was all he said.

With a shrug, a grin and a "What are friends for?" she held the door for Angel and let herself out.

He might have watched her go.

She felt like he was watching.

Wanted to know if he was.

But Iris walked down the beach, shoulders straight and head up, without looking back.

Chapter Nineteen

That first hour Scott was on a high that propelled him around his cottage, getting everything back in order just as he liked it.

He and Iris were good. They'd made it through the fire without getting burned. Singed a little maybe, but the incident had been a lesson to both of them. One that had brought them closer. Making them better. As most of life's lessons did.

Leaning on crutches where necessary, he lightly cleaned bathrooms. Started to move his things back into the master bedroom but had a second thought on that one. He had his independence back. No point in stretching things too far by challenging himself to get in and out of a higher bed when doing so wasn't necessary.

And a little more time to let the memory fade of the night he and Iris had spent sitting up on that bed would probably be good, too.

Those were intimate hours he would never forget. Didn't want to forget.

But the bed, her, him...that part had to go.

Darkness fell and he made dinner. Some of his home-made spaghetti sauce from the freezer, warmed and spread over the pasta he managed to cook and, leaning on his crutches, to drain, too. He was back. Different. But all there. A new and improved version of himself, the back and knee injuries notwithstanding.

His knee still hurt. Joel had told him to expect discomfort for a while as he healed and then worked to retrain parts to work together. In another couple of days, when the stitches came out, he'd progress more quickly. He had no intention of pushing that. One ripped incision in a lifetime was enough for him.

Scott kept busy even after the high from his regained independence started to fade. He did laundry, answered emails, reading case notes as the loads washed and dried.

But as busy as he was, as much as he was getting done, as good as it all felt, there was a pall. A quiet that went beyond physical sound in the house. He could turn on music. Television, even, if he wanted voices. He couldn't bring the emotional needs of another into his home. Not without having another person there.

And while, in that moment, he was missing the companionship, he also fully knew that when he got back to work, was fully engrossed in cases again, in court and judges, with individual members of juries uppermost in his mind, he'd fail to notice those emotional needs, even if another human being was in his home.

He wasn't back in court yet. Wouldn't be at least for another week. Which meant he was going to have to be proactive about keeping his head on straight. Starting with reestablishing the cottage as a place where he could count on being alone. First with Gray's unexpected advent, and then, shortly after the wedding, with Iris's occupancy, he'd begun to get used to having someone else around.

That stopped immediately.

Grabbing up his compression and bandaging materials, he shoved them into a grocery bag, slung it over his wrist and headed toward the back door. Morgan stood there, watching him. Not wagging her tail to go out.

And it hit him. Walking on the beach on crutches would not be prudent. Or in any way helpful to his overall plan to heal as quickly as possible.

"Let's go," he said to the girl, nodding toward the seldom-used front door. Morgan didn't wag her tail, but she did move that time, and stayed beside him during the quarter-mile trek down to Iris's cottage.

He was almost there before he stopped to pull out his phone to let her know he was coming. It wasn't like he could just hang out in the street and wait for her to come out, as he'd have done any other time since he'd known her.

Except that she'd be heading up the beach to his place, not the street.

His thought had been to get there before she left, so she couldn't tell him not to make the trip.

She picked up on the first ring. "If you're calling to cancel on me, forget it." No *hello*. Just that.

Which, oddly, made Scott smile. "I'm calling to let you know I'm almost at your front door. I come armed with all injury care paraphernalia."

He heard her front door open. Saw the ended call on his screen. And smiled again.

They might be facing some struggles, but they were there for each other.

As a bottom line, he'd take it.

Scott had been in her house a total of three times. When she'd had new furniture delivered, to fix an electrical outlet in her office and exactly two weeks before, when he'd come in to have dinner with her while waiting on the real-tor at Sage's old place.

She didn't have time to realize it wouldn't be a good idea to have him in her space. When she'd seen his name come up on her screen, she'd been afraid he'd been calling to tell her not to come, that he'd had Dale come over to wrap him. Or that he'd decided to forgo the wrap altogether. He wasn't wearing it at night. And only for a few hours in the morning and before bed.

While she'd been in his home, arguing with him had been feasible. But now that she was home, her leverage was gone.

Relief flooded her when she heard he was there, and she almost tripped over Angel on the way to the front door.

"You shouldn't have walked all this way," she told him, to keep from saying what was on the tip of her tongue—that she was glad to see him. That he looked fabulous.

That it seemed like they'd been apart for more than just a few hours.

When her hand darted out instinctively to help him over the threshold, she grabbed the edge of the door instead, taking a deep breath. Reminding herself that the intensity of emotion wasn't to be trusted. To let it settle.

"I needed to get out and the beach didn't seem like a good option."

The normal tone, the casual glance he gave her, settled Iris. Taking the bag of supplies he handed her, she motioned him toward the couch, waited while he leveraged his leg out in front of him with one of her throw pillows and then sat down behind him.

They had the routine down pat. He lifted his shirt. Sat perfectly straight. And she wrapped. Being careful not to let her fingers graze his warm skin any more than absolutely necessary.

To think of other things when it had to happen. Chatting about the food portfolio she was working on. She'd sent out a couple of examples to some well-known cooking outlets that afternoon. Print, as well as social media.

He asked to see them, and before she took a look at the back of his knee, she went to get her computer, handed it to him as he turned, propped up on his side, giving her the access she needed to the disfigured wound he'd reopened three days before. With the laptop pushed up to the back of the couch, he scrolled.

The incision was still swollen, but not alarmingly. It wasn't hot or overly red. She worked as quickly as she could, while every part of her was aware of every single part of Scott.

She didn't want to be. Wasn't happy about it. But couldn't seem to get herself out of the space. She wanted him. Right then. Right there.

The man was injured. Not in any state to engage in extracurricular physical activity.

Except that, as she leaned over to slide her hand under the front of Scott's left knee to brace it, she saw just how capable parts of him were.

With her body thrumming she finished her task.

And made up her mind, too.

"We have to deal with this, Scott. It's going to destroy us if we don't." Pretending didn't work. Not for a lifetime.

When he lay still, saying nothing, she continued with words that had been building, and could no longer be held back. From herself, or him.

"I don't like the dishonesty between us. And when Sage and Gray get back, they're bound to notice it eventually, too.

And you know Sage, she won't let it just lie there. She'll ask questions and…"

He moved so swiftly, her heart gave a jump. He'd turned and had his arms around her waist, pulling her down to him, before she'd taken a breath.

His head rose, to meet her lips, and she accommodated the search, lowering her mouth to his with a hunger that shocked her.

Her entire body was on fire. She felt tears rising with the sheer enormity of her need to be closer to him. To take him into her and put them both out of their misery.

His lips were moist. Firm. Demanding in their movement on hers. Their tongues met seemingly of their own volition. Knowing how to move, where to meet. She lost track of everything but him. His warmth. His breathing and arms. The strength that was consuming her. Driving her to a place where nothing mattered beyond what more he could give her.

They were unentangled, consenting adults. Completely free to do what they wanted.

And what they both wanted right then was very clear.

And wasn't going to go away.

As the fire built inside her, swarming in her lower belly, her crotch, Iris lost all will to fight it. Saw no point. Nature was taking its course.

With his injured leg still supported by the pillow, Scott rolled to his back, exposing the shape of his fully engorged penis beneath the thin silk of his basketball shorts.

He glanced down that way, then met her gaze. "It's here, whether we want it to be or not."

His blue eyes burned with an intensity she hadn't seen in them before. Just looking at them shot her flames higher. Hotter. "I know," she told him, and slid her hand down his body to cover his hardened and reaching organ. Only half of it fit in her palm, so she moved her hand up and down, cupping the length with her fingers. Felt the moisture at the tip.

"There's a condom in my wallet." He glanced toward the coffee table.

Iris stood. Loved the intimacy of reaching into his wallet. And felt like she soaked her panties as she pulled his shorts down far enough, got him sheathed and then reached for her own waistband. All her attention was on Scott's face as he watched her pull her leggings and panties down. Off.

His hands reached for her, those biceps bulging, as he supported her weight while she straddled him. He didn't move. He couldn't, not without risking injury to his knee. The feeling of power that gave her, knowing that what happened would be fully up to her, she sheathed him with her body. Sitting on him. Grinding herself against his skin. Clutching him inside her. Holding him as she made a small circular motion with him fully inside.

Keeping her gaze on his face the entire time. His eyes were half-closed. Mouth open. Jaw taut. Unleashed power that she knew she could let loose.

When her own release threatened to happen just sitting there looking at him, she pulled up and sat again. Twice was all it took. She felt him shoot as she convulsed. Over and over. Until sensation was all there was.

Iris collapsed on Scott when it was done, and he held her against him. Tightly. They were returning to earth, and she didn't want to.

Didn't want to face what awaited them.

But as euphoria eased, reality intruded. Most urgently, in the form of the strain on her inner thigh muscles. She had to move. To get up and put her legs together.

And with the help of his hands holding some of her weight, she did so.

But before she reached for her own clothes, she turned back to him. Helped him get his shorts back up and his left leg in position for him to stand with his crutches.

He could have done it alone.

She figured they both knew that.

But what they'd done, they were in it together.

And would pay the price that way, too.

Leaning on his crutches in Iris's guest bathroom, Scott had all kinds of excuses he could make for himself. For her, too.

For a second or two, he was tempted to allow them.

But by the time he limped his way back into her living room, to find it still empty, he knew that the reckoning would come. One way or another.

He could wait for it to arrive of its own choosing. To take them unaware, in another moment they couldn't control.

Or he could deal with it.

When Iris came out of her room, in baggy sweats and an old T-shirt, with worn gray slippers on her feet, he was propped on the couch, in for the long haul.

Judging by the look on her face she was surprised to see him as such but didn't seem unhappy about it.

"We need to talk," he said.

He took it as a good sign that she settled on the opposite end of the couch, not far from his feet, rather than in the chair perpendicular to him. She wasn't afraid to be close to him.

Of course, it wasn't like he could get down there and jump her bones.

Not that he'd done any jumping earlier. Nope, the work

had all been done by her. Just thinking about it had one part of him getting ready to go again.

"I…"

"We…"

They'd both started at the same time. His *I*, her *we*. And his stomach sank a little. Typical for him. He was all *I* while his partner was giving him *we* mode.

Feeling his throat tighten against that *we*, even as his spirits depleted at the thought of losing it, he blurted, "I can't be part of a *we*." And then, as she opened her mouth to respond, he cut her off with "I'm not meant to be half of a couple." As though the verbiage made a difference. Softened the blow.

"I know." While Iris's tone was low, he didn't detect hurt feelings. She took a full breath before she said, "I can't, either."

Right. He knew that. Actually really did know. And understand. "You know that *forever* is just a word," he said.

And when she nodded, he sat up a little straighter. "I know that when I get back to work, I'm going to be single-minded."

"You don't have to explain, Scott. It's me, Iris. I know you. And I've seen you plenty of times when you're neck deep in a case."

Right again. She had. Scott relaxed some. The conversation was going surprisingly well. Too bad it wasn't putting him in a better mood. "So now what?" he asked, as though finding the solution to their problem was all on her.

He knew what he wanted. But also knew it wasn't fair to ask for it.

Her shrug didn't bode well. Nor did the fact that she wasn't popping out answers. If she was waiting for him to be someone he was not…

But...she didn't want that which he couldn't give. She'd instigated the sex. Had clearly wanted and enjoyed it as much as he had. And was sitting on the couch with him. Calmly. Not crying. Or even looking like she wanted to. So...

"You think we can make it work?" he asked.

"In the short go, I'm certain of it." She grinned, but her expression quickly sobered. "Once Sage and Gray get back, it gets a lot dicier."

Right. Because then they were part of a bigger family.

The only family he was ever going to have. Family that needed him.

And that he needed.

While Iris...had lost hers.

And then...had become a part of his.

She could still be friends with Sage, and have Leigh in her life, if she and Scott couldn't be around each other. But not as often. And the holidays...times on the beach...they'd truly become family there on Ocean Breeze.

They weren't a committed couple, but they *were* family. Nonplatonic, where the two of them were concerned. But still family. He would not be responsible for her losing that bond a second time around.

"So we figure out how to throw the dice," he said, fully realizing that the esoteric words were not the solution.

But they were the way to one.

He'd bet his career on that.

Chapter Twenty

Iris wasn't sure how much she believed what she was thinking. Hearing. What she and Scott were getting around to saying. But then, she'd never have believed that sharing her past would free her, either. She'd changed herself to get away from the pain, when, in the end, sharing it had helped.

"You got any ideas?" she asked him. She'd never been all that great at dice throwing. She'd been the practical one. Ivy had been more prone to taking chances, dragging Iris along with her every single time. Usually benefiting them both.

He shrugged. "We continue exactly as we always have, except, when we both are in the mood, we add the sex component."

She nodded. Liked the words. Wasn't at all sure how the concept would realistically play out. "Do we tell Sage and Gray?"

"No." She felt as adamantly about the response as he sounded. And nodded.

"Good," she said. So far, they seemed to be on the same page. She wanted everything she was hearing. He hadn't said anything that she didn't want. Hope started to stir within her.

She tamped it back down. Wasn't ready for that entity to enter her life again. Doubted she would ever be ready.

Hope had no tangible qualities, and therefore, no guarantees. And definitely came with no warranty. It led one to trust it, and then just…disappeared.

"How do we prevent them from finding out?" she asked. "Practically speaking."

He shrugged again. Seemingly in the relaxed mood she liked so much. "We use the street to get back and forth," he said. Then added, "We see each other on the beach, or not, as usual. Everything stays the same. Except, when we want to have sex, one or the other of us leaves again, by the front door, and walks to the other's front door."

No one ever used their front doors on a regular basis. They drove into their garages and entered the cottages through the garage door into the house. It was just a thing.

Guests used the front doors. Deliveries. And if anyone was out front, she or Scott could just wait to hook up.

She nodded. Feeling a smile coming on. Until she thought about Scott at work, coming home after work. Or not.

The not part, if he was working late, wasn't an issue. She had to be able to work as long as she needed as well, without feeling as though someone was waiting on her.

Or like she was letting someone down.

But Scott wasn't always absent from the beach for work.

"I do have one caveat," she said, her chest tight. She wanted what he was offering more than she could remember wanting something in a long, long time. But not if it meant losing what they already had. And if he was sleeping with her and then…

"Let's hear it," he said, as though, whatever it was, they'd figure out a way to make it work.

"We aren't committed to each other for anything. No expectations. Except for one."

Which meant expectation. She saw his eyes dim some, and his tone was a little less...relaxed as he said, "What is it?"

"As long as we're having sex with each other, the sex has to be monogamous." She held her breath, waiting to hear that the condition was a deal-breaker, but also knowing herself well enough to believe that it couldn't happen any other way.

He threw up his hands, and she braced. "Done."

That was it? Done?

Frowning, she asked, "You're sure?"

"Absolutely. One of my rules. I don't sleep with more than one woman at a time. I don't see it as healthy, and it's way too complicated. You're out to dinner with one, run into another..." He shook his head. "I don't need, or want to cause, that kind of grief."

Wow. She barely stopped herself from saying the word aloud. She'd known him three years. And for all three of those years, she'd figured him for having multiple sexual partners on a regular basis. Not that he ever talked about any of them. Other than an older woman he'd dated for a while the previous fall. Just...he'd always been so casual about dating...she'd thought...

Didn't matter what she'd thought.

He was smiling. She was smiling.

And he was only a few arm's lengths away. "You up for a redo?" she asked him, watching his expression for any signs of doubt.

His eyes were already slumbrous with passion as he nodded toward his crotch. "What do you think?"

Iris didn't think. With her hands running up his shirt, caressing his skin as they moved, she helped get Scott off the couch and into her bedroom.

They had all night.

It just made good sense to get comfortable.

Scott and Iris made no plans to see each other over the next week. He drove himself to his doctor visit on Tuesday morning without issue. His stitches came out, though the nurse practitioner who saw him butterflied the small area where his sutures had been ripped apart. And on Tuesday afternoon, still on crutches, he went back to work. And worked late.

He'd been following the Polly Ernst murder-for-hire trial as best he could through email, phone calls and even some video snippets, advising his second chair as he was able, and the prosecution was close to resting its case. He had to be in court on Wednesday to question their final witness, the defendant, Polly. And thereafter, to hear the defense's case, so that he could be ready for final arguments.

And he'd been assigned a new case as well. A county prosecutor was on trial for having a relationship with a juror during a high-profile case. The charges had been filed in Los Angeles County, not in San Diego, but the trial had been moved to his jurisdiction.

Dale was back to letting Morgan out, and feeding her, too, as needed. Except that both nights that he worked late, the dog had run down beach to find Angel, and Iris had taken her from there.

He and Iris didn't eat together at all that week. But every night, they met up. Three times when Angel had run down the beach to her friend and Iris had followed, to find him sitting on his back porch so Morgan could play in the sand. And Tuesday and Wednesday nights, out front, when he'd hobbled himself down to her place to collect Morgan.

Six nights in a row they'd shared a bed. Not all night.

One or the other of them got up before dawn and made their way home. Him crutching it in the dark with Morgan by his side.

Six of the best nights of his life.

Scott knew the sex wasn't always going to be as compelling. And at the same time, couldn't wait for his leg and back to heal enough to allow him to give Iris the pleasure he knew he had to give. To make love to her so thoroughly that she'd never forget some of the moments in his arms.

He also looked forward to getting back on the beach with her. They only had two more nights before Sage and Gray came home, and as much as Scott yearned to see Leigh—and hoped his little niece hadn't grown up too drastically during her month-long trip abroad—he also dreaded the loss of freedom he and Iris had had to enjoy each other without subterfuge.

To just be themselves.

Under Sage's watchful eye things would have to change. The last thing he and Iris needed was to have his sister aware that they were having sex. She'd be all about having them engaged and married before summer.

The possibility loomed, growing so strong, that on Friday night, as he lay in his guest room with a naked and very relaxed Iris, he couldn't just drift off to sleep. Based on the way Iris was running a finger along his forearm, he knew she wasn't done with the night yet, either.

"One more night until Sage is back," he said, knowing that the only way they were going to continue to work was through complete honesty. With themselves and each other.

"I know."

"If she has any idea, gets any hint…"

"I know."

"She reads me…"

"I know."

He nodded. Relaxing some. He didn't have to explain Sage to Iris. She really did know. As well and probably better than he did.

"She'll think she knows more than we do about getting over the hurdles that keep people single." He said what had been on his mind for days. "Because she was right where we were, for years. And then managed to climb hers."

"She already told me, a week or so before the wedding, that she'd never expected to marry. That she'd been unable to love that deeply again," Iris said, her tone soft, but not content. "Trying to get me to be open to the possibility that I, too, might feel differently. When the right guy came along."

He tensed. He couldn't help it. He was who he was. If Iris was about to tell him that the past week had changed her, too, that he was the right guy...

"Sage will say whatever she's going to say. She can believe with all her heart that she's right, but it isn't going to change who we are, Scott. That's all we have to remember..."

His breath came easy again. His body relaxed.

And he felt sad, too.

Which made no sense at all.

Iris didn't want to have to hide. To go back to pretending to be someone she was not. Scott was worried that Sage's opinion, her attempts to interfere with them, to make them more than they were, would somehow come between them.

Iris had a different fear keeping her awake. "We said we'd be honest with each other," she told him.

"Mmm-hmm."

Not much encouragement there, but she didn't stop. "I'm finding that I can't go back to a life of pretense, Scott."

She felt him tense up again, as he had when she'd mentioned Sage's talk with her before the wedding. Tempted to slide her fingers off his arm, to move away, as was her way—to pull inside herself, she made herself stay put. She'd fought too long and too hard to take back her life, to make a life for herself. She couldn't give up herself.

Most particularly not after finding out how much of her was still in there. Taking a deep breath, she said, "I've spent the past three years living only part of my life."

He didn't move. Not toward her. But not away, either.

"Talking to you last week, it wasn't just me sharing my past with a friend, Scott." She lay on her side, with her fingers still on his arm, looking at the wall beyond him. "As it turned out, it was me accepting the past as part of who I am. About bringing me fully into the present. I feel stronger. Healthier. Happier, even, though I know a lot of that has to do with you. But, regardless, I can't go back into hiding."

She raised her glance up to him as she said the last. Afraid. But knowing she was doing the right thing, too.

His jaw was tight. She saw his Adam's apple move as he swallowed. "What are you saying?" His question held no judgment. But there was definite reticence there. A possibility that he wouldn't be on board.

"I'm saying I don't want to hide," she said. "What we do, the choices we make, who we have sex with, where, what it means…that's fully up to us, Scott."

"You're telling me you want to make some kind of announcement to Sage and Gray?" His tone had gotten thinner.

"No. Of course not." The truth. Not said because she could very likely be losing him. "But if we're on the beach, and want to walk to my place or yours, together, we need to do that. Just like we've been doing all week. Sort of. Like we'd be doing if you could walk the beach."

"They'll figure us out the first night that happens."

"I know."

"So how is this different from making an announcement?"

He hadn't left the bed. But then, they were at his place. In the bed he slept in.

"Making an announcement makes it more than it is. Like we've both changed, made a commitment to be a couple. We aren't that. So to do that would mislead her. We just need to be who we are. Show her, don't tell her. Be who we've always been, other than, you know, the naked part." She wanted to touch his stomach then. Maybe move her hand lower. Figured the timing wasn't right. Settled for talking more. "At some point, she clues in to what we're doing, comes to us. We act casual, because this part of our relationship is just that. We tell her that it's not a big deal. She believes us or she doesn't. We have no control over that, nor does what Sage thinks to herself have any effect on whether or not we have casual sex. As long as we're honest with each other, and both keep wanting what we have, we continue as we are."

Iris rolled onto her back as she finished. She'd said everything she had to say. Would stand by it. Feeling good about it.

And she'd deal with what Scott chose to do. Either way.

Figuring she'd give him a minute or two, and then get up and head home, she stared at his ceiling. Looking at shadows cast by the hall light. Joined by the moonlight.

Illumination that met in the dark by chance. Both sources of which would work just fine, be unaffected if they didn't meet.

"I think you're right."

About the moon not being changed without Scott's hall light on? Her first thought covered the shakiness inside her. For a second or two. "You do?"

Turning slowly, Scott propped himself up and reached over to stroke the hair back from her forehead. A touch that seemed to mesmerize her. "I do," he said. "In the first place, of course Sage is going to sense the difference in me, and in us. But more than that, no more hiding for you. And third, no more feeling like we aren't good enough just as we are."

Iris blinked at the tears that sprang to her eyes as Scott's lips came down to hers. And she gave herself wholly up to him as the kiss grew into more, too.

She might have been robbed of the ability to believe in happily-ever-after as Sage did. But she believed in the moment.

And was grateful for every one of them that she could share with this man.

Scott Martin was not her twin.

But, inside, he was a lot like her. He got her.

And she got him, too.

Which was as close to truly happy as she was ever going to get.

Chapter Twenty-One

He'd been the catalyst to bring Iris out of hiding. Scott's system reverberated with the knowledge over the next several days. In his most rational moments, he figured that it hadn't been him, personally, so much as right place, right time. That Sage's wedding had really been the break-free point.

For all his concern that Sage's return was going to completely upend him and Iris, the first week his sister and her family were home there'd been very little difference. As long as he was on crutches, he couldn't be out on the beach, which had always been the backdrop for their together time.

Sage had come down on Sunday, as soon as she'd dropped Leigh and Gray off at home, saying that she hadn't wanted to set the active four-year-old loose in his house until she'd had a chance to assess Scott's condition for herself.

But the whole family had come down for dinner Sunday night. Bringing in a fresh seafood feast. And while he felt better having them all home, and spent a great hour filling up on Leigh's chatter, he wasn't altogether at peace. While he'd been immersed in family, Iris had been home alone. Or out on the beach alone, as he discovered when they met on the road halfway between their cottages, late

Sunday night. Morgan and Angel, who'd been together for almost a month of nights at that point, walked calmly back to Scott's in front of the two of them.

The sex had been mind-blowing, as usual, but the aftermath, not as much. Iris fell asleep with her hand on his chest, and he lay there, absorbing her closeness and hating how accepting she was of being alone.

Of expecting to be alone.

She'd seen Sage and Gray and Leigh on Sunday, too. Had spent an hour on the beach with them that afternoon. There was no real reason for him to be out of sorts.

Yet, through that week, Sunday's dinner kept coming back to him. Him surrounded by family for dinner. Her alone.

He should have invited her down.

Which would have felt odd, too. Looked odd to his sister.

The fact that he couldn't be on the beach, as usual, where they'd probably have cooked out and Iris and maybe some others would have joined in, was the only reason there'd been a private family dinner.

But Iris had become family to him and Sage and Leigh over the years. Yet his sister hadn't mentioned inviting her down.

Truth was, in the past, it wouldn't have occurred to Scott to even have the thoughts. He and Sage and Leigh had shared meals alone at one or the other of their homes many times.

Maybe that point bothered him most of all.

He was changing.

He didn't want to change.

He was comfortable, satisfied, with his status quo. He honestly liked his life.

Or had.

On Thursday night, four days after Sage and Gray's re-

turn, he lay in Iris's bed after a second especially passion-
ate coupling with her, tired, but not at all ready for sleep. It
wasn't all that late. Just past nine. She had a dolphin photo
session at dawn—would be catching a boat out prior to
that—and they'd met up as soon as he'd returned home
from work.

"Joel says I could be off the crutches by the weekend,"
he told her, not sure if she'd want to head home right away,
so she could get several hours of uninterrupted sleep, or
just go home at their more regular predawn time, which, for
her, would be time to jump in the shower and get to work.

Angel and Morgan were already curled up together on
the floor.

"Do you feel ready?" she asked him, sounding…normal.

Holding her in the moonlit darkness, he looked at the ceiling and said, "More than ready." To get rid of the damned
sticks.

And yet, as eager as he was to return to full health, him
being completely mobile again would bring more change
to the little world he and Iris had created over the past several weeks.

Even that thought bothered him. That he was bothered at
all bugged him. That he'd been getting increasingly more
so since Sage's return had him on edge, too.

Lying still so that Iris could get some sleep—she wasn't
making any move to leave so he figured she'd be staying—
Scott told himself that he was just tired of being laid up.
Missing the freedom to walk the beach. To put on his wet
suit and get in the water.

But he suspected it was more than that.

"What's wrong?" The soft feminine voice in the darkness
was almost a relief. Even as he tensed with the question.

"I don't know." He shook his head. Played with a strand

of her hair. She'd laid her head on his shoulder minutes before and rather than putting his arm around her, he'd had his forearm up, lying beside her head.

"You ready to be done?"

Scott froze. Hadn't even considered that possibility. But if she was... "Are you?"

"No."

His fingers returned to fooling with her hair. "I'm not, either," he said.

"You sure?"

"Positive." Maybe to the point of being the exact opposite. He just had no idea what that meant, practically speaking. He wasn't comfortable at the thought of having her at the table for family dinner but felt like something was missing when she wasn't there.

How in the hell did he fix that?

"I heard that Leigh spent a couple of hours with you and Angel the other day, making macaroni necklaces." He'd heard from his sister and then Leigh, not Iris.

"Sage and Gray had a doctor's appointment." And Scott, of course, had been at work and not available to babysit. He'd heard that, too. Not that Sage would have put him in charge of the rambunctious little girl while he was still on crutches, even if he'd been home. He'd have been fine watching her, of course, but Sage wouldn't have thought so.

And Iris watching Leigh was not a new thing. Or even at all unusual. In fact, it was completely normal.

He listened as Iris went on to tell him about some of the things Leigh had said. Including something about having seen Daddy's butt by accident and it having hair on it not smooth like Mommy's and she thought it was gross. She'd scrunched up her nose as she'd said it. Iris chuckled as she shared the news.

Scott smiled, too. His spirits lifted some. Not much.

"I told her that family stuff was private, just between us at home, and not to take that particular tidbit to school with her," Iris said, humor in her tone. "I wanted to say that she'd likely be changing her mind about finding the male body gross in a few years but didn't want to encourage her to grow up too fast. We sure as hell don't want to have to start thinking about Leigh interested in dating for a whole lot of years yet."

We. Iris had been part of Leigh's life—an honorary family member—since the little girl's infanthood. He'd once heard Iris say that Leigh was the love of her life.

He remembered because, since he knew he wasn't going to ever be in a serious relationship and have a family of his own, he'd agreed with her. Leigh was it for him.

Nothing more full time than a niece who went home to her mother's house.

The example of a father that he had to live up to—as all in with him and Sage as his father had been—there was no way Scott would even try to take on that kind of task. No kid of his was going to have an absentee father.

Which meant—no kid for him.

But Iris...she'd make a great mother.

"I get why marriage, or a committed permanent relationship, isn't in your future, but what about kids? You'd make a great mother."

The words came of their own accord. Had he thought about them, he'd never have let them out. But having said them, he relaxed some.

Because they were honest. Right.

He and Iris—they were alike in a lot of ways. And currently their lives meshed well. But current didn't hang around forever. It led to the future.

And *that* was what was bothering him.

He'd had his future mapped out since the year after his divorce. He knew his course—driven by his career. Hoped to be California's attorney general someday. Or something on a federal level. He'd dedicated his life to making the world a better place by putting away those who hurt innocent people. To stop them from hurting anyone else...

Iris hadn't answered him.

She hadn't taken her head off his chest, either.

But he felt a change. Like the air had been infiltrated with something that caused it to stiffen.

Only a week in and they'd reached a fork in their roads.

He'd accepted that it would happen at some point. That had been a given from the start.

But...so soon?

There was still so much...

No. Maybe soon was for the best.

Before they got in too deep. Involved Sage and Gray and Leigh. A breakup would be more awkward then.

As it was, they could just stop visiting each other at night and now that his sister and her family were back, could just go back to seeing each other casually on the beach.

With the possibility of chaperones appearing at all times.

A return to their old normal was probably for the best.

Even in just a week's time he'd begun to include thoughts of Iris in his self-planning. Like the overnight trip he'd scheduled to meet with an attorney in Santa Barbara the following week. He'd made the plans, but had hated that they meant missing a night of Iris. Had even had a split-second thought to invite her along.

Good thing he hadn't yet done so.

Right. Good thing.

There wasn't one damned good thing about ending things with Iris.

But for her…to give her a shot at true, lifelong happiness…he'd give her up in a heartbeat. He cared for her that much.

And for that, he wasn't sorry.

What about kids? Iris hadn't answered his question. She wanted to. Just couldn't find an appropriate response. How did you explain to someone else what you didn't understand yourself?

As the silence lengthened between her and Scott, Iris fought off an onslaught of fear. It was okay if they didn't meet in the exact same place on every level.

If there were truths they didn't have to give to each other.

So why did she feel as though they were already losing the new journey they'd embarked on? Already reaching a crossroads?

The answer that occurred to her fed the anxiety building within her.

Because what they were trying to do didn't work in the real world. You couldn't be casual friends and share the kind of soul-deep physical joining that she and Scott had been engaging in over the past week.

"We aren't casual friends," she finally had to say. The words had been pushing at her for days. Since the day after Sage and Gray had come home, clearly closer to each other even than they'd been before they'd left, and she hadn't been envious.

Or felt herself on another planet.

Living a different kind of life.

She'd felt as though she had what they had. An emotional connection that was bone-deep. With someone who knew her. Really knew her.

Understood the parts of her that most people didn't see.

Scott's silence stretched too long. They were in trouble. She didn't have to hear him say it.

But couldn't make herself get up, get dressed, thank him for the best sex she'd ever had, take her girl and head home.

Because she'd be leaving a part of herself behind.

Somehow, she had to figure out how to get that back before she left. If she kept leaving herself behind, there'd be nothing left.

"'We aren't casual friends'? I'm not sure what to do with that statement." Scott's fingers had stilled in her hair. She'd been concentrating on the movement to still her panic.

"We said we'd be honest, but we were both lying," she said, afraid to speak. And not to. At least if they ended things before they got too messy, before they ended up hurting each other, they could still be friends.

The thought of losing Scott's friendship was suffocating her.

Utter stillness encompassed them. Neither moving, except to breathe. As though, the slightest adjustment of an arm, a hand, could break them. "How so?" His tone sounded more conversational than fully engaged.

"We kept calling each other casual friends, but we haven't been that in a long time," she told him. "Just the way we both reacted after the night of Sage's wedding... both stricken at the thought that we'd ruined our friendship. If we'd just been casually relating, neither of us would have been so bothered by the idea of losing the other."

Funny how truths presented themselves. Not all at once. When one could make appropriate lifelong decisions. But one at a time. In their own time.

"You make a good point."

Iris didn't even take a breath before she said, "Okay, counselor, please approach the bench. We need private talk here, not courtroom correctness."

"I don't know what you want me to say."

"I don't *want* you to say anything. Or rather, I do want you to say something, but not what you think I want to hear. I need truth, Scott."

"I've never lied to you." He didn't push her away. But she could feel his growing distance as though he had. And wondered how they'd ever thought they could pull off the life they'd set for themselves.

And yet…she didn't want to go back, either. Didn't want to just see Scott Martin on the beach sometimes. She wanted to know that he'd be there, somewhere, anywhere, if she wanted to talk to him. Wanted him to want to seek her out, too. Just because he wanted to hear her voice.

Which was all so confusing.

As she lay there, with anguish building inside her, she had to stop. To calm herself. And felt the warmth of his chest beneath her cheek. He wasn't denying her that.

He hadn't actually denied her anything she wanted.

So why had things gotten off track all of a sudden? Why was she dealing with problems before they arose? Who cared if they used the word *casual* to describe themselves? If it worked for both of them, then why ruin a good thing? A great thing?

The best thing she'd had since Ivy died.

Since she'd quit dreaming about the future. Making plans for the life she wanted to live.

"I used to say I was going to have four kids." She dropped the words quietly. He'd asked about kids. She'd freaked out. And had been ready to throw away something vital to her.

In that moment. In that phase of her life. For as long as it lasted. Scott was vital.

The truth hit. She accepted it without panic. He was vital for the moment.

His fingers picked up a strand of her hair. Threaded through it. Delightful, yet comforting, chills ran through her. The kind she got when she first sank into a hot bubble bath.

"Why four?"

"One for each hand." The answer was just there. As though she'd never forgotten she'd once had the plans.

"You were planning to have four hands?"

She nudged his side with the elbow she was lying on. "It takes two people to make babies," she reminded him.

She'd been talking about the past. He knew that she'd changed since then. Wasn't planning on being part of a couple.

Except, for the moment, she *was* part of one.

Just for the moment.

Chapter Twenty-Two

Scott won the Ernst murder-for-hire case. Professionally, he celebrated the win. Knew that the world was a better place for the precedent that had been sent. Polly Ernst had most definitely been wronged by her ex, but being hurt didn't give someone the right to murder.

At the same time, he couldn't get past the fact that he'd once caused the same kind of pain that had driven Polly. He'd hurt his first wife as badly. It wasn't something he could walk away from. The only way to make it right— aside from the generous settlement he'd given his ex-wife in the divorce, allowing her the means to build a good life— was to make certain that he never let it happen again.

And the only guarantee he had of succeeding there was to never get remarried.

A week passed. And then two. He had a couple of new cases. Iris was fielding offers left and right, lucrative, career-making offers. They were both missing beach nights on a regular basis, and yet, they'd only spent a total of two nights apart.

The night he'd traveled to LA.

And another when she'd been in Sacramento for a high-profile wedding.

The beach wasn't what it had once been to him. While

he still craved his time there, he went out, he did a modified version of jogging, which was mostly just a brisk walk with a few jogs in between, he visited with some of his neighbors while Morgan did the same, but he didn't linger for hours.

Because Sage and Leigh weren't out as much. Instead of Sage being a single mother whose only adult companionship had been on the beach, his sister had a husband and daughter in her home to care for, with another child on the way.

Sage had everything she ever wanted. Was truly happy. And Scott was happy for her.

He was also missing the two of them a lot.

And was afraid he could be using Iris to fill the gap.

She didn't seem to mind.

Because she was using him to fill the same hole in her life? Living right next door to Sage and Leigh, Iris had seen them more than Scott had a lot of the time.

Walking with Iris on the beach late one Friday afternoon in mid-March, watching the girls dart in and out of the incoming tide, Scott said, "Nothing stays the same." Just out of the blue. Hands in the pockets of his shorts, head watching his flip-flops sink into the sand, he went from casual friend to baring his soul.

At least it felt that way to him.

They'd just passed Sage's cottage on the way down the beach toward Scott's. Having already walked past Iris's twice, once on the way down toward Gray and Sage's place, and then on the way back. They'd seen lights on in the cottage, but no one had been out.

"And we were so worried Sage would pick up on the fact that we're having sex." Iris's response fit right into his thought process. Not for the first time.

But he'd been talking about more than just afternoon hours on the beach. Though, on the surface, that had been a big part of it. Those hours had bonded a family unit of which he'd been a major part.

And now found himself more an outsider.

"I'm thrilled for her," he said then. "And glad for me, too, if truth be known. Ever since she adopted Leigh, I worried about her a lot. Tried to take up the slack without stepping on her toes and didn't always get it right. And now I can let go, and just be her brother and the uncle that spoils Leigh again. Something I'm much better at." Saying the words aloud brought their truth home to him. In a sense, not having Sage outside, waiting, was a relief.

Because she was finally truly happy. Fulfilled. Not just as a mother, but as a person. Scott could take care of day-to-day responsibilities as needed, but he'd never have been able to fill the hole Sage had carried around in her heart.

"Which fits, doesn't it?" he said aloud. "I'm better at being on the beach with the family, then inside, being a part of them."

"I wouldn't say that."

"You wouldn't be wrong."

Her hand brushed his arm as she sidestepped the tip of a small wave reaching farther upshore than the others. Scott almost reached for her fingers. Held on. But just in time kept his hand in his pocket. They weren't going to lie about their physical relationship, but neither were they inviting anyone to know about it.

"Relationships take two people, Scott," she said, when he'd expected silence to swallow up his words. "I'm guessing you were consumed by your work during your first marriage. You were a junior prosecutor building a future. Not just for you, but for your family, too."

"I'd spend the entire night at the office and forget to call home."

"She could have called you."

Sage had said the same. More than once. "I didn't like to be interrupted."

"She could have texted. Or called anyway, and dealt with your irritation. Not every minute in a relationship, even a great one, is roses. People have bad days, get tense sometimes, don't feel good. They get irritable. Even Leigh. We've both seen her in some less than precious moments. It doesn't mean she's a bad kid, or unworthy of our love. It's just life."

For someone who'd spent her entire adult life living alone, Iris was pretty in tune with how to be a part of a shared life. He was about to tell her so, when she continued.

"Take you, for example…"

"What about me?" he asked, turning his head to look at her. Saw that she wasn't smiling, but still wanted to hear what she thought about him.

"You aren't the cheeriest fellow when you don't feel good."

Oh, that. He'd expected something more encompassing than a moment in time. "I've apologized for that…"

"And you didn't need to, because I understood. I'm just saying…if your ex was in love with you, she'd have tried to understand, too. And if not that, then to at least meet you halfway. Instead, by the sounds of things, she lived her own life, waiting for you to join in, and when you didn't, she left and lived it elsewhere. On your dime."

"You've been talking to Sage."

"She's mentioned things a time or two in the past, but honestly I didn't spend all that much time thinking about your failed marriage."

Didn't. Past tense. As in she *was* currently thinking about it?

"All I'm saying, Scott, is that I don't think you should just automatically deny yourself a chance at something because you have a failed relationship in your past. You act as though the failure was all you. But the truth is, if your ex wasn't in love with you, or was more in love with herself than she was with you, then it wouldn't have mattered if you'd been home every night on time and were available to her every second she wanted you there. The relationship still would have eventually failed because you wouldn't have really been a consideration in it. It would have been only about her."

He'd married a debutante. His ex had been raised to pay attention to herself. So yeah, she'd been a little selfish. So had he.

They'd been a great couple. Two young people with every advantage, hooking up because of who they were, thinking they'd have a great life because they had the same goals. Wanted the same things.

Except that she'd wanted a life enjoying society. And he'd wanted to spend his time making it a better place to be.

"You might have a point," he said, not sure that it made a difference. Not even sure why, when Iris talked to him about his ex, he heard it differently than when Sage had.

Because he'd grown up?

Grown wiser?

Or just because he wanted an excuse to keep Iris in his life?

Iris spent the night at Scott's cottage. In the master suite with him. He'd moved back to his old room the night she'd been in Sacramento.

She was in bed first and didn't wait for him to reach for her. Instead, she climbed on top of him, as she'd done that first night on her couch. She didn't want kissing and foreplay. She needed him inside her. Filling her emptiness.

And when they were done, she lay beside him, ready to sleep. To escape for a while, knowing that he was beside her.

She'd drifted off, had been on the beach, trying to save Leigh from a wave that was chasing the little girl up and down the sand. It was getting closer to her and Sage couldn't get to Leigh. Couldn't save her, when suddenly Scott's hand on her face was her only reality. "Iris." She heard his voice then. Soft and sure.

Eyes open, she looked up at him, seeing enough in the darkness to catch the glint in his eye. The focus. As though he was as much or more a part of her as the nightmare had been.

She stared at him. Unable to get wholly out. Because her current life had been there with her. In the darkness.

She'd brought her past into the present. Sweet little Leigh had been the one that death had been chasing. And Iris hadn't been able to stop it. Death was stronger than anything she could do to stop it from attacking. Any fight she could put up against it. And it always would be.

Scott was up on one elbow. His bare chest close enough that if she turned her head she could kiss it. She didn't.

He leaned over her, his hand on her forehead, brushing hair back from her face. "You okay?"

She nodded. Smiled. He was there. Still sharing moments with her. Probably not for long. They'd known from the beginning that their liaison wasn't permanent.

No expectations, they'd promised. And she had none that reached beyond the present.

But when Scott lowered his head and kissed her softly, she gave herself fully to that present. Kissing him so completely she lost her air and sucked his. He touched her everywhere, and she touched him back. Letting her fingertips learn every part of him. And when they came together, lying on their sides, their gazes joined and held, along with their bodies, until the waves had come and gone. Making memories that they could call up at some point in the future if they wanted to do so.

Iris gave Scott the best of her, hoping that the experience would be a place of joy in his memories, too. That even if they were still having sex a year from then, they'd still be able to remember back and smile at how it had been. And if, as was more likely, they weren't, then they'd both want to look back fondly from time to time because their weeks or months in bed together had given them joy.

Her friendship with Scott had taught her that she didn't have to run from the love she'd lost. But that, after she recovered from the initial pain, she could bring memories of the past's happy times into the future with her. She'd always be grateful to him for that. He hadn't brought her twin sister back to life, but through him, she'd found the courage to keep Ivy's memory actively alive inside her.

When she left before dawn, leaning down to kiss him goodbye, she heard him murmur "Tonight?" against her lips.

And gave him the affirmative he'd been seeking.

They were one night at a time for as long as it worked for both of them.

And for her, it was working better than she'd ever dreamed it could.

Life was working just as he'd designed. His career was flourishing. His successes were gaining him notoriety, which meant higher-priority cases, with tougher fights against powerful opponents. His sister was happy, Leigh was adored, and still made it clear that she wanted some Uncle Scott time, too. His best bud from high school was now his brother-in-law and living permanently on Ocean Breeze. His knee wasn't one hundred percent, yet—he wasn't back up on a board—but it was close. His back had fully healed.

And Scott was having the best sex he'd ever dreamed of having.

So why in the hell wasn't he satisfied?

A month had passed since he and Iris had talked on the beach about his first marriage. The same night he'd slept in his king-size bed with her for the first time. The night she'd had another nightmare. Something they never talked about.

Neither Sage nor Gray had noticed anything different about him and Iris. To their credit, they were newlyweds with a precocious four-year-old on their hands, Gray's new animal clinics opening, Sage's law career booming and a baby on the way.

And when they were around Sage and Gray, Scott and Iris were who they'd always been on the beach. Close friends. He just hadn't realized, until Sage's wedding, how close they'd grown.

He had everything he wanted.

How could it not be enough?

Nothing was missing, and yet, as he drove home from work one Friday in April, heading to a shrimp boil and fry on the beach behind Gray's cottage—a small affair with only Sage's family, Scott and Iris—he approached the evening with an acceptance that wasn't like him.

He was glad to be going.

Couldn't think of anyone else he'd rather be spending his evening with.

He was really looking forward to the food.

And as, changed into shorts and a short-sleeved shirt, he walked down the beach with Morgan, he felt like he was settling, too.

A sense that escalated as Angel bounded toward Morgan, and he looked up to see Iris standing in the distance. She didn't walk toward him, greet him with a kiss.

He didn't want her to. Not on the beach.

And yet...he did.

On the beach.

In front of Sage and Gray.

He had it all.

And he wanted more.

More than the present.

He wanted a future.

With Iris.

The realization hit with the force of a ticking time bomb. He had to disarm it. Save himself from the explosion.

Morgan saved him instead, barking up at him as Angel stood in his path, wagging her tail. They wanted the treats he'd begun carrying in his pocket.

And because he didn't fail those who were counting on him, he handed down the goodies. And came up with a smile on his face to greet the amber-haired, vibrantly alive woman he was approaching. She'd worn her hair down. Had on capri-length black leggings and a short-sleeved tunic that showed him the shapes of every body part he intended to touch that night.

She'd been out of town the night before.

Maybe that had been the source of his gloom. He'd had to go a night without getting any.

If anyone had told him that he could have sex every night

for months and still not be at all satiated, he wouldn't have believed them. Not in real life.

And yet, he was living proof to himself that it was possible.

Iris didn't take his hand when he approached. She didn't lean in for a kiss. But the look she gave him, long and... longing...stayed with him.

Was it possible she was feeling a lack, too?

Maybe it was time for them to just tell Sage and Gray that they were intimately involved. Without any plans to become permanent in any way.

Didn't matter how much Sage tried to make of it. He and Iris were the only decision makers on that one. And neither of them were going to be swayed by Sage's clearly prejudiced opinion.

Marriage was working for her.

But the institution wasn't the right choice for everyone.

Even if Iris was right, that he was taking a failure on himself that hadn't been his, that his marriage had been doomed from the start due to a lack of love, or mutual goals, he still wasn't ready to trust himself enough to try again.

Not if the risk was breaking Iris's heart.

Scott remained steadfast on that one.

Hands in his pockets, he walked beside Iris over the couple of acres of beach and land, the two cottages, between her place and the beginning of Gray's property. Heard her talk about the night she'd spent with her stepmother. A woman she hadn't had anything to do with since she'd left San Francisco.

She and Ivy had never understood how the woman stuck with their father, making excuses for his return to drunkenness after their mother died. A state that had culminated in their leaving his house earlier than planned the day of the accident. They'd refused to stay with him so drunk. But if he'd been sober, if they'd had dinner with him and his wife that night, they wouldn't have been in the intersection when a drunk driver had plowed through it, hitting them head-on.

Iris had told him the details about that fateful night one evening on the beach, a few weeks before. As a prelude to her possibly accepting the invitation from her stepmother to see a play in Anaheim. One that the four of them, her dad and stepmom and Ivy and Iris had seen during a visit when their dad had been sober and their mother had still been alive.

He'd encouraged her to accept. And while the night had been hard in some ways, she was glad she'd gone. And planned to visit again.

Scott opened his mouth to express a desire to meet the woman sometime, but paused as it occurred to him that such an activity might not fit the friend thing they had going on—how did you explain to a stepmother that you were intimately involved with her daughter, but had no intention of committing to her?

Before he got words out, or closed his mouth, Leigh came hurtling toward them, tripping over her feet in the sand. His niece tumbled, stood up and just kept running, her eyes wide with importance.

She reached Iris first, grabbed her hand, saying, "Come on, Miss Iris!"

And then reached for Scott. "Uncle Scott! My baby sister played with me! Come on!"

Scott glanced at Iris, intercepted the affectionate grin she was bestowing on his niece, his breath catching in his chest.

"I felt it!" Leigh was saying, pulling at both of them as they headed up the beach. Gray was standing over a pit with two large pots situated on metal propane stands in the sand—water and oil, Scott knew—while Sage sat in one of the four adult-size chairs positioned around it. Leigh's little chair would move around the circle, as it always did. The little sea urchin knew how to spread her joy.

And spill secrets, too. Picking the child up in his arms, he glanced at Iris and hurried with her up to Sage. "You're having a girl?" Iris half squealed the question he'd been about to ask.

His sister looked so beautiful to Scott, so truly happy, that he felt a brief prick of tears behind his lids as Sage grinned, stood, said, "Yes," and hugged her friend.

His friend, too.

One who was smiling, and also fighting tears. Minutes later, as Scott watched Iris's face as she felt Sage's baby move beneath the palm she had on his sister's stomach, he felt as though he'd been poleaxed. The expression on the beautiful, green-eyed face beneath that auburn halo was almost Madonna-like.

And he knew.

What he was missing. And what she was, too.

He had to give Iris the chance to have what she most wanted and needed. The only thing she'd ever wanted or needed.

A family of her own.

Chapter Twenty-Three

"We need to talk."

Anxiety darted through Iris as Scott's words hit her the second they started back down the beach after a lovely and lively shrimp dinner. Her relaxed mood fled, leaving her instantly on alert. "Okay, talk," she said, keeping step with him.

Had she done something that bothered him back there?

Had Gray said something?

Did his sister and her husband know about the two of them?

Was he ready to move on?

God, please don't let him be ready to move on. Anything else she'd handle. *Just don't make it be that. Not yet.*

He wasn't talking. Her cottage was just ahead.

"Scott?"

His hands in his pockets, his gaze was pointed at the girls by the water as they walked. In the dark, with the moonlight their only way to see any small life that the ocean was bringing in, both dogs watched pretty carefully at night.

"I need you to hear me out," he said.

He was scaring her. The balmy night somehow sent a chill through her. She wrapped her arms around her middle, hiding her hands beneath them. "I'm listening."

"You told me a while back that me seeing my marriage as only my failure was a biased view on my part. You pointed out facts that lead naturally to a conclusion that while the cause of the divorce was partially on me, it was not solely my fault. And not caused by the single-focused man I am, but by a choice I made. And the choices she made, too."

This was about him? He was about to tell her she'd been right? Relief flooded her. "That's right," she said, fully believing, then and currently, in the deduction.

"You saw what I couldn't see myself."

"Yeah." It was hard to take sometimes, having others see your business better than you did. Because you were blinded by a psyche that had opted to protect you. A concept that would be especially hard to swallow for a man like Scott.

And yet, once she'd seen...she'd been free. Strengthened. Largely because he'd been there, a constant, steady, nonthreatening friend, wanting nothing from her, but that she be around when she could.

Her heart swelled at the thought that she could be the same for him. Give him the same freedom from imprisonment that she'd gained because he'd provided her a safe space to set herself free. She'd always love him for...

Iris's thoughts froze midstream. Her entire emotional and intellectual system shut down, even while she continued to be mobile. Walking in step with the body beside her.

Noticing the dogs in front of them.

Her cottage. The thought came through. Provided insulation from anything that might try to penetrate.

She glanced over, ready to click her fingers for Angel to follow, but her cottage wasn't there. They'd passed it by.

On the way to Scott's.

She didn't love him. Couldn't love him.

The word had been a stand in. Part of a trite, horribly overused phrase people used to express liking. Iris loved the boiled shrimp. Gray had loved the fried.

Scott was talking. She tuned in, holding on to his voice to pull herself out of the funk she'd fallen into.

"...in the same vein, I have to say that I see things, too."

Right, of course he did. They were talking about him. Not her.

She had to stop making everything about her.

When had she started doing that?

"I know." Relieved to hear her voice sound so normal, Iris continued with "You're extraordinarily perceptive. Part of the reason you're so good in the courtroom." Was he doubting his abilities to see nuances because he'd missed one of his own?

Because he'd been lying to himself.

She could fix that one for him. "I—"

"Let me finish," Scott cut her off. And then added a very odd sounding "Please. I'm not sure I'll get this out if I don't."

Her heart softened toward him. Feeling him. "Of course." She kept her tone light. Encouraging. Whatever words she had to offer to help him get through his moment could wait as long as they needed to.

Whatever...anything...he needed, she wanted to give to him.

"These months we've been...together..."

Fear struck again as he spoke. He was ending it. Was ready to move on. She wasn't. The possibility had always been there. That one or the other of them would be first. That they wouldn't reach that point together...

He glanced her way. She didn't glance back. *Just say it*, she implored silently.

"You've been so happy, so much stronger, coming out of hiding, as you put it."

"You're right. It's the best."

"But you aren't done, Iris." His speech sped up. "I've suspected for a while, but it became obvious to me tonight. Seeing you not only with Leigh, but with Sage and the new baby, too. If you'd seen the longing on your face…you're meant to be a mother. The instinct is there. The need is there."

She heard him. Kept walking. Tamped down anger. A lot of it. He had no business… They weren't… He wasn't… He had no right…

"And I want it, too." She took in those words. They made no sense. Scott wanted her to be a mother?

"These last two months, with Sage and Gray married… I'm not Leigh's father figure anymore, and I finally realized tonight that that's part of why I've been struggling."

He'd been struggling?

Why hadn't she known?

She'd thought they were doing great. Other than her bouts of fear, which were just a part of who she'd become after Ivy's death, she'd never been happier.

Damn him for not being honest. They'd said they be honest.

"The past four years, I thought I was just being a supportive uncle, helping my sister, but I realized now that I was using Leigh as a surrogate for what I wasn't going to have, a child of my own. Because that's something I really want."

"What about all that stuff you said once about living up to your father's expectations? The example he set? You said you'd never be able to be as hands-on as he was because of the mental focus required by your job…" She was lashing out. Fighting for her life.

"I said I'd never get married again, too."

Right. That. "I know!" She agreed with him. Getting him back on track.

Until he took a light hold on her arm. Stopped walking. And she stopped, too. Rather than just keep going. Leaving behind what she valued most in her current world.

"I'm not saying that anymore, Iris. I think we should get married. We understand each other. If I'm working too much, you'll let me know. When you're struggling, I understand. Maybe with other people, we couldn't make it work, but together, we can do this."

He hadn't mentioned love.

Wouldn't have mattered if he had, but the lack still held her attention.

"Understanding each other is no reason to get married."

"Wanting kids is."

"Sure, but not to each other."

"We're great in bed."

"Again, no reason to marry." She stood her ground without faltering. Could go on all night with the debate.

"We're best friends."

"And we want to stay that way."

His hands reached up to her face, brushing her hair back on both sides, threading his fingers through some strands as he held her, gazing into her eyes.

His touch was light. She could break away. But didn't. He had to understand how calmly serious she was, to help him see how ludicrous he was being.

He was letting Sage and Gray get to him. Feeling his sister's response to them as a couple—were she to figure them out. Every time the four of them were together, the possibility loomed. Tonight's emotional announcement of a new little girl arriving, coupled with the baby's moves being detectable for the first time...he was on overload.

He had to be.

He cupped her cheek with his hand, and she leaned into the familiar touch. Savoring it. They both had their moments. What made them good together was how they hung in there for each other until clarity returned.

"I love you, Iris."

She stepped back. A foot out of reach. Stood there staring at him. Saw him come closer and stepped back again.

"I'm in love with you," Scott said then, standing firm, tall, his arms at his sides. Emoting the confidence that had drawn her to him in the beginning.

She shook her head. Against the words. Him saying them. What he was doing to them.

"And the thing is, I'm fairly certain that you love me, too."

The words brought a flash from moments before. Her silent remuneration about loving him for being there for her.

Nausea threatened, her muscles felt weak and Iris took another step back. Shaking her head.

And had to go. Get out.

"I've tripped your panic button." She glanced up at the words. Saw the way he was watching her so intently. Backed up another step.

"I love you, Iris. I know you can feel it. Let me help."

He wasn't helping. He was ruining everything.

"If you can't bring yourself to love me, at least believe that I love you."

Those last words, the tone, the pained look in his eyes,

darted inside the wall of ice encasing her. The barriers that protected her so that she could live a good life.

And she found her voice. "How do you believe in something you don't believe in? You're asking the impossible of me."

The night of Sage's wedding, he'd stated his truth.

He believed in love.

She didn't.

There was no way to fix that.

Without a single backward look, Iris called Angel and trod the sand with strong steps, not stopping until she'd reached her cottage.

At which point, shaking…everywhere…she sank to the ground and fell apart.

Her time with Scott was through.

Scott didn't follow Iris on Friday night. Nor did he try to contact her over the weekend.

He'd taken a chance. Played his entire hand.

And had read her wrong.

Still, he stood by his decision. As he'd sat on the beach with her and his family Friday night, he'd seen the potential for failure. And had also realized that the bigger failure was in not trying. A lesson Iris had inadvertently taught him.

She'd been right. Failing wasn't a bad thing. It was to be celebrated because it meant you were trying. You didn't learn to walk unless you tried again. Not trying…that was the failure he had to avoid.

He'd seen something else, too. That while Iris had taken a huge step over the past few months, and was growing in her newfound freedom, taking up the reins of life again, she was also continuing to hide. She'd acknowledged who she was. Had found a way to bring her past with her as she moved on to new ways to be happy.

But she was still hiding. Refusing to let herself love again. To make the family she'd always envisioned for herself. By going along with their plan to never commit, to never be more, to never let their relationship grow, he'd been helping her to continue to hide from her own heart. Giving her the means to flatline.

Scott was done hiding.

Turned out, his father had been wrong. Failure wasn't the worst thing. Not trying was.

When Saturday passed with no word from Iris, and no sign of Angel on the beach, and Saturday night came and went with no word from her, he hurt. A lot.

But knew he'd done the right thing.

On Sunday, he went surfing.

On a long enough board to sustain his height. With a thicker tail making it easier for novices to get up on top of a wave. At a spot where beginners learned to surf. He didn't ask himself to take on anything big. Didn't swim far out. He just stood and glided.

Because he loved the waves and wanted to be one with them. Because he wanted to learn to surf. Not because he didn't want to fail.

He'd probably never be a champion. Or even a noteworthy surfer.

But as long as he had the desire to surf, he'd be out there trying. Baby steps one at a time. Like learning to walk.

Toddlers didn't run marathons. But after innumerable falls on their butts, they learned to stay on their feet. To balance without holding on. To take steps. To walk. And then to run.

Even then, not everyone had the physique, the musculature or the desire to run marathons.

No one could excel at everything.

And failing didn't make you a failure, either.

Not trying for fear of failure...that was the thing to avoid.

Sitting on the beach Friday night, it had all become clear to him. And with clarity, he'd done what he'd known he had to do.

He'd tried.

He'd lost Iris.

But he'd tried.

Had he not tried, the woman would likely still be sleeping in his bed, but he'd have been losing her at the same time. Even if she'd stayed in his bed for the rest of her days.

She'd quit hiding from her loss. But she was still hiding from the fear of the pain that the loss had caused. And he'd been making it easy for her to continue to do so.

None of which helped ease the incredible ache he felt as he walked Morgan on the beach late Sunday afternoon. He'd never have believed it was possible to miss someone so much.

To feel a grayness inside while standing under pure blue skies with sunshine pouring down all over him.

But there it was.

The result of trying.

And he was still glad he'd done so.

Chapter Twenty-Four

Iris had to get off the beach. For the first time in three years, she found no solace there. Taking Angel with her, she spent Saturday driving around San Diego, visiting a few of her favorite parks, driving over to Coronado Island, taking pictures of her sweet girl in every spot they visited. And when nighttime came and her heart sank at the idea of heading back to Ocean Breeze, she called her stepmom.

She and Ivy had never given Diane a chance to be any kind of a mother to them—they'd had their own, and after she'd died, had hugely resented anyone who thought they'd take her place.

And, like their father, she'd been a recovered alcoholic. As teenagers, filled with their own knowledge, she and Ivy hadn't understood enough about the disease. Number one, that it *was* an illness, not merely a choice.

And that those who suffered with it, didn't want to be that way.

They'd only known how their father's drinking had hurt them personally and destroyed their family. And had seen Diane as potential for more of the same.

But as Iris opened herself up to the past, she'd been re-membering more and more about the early days after the accident. She might not have survived, or had the will to fight to learn to walk again, if not for Diane's presence beside her hospital bed, day after day, week after week. Twenty-four/seven during those first touch-and-go weeks.

In the six months she'd been in hospitals and rehabilitation facilities, Diane had never missed a day's visit. Not one.

But as Iris had moved from hospital care to strictly psychological healing, she'd blocked Diane's presence as much as she'd shut out everything else that she couldn't take with her if she was going to survive.

The pain had buried her. And could again.

That's what Scott didn't get.

She hadn't had a choice. She had to walk away.

She was good being with him, as long as it stayed within boundaries that kept her healthy. Love didn't do that.

It destroyed her.

She'd been there.

She knew.

Diane met her at a hotel lounge halfway between San Diego and Anaheim, and over dinner and a glass of wine, she listened as she'd always done, while Iris unloaded on her. About finally being whole again. The journey she'd been on to get there. How good it felt to have arrived.

Until Iris got a look at herself, peering down at the two of them from some perch above. Or maybe Ivy, looking at them from her perch, gave her a strong nudge.

"I'm sorry," she said, then, knowing deep inside her that that's all she'd come to say. Looking into the woman's big brown eyes, filled with the same honest caring she'd always shown, Iris teared up. "You've been nothing but kind and welcoming since the first time Ivy and I met you and we wouldn't let you in and I'm just so sorry."

Diane smiled tenderly, shook her head, patted Iris's hand and said, "It's all part of being a mother, sweetie. I only got to do it secondhand, but I'm grateful to have had the chance." Her lips trembled, though, showing Iris some of the pain she had to be hiding.

"All those months I was in the hospital... I just need you to know...you being there saved my life."

Tearing up in earnest, Diane continued to smile. Nodded. And reached her hand out across the table. Iris didn't hesitate at all as she took hold of the soft fingers and held on.

Sage called Scott late Sunday afternoon, asking him to come down. He didn't answer right away. Wasn't sure if he was going to go or not. He had work inside his home office, waiting for him. Briefs to go through, some case law to verify. All needing to be done before morning.

And work was an excuse Sage would take without question.

Unless it was a matter of life and death, or Leigh had an immediate need for which Sage couldn't provide, his work always came first.

The big question was, would Iris be there?

He didn't ask.

He did take Morgan back out for another opportunity to do her business, though, as he considered Sage's invitation.

Looking, again, for Angel on the beach. If she showed up, problem solved.

But Angel didn't show.

But in the end, the possibility of seeing Iris, within the safety of the small group they'd existed in since they'd met, was too much to pass up, and when Morgan had done her business Scott headed down to the end of the beach.

He took it slow. Not waiting, exactly, but watching for Angel to come bounding up to greet them. And made it all the way to Sage and Gray's back porch without encountering either the dog, or her owner.

The newlyweds were waiting for him outside. In two of the really nice chairs they'd picked out as part of the cushioned furniture they'd bought for the space. Making it more an outdoor living room than a beach porch.

His twin handed him a beer as he stepped up on the newly built expanded deck.

He could hear the television going inside. Emitting childish, cartoon voices.

Computed that Leigh had been told to stay put, as he opened his beer. Sat. Raised the can to his mouth, looking over the rim of it at his best friend.

He'd barely taken his first sip, when Sage, whose gaze he'd probably been subconsciously avoiding blurted, "Iris is moving." Her tone stopped short of accusation, but not by much.

He frowned. Shook his head.

And Sage just kept spewing in his direction. "She put her place up for sale this morning. Is already packing. She offered me all the things she's collected over the years to entertain Leigh when she's visiting. Even the little toddler bed she uses when she spends the night. Said I could use it for the new baby..."

He took the hits hard. Probably more so than his sister had intended. Sage was upset. A bit panicky. She wasn't mean-spirited.

And... Iris was moving? Just like that?

She'd already put her place on the market? She loved Ocean Breeze. The cottage.

Love. Iris didn't love *love.*

She couldn't allow herself.

And was refusing to let herself have any of it in her life

from others, apparently. He hurt for her. Significantly. More than he'd ever imagined. Took a sip of his beer. Then another, and said, "I'm sorry to hear that."

He shouldn't have come down. The conversation he'd inadvertently walked into would have been much better coming over the phone.

"I know you're in love with her," Sage said. "That you two have had a thing going for months."

Iris hadn't contacted him at all, but she'd told Sage about them? Blaming him?

He couldn't wrap his mind around that, either.

"She told you?" he asked, still trying to catch up. Iris was *moving*?

He hadn't seen that coming.

Sage's glance at Gray, her knowing nod, clued him in. "She didn't tell you," he said then, reminding himself who he was talking to. Not just his twin, but a top-tier lawyer just like himself.

"We figured it out while we were still in Europe," Sage said.

Scott's gaze swung to Gray, pinning him. The other man threw up his hands. Shrugged. Shook his head.

As smart as always. Not getting in between the Martin twins.

"Don't blow this, Scott. Your first marriage, she was a selfish daddy's girl looking for someone to support her in style. And you were too young and focused on climbing the ranks in the prosecutor's office. You needed a wife, she needed a husband, but you weren't in love and it didn't work out. But that's not this. You've got a once-in-a-lifetime shot here..."

He nodded. Held his beer on his knee until he could be

fairly certain he'd get the swallow down, and then took a long swig.

"I'd already worked through all that," he said after a brief silence. "And I tried."

He didn't go so far as to say Iris had turned him down.

It hadn't been that clear cut.

And was far worse than he'd realized.

Iris was *moving*?

He looked over at his twin, seeking not sympathy exactly, but in need of a dose of the compassion she'd been salving him with throughout their lives.

Sage's look held little understanding. Eyeing him with determination, more than anything else, she said, "Fix it, Scott."

He got it. The woman was losing her best friend because Scott had slept with her. Of course, the other side of that was that Iris had slept with him, too. He looked over at Gray, knowing his friend would at least try to back him up.

Gray met his gaze, and said, "Fix it, man."

Scott quit looking at the other two people on the porch. He reached down to pet the girl at his feet, sat back and drank beer.

Finished off the can. And stood.

"Scott, please." Sage glanced back at his chair. He didn't sit back down. But he didn't leave, either.

Sage's gaze had softened as she looked up at him. "If there's one mistake you made in the past it was that you didn't fight."

"She's right about that, man," Gray piped in, and Scott's gaze swung in that direction, half wondering who the man was who'd invaded his buddy's body. Until Gray said, "Your ex told you she'd moved out, and you didn't ask her to reconsider. To move back and give the marriage a chance.

You didn't ask what you could do to make things work. You just took the blame—some of which was yours to take, but not all—and branded yourself a failure."

That's what he got for drinking too much one night at some bar in the city and pouring out his woes. Your best bud poured them back on you when you least expected it.

Sage sat forward, drawing his attention. Scott was beginning to feel like a Ping-Pong ball being batted back and forth between two paddles as Sage said, "Yeah and then when she served you with ridiculously one-sided divorce papers you just signed them. At the very least, the divorce needed to be an even split," Sage continued. "But instead of fighting for yourself, you just walked away."

When he'd done nothing wrong except work hard to begin to build a future for his family. And neglect his wife.

He'd had some fault in the matter.

As he was sure he had with Iris, too. Maybe if he'd chosen different words. Different timing…

Kept his mouth shut altogether…

Sage's hand reached out to his, hanging loosely at his thigh, and held on. "Don't just walk away again, Scott. You don't get many chances like this in a lifetime. You and Iris are so good together. And for each other."

Clearly Iris hadn't told her anything about what had happened. Sage didn't know she was preaching to the choir. "I tried, Sage. Trust me on that one. But the choice is hers to make. I can't force her. I wouldn't even try. And I'm not going to beg, either. She has to want to stay. Anything else would end up…ending just like this. Only sometime in the future. When we'd both be hurt even worse."

Those words came rote. He'd been having the conversation over and over with himself for the past two days.

"No, Scott." Sage stood, not as tall as him, but, he believed, every bit as mighty. "No." Her eyes were inches from his. He couldn't avoid their stare even if he wanted to. So he met her eye to eye. Strength to strength as she said, "Do you take the first no you get in court? Or the tenth? You listen to the argument. You process. You consider all the facts, and you come back again. Winning way more times than not." Continuing to study eyes the same color as his own, read more than the intensity shining up at him, Scott sighed. Didn't have any argument left.

"You know her, Scott," Sage said, as though the four words held all the answers he'd need. "Fix it."

Iris was in her workroom late Sunday night, editing photos she'd taken of Angel the day before, avoiding going to bed. She'd slept on the leather sofa in her workroom Friday and Saturday nights but knew that it wasn't healthy to do so.

She couldn't hide from the inevitable. Nor was she going to be wasteful and buy new furniture when hers was only a couple of years old. She was going to be sleeping alone, again.

In the bed, the room, she'd shared with Scott.

She needed to just get in there and get on with it.

Already in the cotton pajama shorts and short-sleeved shirt she intended to wear to bed, she called to Angel and headed toward the door for the girl's last duty call.

The front door, not the back. No way was she taking a chance on Morgan being out. On the girls creating a horribly awkward situation for her and Scott.

She'd already set about taking care of that situation. Had spent a good part of the afternoon looking for another place to live.

Angel was whining before Iris even got the door opened. Frowning, wondering if the girl wasn't feeling well, Iris let

Angel head out first, to get to the small patch of artificial grass Iris had laid for her to use, only to see her running down to the cemented post mailbox at the end of the drive.

That's when she noticed the man standing there, leaning on the post.

Turning, ready to go back inside, she heard Angel's yip as she greeted the best friend she hadn't seen in two days. And knew that she couldn't run. Or hide.

She wasn't going to desert Angel.

But she could take the offense. Get through the difficult moment she'd tried to avoid and be done.

"What are you doing here?" she asked, when nothing better came along.

"Waiting to see you."

"You could have called."

"Would you have answered?"

Probably not. Since his question implied the obvious, she left it alone.

Tried another stance. "I saw Diane last night. Apologized for how I'd treated her when I was younger. And let her know she'd saved my life." Just to let him know that she was healthy. Strong. And willing to admit to her mistakes.

Like the one she'd made when she'd walked away from him without giving him the same?

"I'm sorry for the other night, Scott. I handled it badly."

With his hands in the pockets of his shorts, his biceps oddly highlighted by the streetlight just above them, he remained by the post and said, "Sorry for how you handled it? Or for your response in general?"

Both really. The admission did nothing but prolong the inevitable.

"I'm moving," she said then, figuring Sage would have

already told him. Guessing that was why he'd shown up. She'd wondered if he would.

Had hoped not.

"You and Sage were here first. Ocean Breeze is your home. It's right that I be the one to go."

She thought he nodded. Couldn't be sure. Saw Angel pee, and was glad the awkward goodbye was almost done. "Anyway, I just wanted you to know, I'll remember you always, with utmost fondness. I'm glad I knew you, Scott Martin," she said and, clicking her fingers for Angel because she didn't trust her voice to get out another coherent sound, turned to head toward her new life.

Whatever it would be.

Wherever it would lead her.

Fix it.

Sage's words screamed inside Scott's head as he watched Iris turn to go. He had no magic bullet. No solution. He'd come home via the street because he'd figured that's where Iris would be taking Angel to do her business to avoid him and Morgan. He'd planned to stand there as long as it took for her to come out.

And that was all he had. He'd just stood there.

Until he saw the one woman for him turning her back on him. It was as though the jury had all left without rendering a verdict, the judge had quit, the defendant was going to win. He couldn't let that happen. "If you don't believe in love, why are you so afraid of it?" His delivery was louder than it should have been.

Otherwise, he stood by his words. And wasn't going to let her go without answering to them. Even if he had to text her, write to her, for years to come...

She continued to her door as though she hadn't heard him.

But she had. He'd seen the way her back had stiffened. Noted the oddly unmoving tilt of her head. The way she got when she was fighting off fear.

"When you figure it out, I'll be waiting," he said, his tone bedroom soft. "Because that's what love does. It doesn't die. It doesn't leave. It waits. Sometimes we don't get that until eternity gets here, but the love, it's always there."

His father's never-ending love for his mother had taught him that. The years without her, his father had always played her favorite song on her birthday. He'd learned to make her special recipes. He'd talked about her.

And, Scott suspected, had talked to her, too.

Because Randolph Martin was a man who gave his all to everything he did. He'd been strict. Had had seemingly impossibly high expectations. And yet, he'd always been there to wipe up spilled milk, too. To tend to wounds. To pick up the pieces.

That's what love did.

As Scott watched Iris's straight back disappear inside her cottage, saw the door close, he stood there with tears in his eyes.

But no regret for having loved her.

Iris made it into her bathroom before her tears fell. She brushed her teeth through blurred eyes. Turned out the light. Got into bed. Called Angel up to cuddle with her.

Wrapping her arms around the warm girl, she promised herself she wouldn't cry anymore. She didn't want to wet Angel's fur.

She just wanted to sleep.

To get a break.

To wake up refreshed and move forward.

Except that the tears didn't stop. Which meant she couldn't sleep because she had to keep blowing her nose.

And Angel kept staring at her. As though expecting something more.

Or was worried.

Rolling onto her side, she pulled the girl right up to her face, and said, "You're going to miss Morgan a ton."

Should she leave Angel behind? Gray and Sage were looking to adopt a puppy for Leigh.

It would be the right thing to do. Iris had no idea where she'd be in the short go. Didn't know what kind of yard Angel would have. Or have anyone to watch the girl when she had to work long hours.

Knots twisted her stomach as the thoughts piled on. Angel crawled a couple of inches forward and licked her nose. Twice. Then lay her head on Iris's face. Right there, neck over the bridge of Iris's nose.

Loving her. Even as Iris had been planning to give her away.

To leave her behind.

Loving her.

Oh God.

Oh God.

Her heart pounded, she started to shake and wrapped her arms around the miniature collie's warmth. People couldn't get through to her.

She'd closed her heart off tightly to that source.

But the dog…her precious little girl…

Was showing her the truth that Scott had just challenged her to see.

If you don't believe in love, why are you so afraid of it?

She *was* afraid. So afraid that she couldn't let herself…

A vision of Ivy's knowing smile crossed her mind's eye

and in that instant, Iris recognized it for what it was. Not just a memory from the past.

But a living entity that surpassed understanding.

Ivy's body was gone. Her love was not.

Nor was Iris's capacity to feel her. Or Angel.

Or...

Out of bed in an instant, Iris slid into a pair of flip-flops, grabbed a long sweater from the hook on the back of her bathroom door, clicked her fingers for Angel and ran out the front door.

Scott had said he'd be waiting.

He wasn't there.

But she knew where to find him.

Jogging as best she could with foam flapping at her feet, she was sweating by the time she got to his front door. Heard Morgan barking inside.

Followed by Angel's bark beside her.

Leaving no doubt to the man inside about who was pounding on his door after midnight when he had to be up early for work in the morning.

When he opened the door, she met his gaze, and said, "I could have waited until tomorrow, but what if something happened to you on the way to work in the morning? Or before you made it home? What if something happened to me?"

His gaze soft, he stood there, bare except for the briefs, and said, "You trying to tell me something?"

"I do want to be a mother. But the thought of bringing a child into the world and then dying on it, hurting it like that when I have no control over such a thing, or having it die on me, scares me so much I can't breathe."

"It's all part of being human," he said. "You don't get to control that, either. You're human. Not something you can change."

He'd changed. Was as calm as she was agitated.

"Anything else?" he asked, crossing his arms as he leaned against the doorjamb. Not shutting her out, at all. He seemed really interested in anything she might have to impart.

But he wasn't inviting her in.

"You didn't take pain pills. No matter how bad your pain got, you'd made a choice that you'd deemed vitally important, with implications beyond your ability to endure physical pain, and you stuck to it."

"Okay."

He already knew that.

"That's what I can trust," she said. "And what I want to give to you. That bone-deep knowing that as long as I'm alive, I'll endure whatever pain comes my way in order to keep loving you."

His chin quivered, but he still didn't move. "You're telling me you believe in love?"

Crying again, Iris smiled, too. "You deserve your pound of flesh, counselor," she said in a voice that wavered almost beyond comprehension. And then, with a deep, calming breath said, "I love you, Scott Martin, and if you'll have me, knowing that I get weird sometimes, and that I will probably always struggle with bouts of fear, I would like to marry you and have kids with you."

The words rushed out through a wall of fear.

But once they were out, as she watched Scott stand up straight, saw his arms reaching for her, she had no anxiety at all.

No heaviness, no dread, no shards darting through her. She saw light, the light in Scott's eyes, and felt warmth, the warmth of his embrace, and knew that her answers had been right there, waiting for her all along.

Bad things happened. Life hurt sometimes.

But love really did have the ability to heal even the worst tragedies.

The human heart was capable.

It was just up to individuals to let it happen.

When Scott picked Iris up, kicking the door closed behind the girls as they trotted in, she held on to his neck, eager for the ride.

Knowing that she would have his love with her for every minute of the rest of eternity. Whether he was in bed with her, inside her, at work, or gone farther away, the love that was engulfing them would never leave her wholly alone.

Their lovemaking that night was rushed, almost desperate, and then, softer, sweeter. And when she finally lay down to rest, her head on Scott's chest, Iris sighed.

"You're my first and my always," she whispered in the darkness.

"And you are mine," he whispered back, the words following her into a peaceful rest that had been eluding her for years.

She woke once in the night. Lay there with her head next to Scott's watching him sleep, thought about what she'd do if she ever lost him and swore that he smiled a little.

Because she was who she was. She'd experienced a trauma that would always be a part of her. And love was what it was. She could fear. But love would win.

With a smile of her own, Iris promised herself, and Scott, that she would never hide again.

And knew that if she did, Scott would always find her. Always.

* * * * *

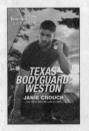